CITY OF ASSASSINS URBAN FANTASY COLLECTION

CONNOR WHITELEY

DEDICATION
Thank you to all my readers without you I couldn't do what I love.

CITY OF
DEATH

CONNOR WHITELEY

CHAPTER 1

Everyone will die. But whether or not I will kill you is down to you.

Breathing in the smoke filled air, I pressed my body against the cold wood of a bakery as I scout out my next location.

I always like to be near a bakery because sometimes you can easily steal something and dash off into the distance. Granted I normally give the stolen good to a starving child but I still love stealing.

Wearing my thick black leather armour and black cloak, I made sure my smooth face was covered up. I was not going to be recognised here, especially with all those crazy bounty hunters who want my head.

Looking forward, my eyes narrowed on the busy street full of busy common people walking past in their smelly clothes. I wish some of these people would take a bath, but I guess they aren't, and that's why I do what I do.

I want to help people.

As I looked past the crowd in the busy dirty street, I turned my attention to the massive solid grey stone wall ahead in between two bigger towers. I smiled and placed my hands on the hilt of my two long black swords.

The sounds of the people chatting and talking filled my ears as I focused on the wall ahead. I needed to focus and analyse my target, a lot of people would have said how I analyse buildings and people is flat out weird. I prefer to think of it as making sure I stay alive.

Two entrance points by ladders about twenty metres away. A large crowd in my way. Definitely not my favourite conditions to get to a target but not my worse and these people in the street were hardly enemies.

Stretching my neck a little, my eyes narrowed on the grey armoured guards on the wall. Six guards, that should be easy enough to kill but I needed to do it quickly.

Then I smiled as I looked at what my real target was, from where I was standing I couldn't see it perfectly clear but it was enough.

Looking at the large brown crates with wooden bars across the top, my smile didn't stop as I imagined the birds inside. I needed only one bird but that was risky.

Making sure my hood was up, I walked into the street carefully, trying to blend into the crowd (and trying not to gag on the body odour of these commoners!). In the back of my mind, I knew I had to succeed here or many great people would die.

As I passed through the crowd towards the massive grey wall, I couldn't believe I was doing this in all honesty. For my entire life I have been a cold, calculating assassin. Killing for a paycheck and loving every moment of it. But damn that Rebellion with their kind words, warm hearts and their cause. They hooked me in tightly so when I learnt on my last mission that stupid, tyrannical Overlord had sent an army to kill them.

I sadly grew a damn conscience.

So I rode here, wrote a warning note and now I want to, no have to attach this to a bird and release it. The Rebellion has to get my note, they have to live.

Another breath of horrible sweat made me cough, and oddly enough it reminded me of the juicy salt bacon breakfast my mother use to make.

As I got closer to the wall, I gripped the hilts of my swords as I noticed two grey armoured guards next to the ladder. I saw two other guards take the other ladder away. I was not impressed!

The two guards started to look at me, under my hood I started to wonder what to do to them. Should I kill them quickly? Stab them in the liver and let them bleed out slowly?

I rolled my eyes as I realised because I had to save my friends and all the other Rebels, I sadly didn't have time to play with my prey.

I walked up to them.

3

The Guards frowned.

Reaching for their swords.

I whipped out mine.

Slashing their throats.

Someone shouted.

I charged up the wooden ladder.

A Guard charged at me.

I jumped into the air.

Kicking him in the head.

He fell off the wall.

His corpse smashed below.

Another two Guards attacked.

I looked at the crates.

I needed to move.

The Guards swung.

I dodged.

Leaping back up.

Thrusting my swords into their heads.

I charged to the crates.

Got out my note.

An arrow hit the ground.

I spun.

Two Guards fired.

I grabbed the arrows.

Snapping them.

The Guards stopped.

I charged.

Jumping into the air.

Another Guard fired.

I caught the arrow.

Thrusting it in their head.

The arrow exploded out the back.

Blood gushed out.

I landed on the Guard.

Wrapping my legs around her neck.

I swung my body weight.

She fell.

Slamming onto the ground.

I snapped her neck.

One more Guard.

I jumped up.

The air moved.

I ducked.

A blade rushed past.

I slammed my fists into his face.

He whacked me.

He swung his sword.

I jumped.

Leaping over the sword.

I swung my swords.

Slicing off his hands.

He screamed.

I silenced him.

I smashed his skull in.

Common people stared at me.

I had to act.

I rushed to the crates.

Opening them.

I heard more Guards coming.

Grabbing a little grey bird.

Attaching my note.
I threw it into the air.
It flew.
Arrows flew through the air.
The enemy were attacking.
I looked at the crate.
There were more birds.
I had to protect my friends.
I launched all the birds.
Twenty birds flew into the air.
Arrows roared through them.
Birds were slaughtered.

As I watched the little corpses fall to the ground, I smiled as I watched the bird with my note fly off far, far into the distance.

Maybe my friends would be safe and maybe my warning would be enough, but I had to make sure they were safe, and for that I needed allies.

CHAPTER 2

Commander Coleman stared out over his amazing valley and mountain range that surrounded his Rebel stronghold. He loved it here, he loved everything about it.

Coleman wasn't exactly sure what his favourite part was but he sure loved how the sharp dagger-like black mountains in the distance provided some protection for his stronghold.

Feeling the cold, hard rock under his feet, Coleman knew he needed to be prepared. He couldn't place the feeling, everyone else thought he was mad, but he felt like something was coming.

Something to end them all.

Coleman checked report after report about the horrific activities of the Overlord and all his puppet Kings. There was nothing in the reports. Coleman still had that nagging feeling.

Smelling the fresh, crisp air of the mountain, Coleman smiled and turned his attention to admiring the stunning valley between the black mountains and him. It was amazing watching the little rabbits and deer run and hop and eat down there on the lust green ground.

Coleman wished his life was that simple but as he turned around and looked down from his watch post. He smiled for a different reason as he remembered how he wouldn't have it any other way.

Looking down at the twisting, turning rocky mountain that the Rebellion called home, Coleman felt a wave of pride wash over him. He was proud and he loved this mountain, it was where Coleman could change things and help people live better lives.

That's what he loved.

Coleman had picked every man and woman in this base, he had trained them and from here Coleman loved how he was trying to change the fate of the Kingdom.

Listening to the gentle howl of the cold wind, he remembered a woman once asking him why he bothered fighting the Overlord and why doesn't he just stay in the mountain and live in peace.

Sometimes Coleman laughed or smiled at that memory but it was so important. It was important that Coleman remembered why he did this. He didn't do it because he wanted to rule and have subjects.

Coleman wanted people to be free and choose how they lived their lives. Instead of being forced down a particular path depending on which City the person lived in.

He shuddered as he remembered where he lived before he formed the Rebellion. Coleman hated how the City of Pleasure in the North made him train for hours each day to make sure he had the correct body for his purpose in life.

Even now Coleman's hands formed fists as he remembered how everyone common man and woman in the City of Pleasure was destined to become a sex object.

That's why he did what he did. No one, absolutely no one should have to do that.

Turning back to staring out over the valley and the mountains beyond, Coleman tried to think about what to do. He couldn't do anything military related because he only had a hunch and Coleman could never, ever risk the lives of his friends without it meaning something.

After a few moments of thinking and wondering about how to prepare for this invisible threat that was coming, Coleman's stomach twisted into a tight knot.

A small part of Coleman couldn't get that beautiful, mysterious assassin out of his head. He knew it was silly, after all she was a dangerous assassin who only killed because he paid her.

But he loved that smooth, pale face and that long brown hair. He loved how confident she was, but Coleman tried to push those thoughts away as he knew they were fantasies. He couldn't act on them and even if he did, he sadly knew he would be putting the cause at risk.

As Coleman turned and started to walk away (hoping he could form a plan in his office), he heard a strange shrieking, and he smiled as he saw a little green bird land on his shoulder.

It shrieked. Coleman forgot how loud and annoying delivery birds were.

Then he cocked his head as he noticed a small thin piece of parchment on the bird. Taking it off, Coleman rolled his eyes and his stomach relaxed a little as he saw the name on it.

The Assassin.

Coleman felt his cheeks turn rosy at the idea of his Assassin writing to him and maybe it was a love letter. Coleman laughed at that idea, of course it wasn't.

Opening the parchment, Coleman's eyes narrowed as he realised this was not a love letter in the slightest. He was right. Something was very, very wrong.

Coleman ran down the mountain. "Call the War Council!"

CHAPTER 3

Rain lashed and slashed at me as I rode along the long twisting dirt road towards my next target. I needed to see an old friend, a warlord in fact.

As I felt my beautiful (stolen) brown horse moan and trod along, I took a moment to relax a little and consider my next moves, but the air did have a wonderful crispiness to it and a hint of cedarwood and dry pine.

Looking ahead, my eyes narrowed as I saw a large bend in the dirt road and the fact that the road was lined with thick dense trees didn't help the matter. The last thing I wanted was to be ambushed.

Just in case I placed a hand on the hilt of my long sword, I was going to be prepared. I raised the black hood of my long black trench coat and cloak to be on the safe side.

If there was an ambush I didn't want these stupid ambushers to recognise me and see a payday riding towards them!

Listening to the awful singing of birds and the rustling of the leaves in the gentle cool wind, I remembered the first time I met Lord Baron Huin, it was on a mission and I had been sent to slaughter his wife for a client (not the Rebellion) and well... he was hardly impressed. So we fought, I sliced off his hand and I did my mission.

It took another two years for us to meet again and become friends. It turned out I did him a favour. It's strange how these things work out, but that's part of my job as a female assassin, I kill for the money and sometimes (damn the Rebellion) I kill for a good cause.

Even now, I still can't believe what I'm doing, if it was anyone else I would have learnt they were in trouble, sent the note and be done with it. There are plenty of people who would hire me and pay me well to kill for them.

And if I was really, really pushed for work and money (Like that would ever happen!), I suppose I could always ask the Overlord for work and explain I only killed all his people because it was my job. And if he refused, well, I would have to kill him.

The birds started to fall silent.

But that Rebellion and their goody tooshie cause, it definitely makes you a fan so I have to ride on and I have to get my old friend to help us.

My stomach tightened as I thought about my note not getting to the Rebellion, and that's another reason I have to get my old friend to help us. If his war party, or whatever he calls them these days, can reinforce the Rebellion, then there's an extremely slim chance we would win.

And maybe, just maybe I'll be able to see that hot Commander Coleman again. I smiled as I remembered that amazing, attractive man with his large muscles, smooth square face and a strong jawline. Maybe I was doing all this to save him, and him alone. I would like to think not but you never know.

A twig snapped.

As I got closer to the bend in the road, I drew out my sword just in case. The air felt off here. Like it had been disturbed.

I heard something step out of the trees behind me. As I turned I stayed calm, there was no point getting angry here.

Cocking my head, I had no idea what I was looking at as I stared at a tall man cloaked in darkness and black cloaks. Almost like he was half man, half shadow. It didn't make sense, even his face was shrouded in darkness.

He drew out his sword. I frowned. It sounded like the blade was quietly screaming.

I hopped off my horse. Two more shadowy people stepped out behind me. I was surrounded.

"I know a pretti bag of goldie for me and ya head," the first shadowy man said, his vice dark, twisted but had a weird angelic edge to it.

"Sorry to disappoint you!" I shouted.

I whipped out my other sword.
I charged.
Flying through the air.
My swords swung.
The shadow man swung.
Our swords clashed.
Locking our swords together.
Lightning shot out of his.
Annihilating a tree.
Other trees burned.
The other men charged.
I kicked the shadow man.
He unlocked our swords.
I swung.
Slashing his shadowy cheek.
Nothing happened.
The air moved.
I raised my swords.
Meeting three blades.
I jumped into the air.
Kicking them.
Icy coldness shot into me.
My feet turned numb.
I wasn't kicking them again.
I turned to run.
I couldn't run properly.
The shadow men charged.
I tried to hop away.
I couldn't.
The men swung.

I rolled forward.

Dodging the attacks.

I tried to stand up.

I couldn't.

My feet were numb.

The men rushed over.

Raising their swords.

Feeling returned to my feet.

Not enough though.

I needed more time.

Lightning buzzed from their swords.

The air smelt burned.

I swirled my swords.

The enemy jumped back.

My sword sliced one of them.

Nothing happened.

No scream.

No blood.

No nothing.

The enemy swung.

I could feel my feet.

I rolled back.

Missing the swords.

I jumped up.

Thrusting my swords into their backs.

Two corpses dropped.

The last one stared at me.

After a second or two, I realised he was pointing and gesturing me to look at the two corpses I had made.

Taking a few steps back I did, the black shadowy corpses laid there as dead as any of my other targets. There was nothing special about them.

Small amounts of lightning buzzed around the bodies and they moved.

My eyes widened in horror as I realised what these creatures were. These weren't any humans or mortals they were Hunters. Some people called them demons. Others called them warlocks.

I didn't care what they were called but they were horrific foes.

I flew forward.

Kicking them in the head.

The lightning disappeared.

The other shadowy figure screamed.

My ears bleed.

I spun.

Rushing to my horse.

I jumped on it.

I escaped.

As I rode away as fast as I could, I couldn't deny the thought of having Hunters after me, scared me more than anyone could ever know.

CHAPTER 4

Commander Coleman felt the cold black leather chair he sat in moulded to his body as he looked at the large cave office ahead of him.

Coleman smiled as he remembered how many newbies to the Rebellion had come into his office and commented on how underwhelmed they had been to see this was the amazing, grand office of the Rebellion.

As Coleman looked around at the rough domed walls of the cave and the rough grey floor of the office. Coleman understood why people weren't impressed with his office, but as he always said to them he didn't want to spend money on an office. He would rather spend the money on the starving people that were being abused and sometimes raped by the Overlord's people.

Yet there was something about his office that Coleman loved, he just couldn't place his finger on. Maybe it was the sweet smell of the sugary piney incense that was burning in the corner. Maybe it was the large brown table he sat at with a massive map of the Kingdom covered in little wooden eagles and men.

He didn't know in all honesty, Coleman just loved it. Especially as he turned his attention to the map out in front of him, there were so many wooden men on the map showing all the Overlord strongholds and the Cities the Overlord still held.

There were too few Eagles on the map. His favourite animal.

A part of him doubted this could ever work and Coleman knew he would never win against the Warlord. The only reason there were the eagles on the map was because of that beautiful Assassin.

Coleman smiled as he thought about her long black trench coat and her amazing figure. She was stunning.

A small part of him knew it was silly but he really wanted to believe she had sent the note for only him. To protect him and show in her beautiful assassin way, she was trying to protect him so she could have him later on. He knew it was silly but he hoped it was true.

The sound of the knocking on heavy wood and muttering outside of the office made Coleman rolled his eyes. As much as he loved leading the Rebellion, Coleman really didn't enjoy these meetings or so-called War Council.

"Come in," Coleman said.

The heavy wooden door opened and Coleman gave a small grin as one man and two women wandered in. All wearing thick, heavy metal armour.

Nodding his respect to the two women, Coleman admired how these two amazing sisters (Abbic and Barbic) always managed to look so stunning for these meetings with their long perfectly straight blond hair and their smooth faces.

Coleman stopped that train of thought as he remembered them on the battlefield. He knew (from personal experience) how deadly and aggressive these two were. He wasn't going to underestimate them like so many enemies did.

"Commander," the man said, his voice rough and deep but Coleman liked Captain Dragnist with his long black bead and scars covering his face from gods know how many battles.

"Me Lord, why did ya call us?" Abbic asked.

Coleman loved how smooth her voice was and wanted to laugh because it made her sound harmless.

"Thank you coming all of you. I received this note from the Assassin earlier," Coleman said, passing them the note.

Barbic cocked her head. "This Assassin is warning us of some invasion. Oh please. She is a no good trouble maker,"

Coleman's eyes narrowed. "You think she is lying?"

"Of course, dearest Coleman. She is a dirty Assassin. No good. She is a troublemaker, this is

20

probably fake,"

"I donna know Sis, this note looks gooda to me,"

"Seriously Abbic? This Assassin says the enemy will launch themselves from the City of Death. That's rubbish. The City of Death hasn't been stepped foot in for a thousand years,"

Coleman rolled his eyes as he knew that was completely wrong. He had walked in the City a few years ago but Coleman would never, ever do it again. He felt there was a good reason why no one lived there anymore. He just might have been too scared to find out.

Dragnist frowned. "That not true and yo know it. Overlord use it mining stuff,"

Coleman nodded. "Whatever is going on with the City of Death. I am not taking any chances and I do believe the Assassin because-"

"Dearest Coleman, we all know you have a soft spot for her but she is a dangerous no good Assassin. She will kill you. The Overlord only needs to pay her enough,"

Leaning forward Coleman stared Barbic dead in the eye.

"I am in charge here. I will defend the Rebellion to the end. My question to you is what should we do about it? I would send a scout party to the City but I don't want to waste manpower,"

"Bossie and if tha Overlord is there. We don't wanna get them slaughtered,"

"No Sister we don't. I propose we get allies,"

Coleman leant back in his chair and smiled at that idea. Barbic must have seen his smile as she passed him the Assassin's note and pointed to the bottom.

"Dearest Coleman, you see here,"

Focusing on the note, Coleman looked at the little word on the bottom of the parchment it meant nothing to him. It was a single name of a town tens of miles away. It was abandoned for all Coleman knew, it wasn't important.

"So?" Coleman asked.

Barbic rolled her eyes. "This is a town twenty miles away,"

"I know but it's abandoned,"

"Na it isn't bossie. Ya old friend lives there. Ya know, Lord Baron Huin," Abbic said.

Coleman couldn't believe he was hearing that name again, it had easily been five years maybe longer. Coleman had no idea why the beautiful Assassin would be going there. But he wanted to see her and maybe Coleman could get the Lord Baron to help them.

He had to try.

"You three can control whilst I'm away. I have to see Huin," Coleman said, walking away before anyone could argue.

As he walked out the heavy wooden door, Coleman felt his stomach fill with butterflies as the idea of seeing his beautiful Assassin filled him with excitement.

He just hoped she would feel the same.

CHAPTER 5

I was hoping not to have to use my backup plan but it seems worth it now. There was a very special reason why I chose to ride across this stretch of the dirt road.

Sliding off my strong brown horse, I made sure my long black leather trench coat and cloak covered my body and face, as I felt the soft mud move under my feet.

Well, at least I hope it was mud but judging by the strong smell, I doubt it.

As I pretended to tie my horse to a wooden post, I looked around and studied the dirt street in this small town. It certainly wouldn't have been my first choice as places to hide or concoct some sort of scheme but it was okay. And to be honest, anywhere I can kill someone is okay to me.

My eyes narrowed on the large dirty muddy square surrounded by little wooden houses. They didn't seem dangerous and I doubted the Hunters

would have got here before me so I should be safe
for a few minutes.

Turning my attention to the crowd, I rolled my
eyes as one man's mouth dropped as he looked at my
assets. I hated men like that, maybe I should
accidentally swing my blade later on.

Listening to the talk of the crowd and the high
pitch laughter, my eyes were drawn to the tall women
dancing in the middle of the square. I cocked my head
as I realised there wasn't any music or anything to
dance to. Why were they dancing?

I checked again if my hood was covering most of
my face and when I knew it was, I slowly walked
through the square. Smelling the oddly perfumed air
from the women I passed and the disgusting hints of
alcohol I got from the men I passed.

As much as I hated walking through the crowd
that was getting increasingly busy as the dancing
continued, I needed to wait until the Hunters got here
to fight back. I had a feeling they were tracking me
somehow.

I just needed to test it.

In the back of my mind, I could feel myself
wanting to scream out for help and panic at the idea
of the Hunters after me. In all my years of being an
assassin, I had heard rumours of these supernatural
killers that massacred people and entire Cities for the
Overlord. But I never believed them.

I'm not exactly sure why, but I think it's because
after the Overlord annihilated the Temple of

Assassins and killed all my friends and mentors. There are just so few assassins anymore.

I smiled at the idea of being the last of a dying breed and maybe I was. Despite popular belief, assassins aren't typical commoners trained to kill.

My stomach twisted at the memories of the witchcraft, the positions, the training and slicing of my flesh. All to make me an assassin.

As I forced those memories away, I could understand why the Overlord destroyed the Temple and my friends. But I won't ever forgive him for killing my brother, my beautiful sweet, little brother. And that's why I'll help the Rebellion to kill the Overlord.

Someone touched my ass.

"Ello love," a creepy man said, grabbing me from behind.

Without even looking at the foul man, I knew it was the man who was staring at me earlier.

"Release me now and I let you live,"

"Come on Love, let's get down and dirty," he said, humping my back.

I spun around.

Whipping out my swords.

Slicing off his hands.

I grabbed his manhood.

I ripped it off.

He screamed as the blood rushed out of his lower body, turning the mud a beautiful deep rich red.

I did warn him.

Putting my swords away, I looked towards the entrance to the little town and saw the dancing had turned faster and more dramatic. I knew this town was a little strange and I didn't really want to be here.

Remembering the rumours of the witches and warlocks living in the town and their rituals to their gods, I knew I had to leave but I had to wait for the Hunters to arrive.

Someone screamed.

Knowing I was hardly in any danger for the next minute, I stared at the entrance of the town as the three shadowy male Hunters advanced into the town.

Ripping the souls out of the living.

I cocked my head at the new way to kill. I had no idea they could do that but now I really didn't want to be here.

One Hunter disappeared.

Someone slammed into me.

Tackling me to the ground.

I rolled up.

Holding up my arms.

I blocked a punch.

Then another.

Then another.

I kicked the person.

It was a Hunter.

I kicked him again.

His grip weakened.

I threw him off.

I punched him.

He jumped up.

Whipping out his hand.

Pain flooded me.

I felt my body being ripped apart.

I screamed.

I could feel him smile.

He gave twisted laugh.

I stopped screamed.

I focused.

I charged.

Knocking him to the ground.

I whistled.

Grabbing his head.

I smashed it to the ground.

My hands felt icy.

There was screaming.

The people were being slaughtered.

I heard something else.

There was singing.

There was shrieking.

The other Hunters were screaming.

The witches were attacking.

That's what the dancing was.

The Hunter whacked me off him.

I heard a horse.

The Hunter paused.

He screamed at me.

Whipping out his hand.

I jumped up.

Jumping into the air.

I landed on my horse.

I rushed away.

Leaving the Hunters to the witches.

CHAPTER 6

Commander Coleman took a long deep breath of the fresh, crisp air with hints of dry pine as he walked into the small ruined town.

Coleman hadn't been here before but he already knew that he wanted to be done with this place. The town was a small dusty ruined place with the rows of wooden houses infected with mould and damp and most of them were falling apart.

Even the semi-circle of houses that faced the entrance to the town was half destroyed. Coleman felt a wave of unease wash over him as he walked further.

Feeling the soft sandy ground crumble under his feet, Coleman focused on the surroundings and hoped this wasn't a trap of some sort.

It still bought Coleman comfort that he was wearing his large, thick grey armour that covered his entire body. Coleman didn't want to wear the helmet, it messed up his longish black hair.

As Coleman stopped in the centre of the circle of

houses, he noticed there were already a ring of guards stepping out of the half destroyed houses.

A part of Coleman wanted to laugh at the idea of calling them guards, they looked like young adults they were given a sword and sometimes a bow and told how to fire it. These weren't soldiers or guards.

If he was as callous as some of his friends, Coleman might have wanted to say these were hardly the people he wanted to help the Rebellion. But he hardly had a choice, if the Overlord was sending an army to kill them all. Then Coleman knew he couldn't be choosy about who he picked.

Hearing the guards click and mutter to themselves, Coleman tried to understand it but he couldn't. He remembered something about the clicking language of a northern tribe but he never learnt it. He didn't need to.

Yet as Coleman heard a few more clicks and the clicks getting faster and faster, he wished he had learnt.

Everything fell silent as Coleman smiled at a large heavy set man walking towards him. The Lord Baron Huin was a large man wearing thick leather armour that was far too small for him.

Coleman hoped the Lord Baron had better armour for when the Overlord came. The Baron couldn't last five minutes wearing that excuse of armour. But Coleman knew he was far too kind to say it.

Subtly looking around Coleman frowned slightly

as he couldn't see the Assassin anywhere. He really wanted her to be here and Coleman wanted to see (and feel) her long black leather trench coat and cloak. She always looked amazing in it.

Focusing on the Lord Baron's large, bearded face, Coleman smiled and nodded his respect towards the Lord.

"Commander Coleman. It's been a while," Huin said, his voice deep but sickly.

Coleman noticed the guards were still walking towards him.

"Lord Baron it is an honour to see you,"

"I would hope so. You own me,"

Coleman's eyes narrowed. "For what?"

"You costed me two thousand coins boy!"

Coleman shrugged. He had no clue what the Lord Baron was talking about. The guards were still getting closer.

"Last time we met. We raided a warehouse,"

Coleman frowned deepened. He knew where this was going. He remembered.

"Then you, Commander Coleman, burned all the fabrics and explosives and more!"

"That warehouse had to be destroyed,"

"Why! So you could save the innocent? I need to sell things and make money,"

"You would have sold it straight back to the Overlord,"

The Lord Baron smiled. "Given the right price of course. There are no sides in this war. Only money,"

Coleman spat on the ground. "That is where we are different. I want to protect the innocent. You want to kill them if it makes you money,"

The guards stopped a few metres from him.

"Coleman not all of us can live for free or live off pity donations,"

"Pity donations? People give us things because we are right. We want to make a difference,"

Huin and the guards busted out laughing.

"Coleman, people give you things because they pity the stupidity of your cause,"

A tiny part of Coleman wanted to nod at that. He knew the few free tribes that roamed the Kingdom thought his mission was silly and pointless. Even the Cities the Rebellion had claimed and freed didn't want the Rebellion there.

And that was something Coleman could never understand. He couldn't understand how people could allow themselves to be enslaved, tortured, forced to do horrific things and be okay with it.

"I will not stop trying to save them," Coleman said.

The Lord Baron nodded and waved away the Guards.

"One day you're values and your naivety will kill you,"

Coleman nodded. "That day maybe today or tomorrow, old friend,"

The Lord Baron walked up to Coleman. "You need by help, don't you?"

Coleman was about to speak but the Guards looked at something.

The Guards shouted.

They charged over to the entrance.

Coleman spun.

His eyes narrowed.

There was something coming for them.

The Guards aimed their arrows.

Then stopped.

Coleman cocked his head as he saw a strong brown horse ride into the small town without a rider.

He felt a blade against his throat and he smiled.

"You took your time, Assassin," Coleman said.

Feeling the blade leave his throat, Coleman turned around and his mouth almost dropped as he looked at the Assassin's long beautiful brown hair that looked so perfect and life filled.

Coleman felt his mouth drop slightly as he looked at her smooth, round, perfect face with her deep rich emerald eyes that he would happily get lost in. And he loved her black trench coat too.

Knowing that his beautiful Assassin was here, Coleman couldn't help but smile and imagine a time fighting side by side with her, and hopefully saving the Rebellion.

Then the question always would be, after that was done, would she want to stay around him? Or would she leave?

CHAPTER 7

As I took my cold blade away from Coleman's throat as he slowly turned around and smiled. Of course, he probably thought he was being careful and subtle in his love for me. But he really, really wasn't.

He must have loved the fact I had pulled down my black leather hood so my long brown hair covered my long black leather trench coat for to see. Some might say it was petty of me to make sure Coleman could see me. But a small part of me wanted to be admired, and it wanted to only be admired by Coleman.

Breathing in the fresh, crisp air with a hint of dry pine leaves, I have to admit he's great to look at too. But I'm naturally a lot better at containing my affection, the last thing I wanted was to give the Lord Baron a weakness to use against us. I wasn't having that!

But as I stared at Coleman's thick wonderful armour, I almost smiled at the memories of that amazing v-cut body beneath and those muscles. And I suppose his strong jawline and square face is another great feature of his.

As much as I didn't want to admit it, he was beautiful.

Making myself forget about him, I turn to face the overweight, ugly Lord Baron Huin, he hardly looked impressed to see me but I hardly cared. It would take me a second to chop off his head.

It would only take me an extra to spill his guts but I didn't want to ruin his horrific black leather armour. It was ugly, and against me, well, it would hardly offer him protection.

Feeling the soft sandy ground beneath me, I made a mental note about the ground in case I needed it. From past experience, I knew throwing sandy soil in people's eyes was effective. Forcing it down their throat, even more so.

As I subtly looked at the young guards dressed in rags that were eyeing me up and down, I put my little dagger away and I placed my hands on the warm hilts of my long swords. The young guards seemed to smile.

If I was a rude assassin, I probably would have called them out on their want for a challenge and called them stupid, for wanting to fight me. But I pretend to be polite most of the time.

Listening to the guards' click and mutter, I smiled at them as I heard them planning something. These pathetic guards probably didn't realise it was the

Temple of Assassins that created the clicking language and its various offshoots.

"It's nice to see you again," Coleman said.

It was times like this that I wished the Temple had let me keep most of humanity and my emotions. A normal person would have acted on the emotion in his voice, but I wanted to roll my eyes. I didn't have time for his affection.

I ignored him. "Baron, has Coleman told you the situation,"

"No, I was about to but that's when you arrived," Coleman said.

The guards clicked a little more. Something about an attack.

"I killed one of the Overlord's Puppet Kings. He told me the Overlord is sending an army to destroy the Rebellion. They're using the City of Death as a staging ground," I said.

The guards stopped clicking.

"And why do you both want me?"

"Because Huin, you have men and women. Fighters. We need them all," Coleman said.

I was a little impressed that he sounded forceful with that comment.

"What makes you think I will fight for the Rebellion? And you Assassin, what's your stake in this?" Huin asked.

I opened my mouth to speak but I closed it. I didn't know what I could say, I was an assassin who went around slaughtering targets for money. I couldn't say I was doing this out of the good of my black heart. I do have a reputation to protect.

So I said the only thing that sounded natural.

"Ask me again and I'll gut you," I said.

The Guards clicked a little faster. Something about prey. My hands tightened on my swords.

"Tell me, Assassin, Coleman, how many soldiers do you think the Overlord has?"

I shrugged. This wasn't my concern.

"We don't know but if they're using the City of Death then it's probably a few thousand," Coleman said.

"Exactly, Coleman. You actually think you can win. Flee. Go now. Leave your mountain and fight another day,"

I stepped forward. "What are you afraid of Huin? The once great Lord Baron, Ruler of the Huinian Kingdom and Family Ruler,"

As the Lord Baron's eyes narrowed and I saw rage build within him, I couldn't help but think about the Overlord and all the destruction he had done when he first took over the area fifty years ago. I was glad I wasn't alive to see that bloodshed.

I stared at Huin. "You had the choice to become a Puppet King for the Overlord. You could have ruled your region and lived. Why give it up?"

Huin's eyes widened, and I saw something in them. Conflict.

The guards started clicking more and more. Something about death and destruction and devastation.

"We have to go!" I shouted.

I grabbed Coleman.

We ran for my horse.

The three shadowy Hunters appeared.

All the guards and Hunters pointed their swords at us. I wasn't going to fight them all just yet.

Turning to face that traitorous Huin, I asked a simple question, my voice cold and flat and a bit psychotic.

"Why?"

"Because I never left the Overlord. I was given a higher purpose. Long live the Overlord!"

"Long Live the Overlord!" the guards shouted.

CHAPTER 8

Coleman stared at all the shiny swords pointing at him and his beautiful Assassin as they were surrounded by guards and now three shadowy Hunters.

His eyes widened as he looked at the Hunters, he couldn't believe how these things existed. Half human, half demon sounded made up but as he stared at their black shadowy faces and cloaks. Coleman knew they were real.

He knew they would kill him given the chance.

Taking a deep breath of the fresh air filled with the smell of dry pine leaves, Coleman felt the soft cold sandy ground under him. He needed to be prepared to move and run.

Coleman knew he couldn't afford to slip or fall during their escape. He had to be ready, his Assassin would be so he had to be ready. Coleman wasn't going to look like a fool in front of her.

As he turned to face that disgraceful Lord Baron

Huin, Coleman spat at him. Coleman always knew he had hated Huin, he was useless at the end of the day.

And it actually didn't surprise Coleman that Huin was working for the Overlord. It made sense why Huin got so annoyed at him for burning the explosives and other supplies.

Listening to the guards clicking and the cool wind gently howl past, Coleman placed his hand on his sword. But the Assassin's leathered gloved hands stopped him.

He knew the touch was through gloves, but it still made his stomach fill with butterflies.

He had to protect her.

"How much?" the Assassin asked.

Coleman wanted to kick himself at the Assassin asking that. He was the leader of the Rebellion and according to almost everyone he was the greater mind when it came to these things. So Coleman knew he should have asked that simple question first, he had to focus. He needed to act how he normally did, confident and firm.

"This wasn't about money Assassin. It's about the truth. The Truth you will die and the Rebellion will fail,"

The Assassin grinned at that. Coleman hoped she didn't think of him as a failure and a doomed cause.

"As I said Coleman, there are no sides. The Overlord is supreme and must be worshipped,"

Coleman laughed at that. "You really are deluded old friend,"

The Assassin looked around.

"No Coleman, it is you who are fooled. You cannot win. The Overlord will lead the charge and you will dead by his righteous hand,"

My eyes narrowed. "What? The Overlord has left the Capital for the first time in thirty years,"

Huin nodded.

Coleman looked away from the Lord Baron, he couldn't understand this. The Overlord was meant to be this god amongst men, a slaughterer, a butcherer, a master of arms. Coleman couldn't let his Rebels face him, they would die. Something Coleman couldn't allow. He had to do something.

The Assassin looked around.

"Baron Huin. Where is he?" she asked.

"The City of Death,"

Coleman was about to speak but he noticed the air behind him felt colder than before. He turned around and frowned when he saw the Hunters were getting closer to them.

Placing his hand firmly on his sword, Coleman said.

"Tell them to back off,"

Huin laughed. "I don't control them. I wouldn't dare offend the Will of the Overlord,"

The Lord Baron knelt on the floor and bowed to the Hunters. Seeing the Assassin was licking her lips at the kneeling Huin, Coleman hated to think what she was planning.

"Assassin dearest, are you done scheming?"

"In a moment," the Assassin said.

Coleman looked at the traitorous Baron and he was a little surprised Huin didn't seem concerned by that simple question. Was he really that silly?

The Assassin's eyes narrowed. "Huin, how did the Hunters know we were coming? You would have turned us in any way. But even you wouldn't have the Hunters come here,"

Coleman rolled his eyes as he saw Huin given a slight nod, to Coleman that added to the weirdness of it. Why would Huin fight for the Overlord if he was so scared of him?

"The Hunters grabbed the bird you sent. They read the note, not changing it and sent the Rebellion another bird,"

The Assassin smiled and nodded.

Coleman looked at her. "Done now?"

"Of course," she said smiling. "Ready?"

The Hunters tensed.

Coleman nodded.

The Assassin rammed her sword into Huin.

His corpse fell forward.

Coleman whipped out his sword.

Charging at the Hunters.

He jumped on one.

Icy pain shot into him.

He slammed his fists into one.

The Assassin slaughtered the guards.

They screamed.

Their bodies shattered.

Their blood gushed out.

Coleman jumped up.

Swinging his sword.

The Hunter met it.

Lightning shot out.

Coleman's sword glowed.

He jumped back.

The Hunters charged.

The Assassin grabbed him.

They ran to the horse.

The air buzzed.

It crackled.

Lightning shot towards them.

The ground exploded.

Kicking up sand.

Coleman covered his eyes.

He tripped.

Falling to the ground.

He opened his eyes.

The Assassin kept running.

The Hunters touched him.

Coleman screamed in agony.

Crippling pain filled him.

He felt his soul being drained.

Coleman swung his sword.

Slicing a Hunter.

The Hunter shrieked.

The air crackled.

Coleman swung it as hard as he could.

It sliced into the shadow.

The Hunter fell.
The other two released him.
Coleman rushed forward.
The Assassin rode to him.
Grabbing him.
Throwing him over the horse.
The Hunters screamed.
The air crackled.
They were gone.

CHAPTER 9

I love watching.

Some people would say that I watch too much or for too long before moving on them. I disagree as I know these people clearly aren't assassins or they're only wanna be assassins, I remember at the Temple of Assassins that the longest a Master Assassin had waited and watched before killing a target was five years. I don't think I would watch for that long, but watching is critical.

Staring out over the massive grey sandstone valley between our mountain and the City of Death, my eyes narrowed and I blocked out all the sounds around me, from the singing of birds as the sun set to the rustling that Coleman was making.

A part of me wanted to talk to him but I oddly enough felt nervous about it. Just the thought of having a real conversation with that beautiful, handsome man made a drop of sweat roll down my back.

I know it's stupid and I know I shouldn't be like this but it's happening. This is why I like to work alone and I hate working with other people, because sometimes these other people are beautiful, handsome and stunning.

And I don't need them distracting me from my work.

Focusing on the City of Death ahead, I understood why it was perfect for mining. The massive black rocky hill in the middle of the valley shone slightly in the dying sunlight, it was rich in ore that was a fact.

I moaned under my breath as I couldn't see anything more than that. I hated how the City of Death was a City inside a black rocky hill. The only thing I could see of the City was the top of a spire. Maybe a Church, maybe a watchtower. I couldn't tell.

Breathing in the cold, crisp evening air, I pulled my long black leather trench coat and cloak over me tight. The last thing I wanted was to be remembered as the best assassin who didn't die from a blade or a bow, but died by freezing on a mountain.

I felt Coleman walk up to me before he stopped about a metre from me. I didn't need to turn around to see he was probably considering whether or not he should comfort me or hug me for warmth.

A part of me wondered if I wanted it, Coleman was handsome and he did have large strong muscles that were probably very warm. But could I allow him to see me vulnerable? What if he tried to kill me?

I almost laughed at myself but I remembered a game or mission we played through our years at the

Temple. We were to get with people we found attractive then try to kill them when the time was right, and if we died or we killed them we won the game, and the dead one wasn't a worthy assassin.

That was fun! Twisted but fun!

As I knew I was being silly and acting strange, I was about to turn around but Coleman sat next to me. He looked so handsome in his thick, heavy metal armour but I stared into the deep emerald eyes and I relaxed. I felt... safe. The first time in a long time.

"Thanks for saving me again," Coleman said.

I smiled. "You didn't do so bad. You saved yourself sort of,"

As bad as that must have sounded (I knew it sounded cold) Coleman didn't seem upset or put off.

"I felt something was off so I was glad to get your note,"

"Coleman, please I know you want to say something,"

He took a deep breath.

"I've missed you,"

A small part of me wanted to say the same but I couldn't get the idea of him wanting more from me out of my head. I liked Coleman a lot and he was handsome but I couldn't deal with those feelings right now. I had to complete my mission and save the innocent rebels that (damn them) I care about.

"I missed you too but I am an Assassin,"

"So?"

"Coleman, I kill people. You lead them. nothing

can ever happen between us,"

I rolled my eyes as I realised that went from letting him down gently to throwing him away quickly.

Coleman smiled. "So you do have feelings for me?"

For some reason I smiled at his question, he wasn't giving up on this strange fantasy of his and I respected that.

Coleman leant in closer to me. I wasn't going to move away, a part of me wanted Coleman just for a moment, just so I could always have this memory of a kiss before I forced myself to go back to my assassin ways.

But that wasn't fair on him, he wanted a moment to happen and last forever. I couldn't hurt Coleman like that, he was too good of a man for that.

I pulled away.

"Coleman, I'm not going to ask that,"

He nodded, a little sadness in his eyes, but he seemed okay.

Looking out over the valley, I pointed towards the City of Death with little fires lighting it up now as night descended.

"We need to check it out," Coleman said.

I was a little surprised by his bravery at that suicidal mission, but I respected him.

"If the Overlord's there. He'll be guarded," I said.

"I'm not worried about the Overlord. We need

to know what we're dealing with,"

"Wait, you don't want to kill the Overlord. This is the first shot the Rebellion's had in thirty years,"

Coleman nodded and shrugged.

"Fine, Coleman. We'll do a quick sweep and escape back to the rebel base," I said.

Watching those deep emerald eyes nod and agree with me, we stood up and started to ride down the mountain.

I just didn't have the heart to tell him I was an assassin and I never miss an opportunity to kill someone. Even the Overlord.

CHAPTER 10

Commander Coleman crouched as him and the Assassin advanced in the City of Death. When they stopped behind a large boulder Coleman looked around, he wanted to study every detail.

He wasn't impressed that the two of them were deep within the City of Death without any help. Coleman hated the look of the sharp, rough black rocks all around them.

The odd thing about the City of Death was, it was the only City in the Kingdom to be built inside a mountain that Coleman wondered whether it was a dormant volcano. Since most of the City was inside a large dip in the mountain.

That fact still didn't make Coleman feel any better as he focused on the sharp, rough black rocks that formed the slopes. He hated the idea of slipping and the sharp rocks ripping into his flesh.

Breathing in the freezing cold air with hints of coal and smoke, Coleman popped his head out from the boulder and studied their surroundings. He cocked his head as he realised there was no one here.

The sounds of a fire roaring in the distance, probably one of the distant tunnels, was the only sound here. Considering there was meant to be thousands of angry Overlord men here, it was too quiet and empty.

Coleman's eyes narrowed as he looked on the large patch of smooth flat black stone that made some kind of floor at the bottom of the dip, with nothing else there except a wooden hut in the middle.

A small part of Coleman wanted to go inside but something felt very off. It made no sense for the army not to be here with all the intelligence and information saying so. It made even less sense to Coleman why the Overlord would tell all his men one thing, but keep the actual army in another location.

The army had to be here. But they weren't.

Coleman placed a hand on the icy cold hilt of his sword and took a freezing cold breath again. He was going to be prepared.

Turning his head slightly, Coleman looked at his beautiful Assassin crouching there in her beautifully long black leather trench coat and black hood. Coleman loved it how she was almost invisible in the darkness.

For a moment he remembered what she had said to him about a relationship. Coleman smiled at her confessing (in a weird way) she had feelings for him and that had filled him with happiness. He had been wanting to hear that for so long.

Now he just needed to convince her it was okay if they got together and it wasn't some weakness to be used against her. And Coleman also wondered what her name was, it had to be a beautiful name knowing her and she had never told anyone.

Hearing the Assassin move into the open, Coleman carefully followed and he whipped out his sword. He followed her to the wooden hut as she inspected it.

Coleman wanted to kick him, he knew she wouldn't come here for a quick scouting mission like he ordered. If it was anyone else, he would have been firmer and he would have left now. But Coleman knew he cared about the Assassin too much and now he feared it might come back to bite him.

Seeing the bright orange light of fire at the end of a nearby tunnel, Coleman felt his stomach tighten. This was too close for comfort, one sound and Coleman knew the enemy would hear.

"What are you doing?" Coleman asked, his voice barely audible.

"I'm doing my job,"

"No your job is to-"

"Coleman I am an assassin. I kill people,"

"If the Overlord is in there let's be prepared,"

The Assassin shook her head.

"Assassin this is not an argument. We are leaving," Coleman said, firmly.

The Assassin stopped and slowly turned to him.

As Coleman stared into her cold, dark eyes he felt a drop of sweat run down his forehead.

"You're. Ordering. Me?"

Coleman had to stand up to her. He was not a coward.

"Yes. We are leaving. We have what we-"

The Assassin slapped him.

"I am not yours Coleman. I am not one of your Rebels. I am not your girlfriend. I am not property. I thought you were different,"

Coleman felt his spirit and body lower a little as he listened to those words, at first he thought the Assassin was taunting or mocking his feelings for her, but as he listened to her words they weren't mocking or judgemental. They were truly sad with an edge of disappointment.

As he watched the Assassin scout out the rest of the wooden hut, Coleman wanted to kick himself hard. He wasn't the bossy, overprotective type, he always worked with his friends.

Coleman walked over to the Assassin. "I'm sorry,"

The Assassin was silent.

"I didn't mean to be overprotective,"

The Assassin hissed.

"I-"

Rocks fell down the slopes.

Coleman looked up. Shadows were moving.

He raised his sword.

The Assassin jumped up.

Swords raised.

The sound of tens upon tens of heavily armed men and women marching out of the tunnels made Coleman roll his eyes as him and the Assassin lowered their weapons.

They both knew it was useless fighting this many warriors but as the warriors surrounded them and took their weapons.

Coleman's stomach twisted and sweat dropped off him as he saw a tall man in thin glowing silver armour.

The Overlord had come.

CHAPTER 11

My mouth dropped as I stared at the tall angelic man who walked towards us. I could only stare as I looked at his smooth youthful skin and his killer smile that would make women fall over him and straight men gay. His long blond hair was stunning and I felt all energy from my body leave me.

Of course, as soon as I realised this, I stopped thinking like a common woman and instead my assassin training kicked in. I wasn't sure what magic this idiot was using, but it was powerful I'll give him that.

I wasn't a fan was of thin silver glowing armour. I would probably guess it was a combination of normal steel armour and some kind of magical blend. I doubted my swords would pierce it, so I'm afraid I might have to leave him.

I so badly wanted to smash his skull in.

Turning my attention to the guards and warriors, I smiled at each of them as I looked at their thick grey armour and their longswords, bows and even something called a crossbow.

This killing was going to be fun.

My smile deepened as I noticed the sharp black rocks on the slopes of the City of Death, I wouldn't object to ripping someone's flesh on them.

The sounds of clicking and metal moving made me shook my head, I couldn't believe no one knew that the clicking language was made by the Temple of Assassins. Ridiculous!

Staring at the warriors, I clocked their eyes were wide and focused. They were scared of me and I loved that. So to show how contempt I was, I took a long freezing cold breath (almost coughed at the hints of smoke) and breathed it out. Forming a long column of vapour, as simple as it sounds I smiled as the warriors took a tiny step back.

The Overlord clapped his hands.

The warriors pointed their swords at us.

They advanced.

As we walked backwards I heard some fool open the door to the wooden hut, I hadn't noticed the door was iron before. We walked into the hut and the door slammed shut with a heavy click of the lock.

I ignored the wooden hut for the most part. It was a small empty wooden room with rough wooden walls.

Instead I focused on the iron door and I stared at the three bars running across the top forming a window of sorts.

The Overlord stepped in front and smiled. That stupid killer smile, I was definitely going to slice that smile open at some point.

"At Jasmine you are safe," the Overlord said.

My heart dropped and my mouth fell to the floor as he said my name. The name only I truly knew, well, there was a reason he knew but I hated him.

If I could, my hands would shoot through these bars and rip his throat out right now.

"Jasmine?" Coleman asked.

I wasn't even going to look at that beautiful idiot who felt so overprotective of me like I was his property.

"Oh yes Commander Coleman, Jasmine is her name. Didn't she tell you? She probably didn't even tell you I'm her father,"

My eyes widened as he dared to speak those words. I was going to shred his skin one day.

"You are not my father. You threw me in a river. My family is not you,"

The Overlord smiled at that. It took everything I had not to lash out.

"I am still your father. I raised you for a month before I threw you in that river. It's a shame you didn't drown but here we are,"

I could feel Coleman coming closer to me. If he hugged me, I swear to the gods I'll punch him. (I didn't want to though, I didn't want to slap him either)

"Jasmine, your adoptive parents and brothers and

sisters are dead. The parents burned screaming out your name as they tried to warn you I was coming,"

My eyes narrowed.

"And well, you know what happened to your true brother and your adoptive sisters,"

I walked straight up to the metal bars. "Why kill us? Why threw us in the river?"

The Overlord pressed his head against the bars. Our noses touched.

"Because… it was fun,"

I chomped his nose off.

Spitting it on the ground.

The Overlord shot back.

Laughing.

The bastard was laughing!

I looked at Coleman for a brief moment, a small part of me wanted to just fall into his strong muscular arms and kiss him.

But as I looked at him, he wasn't staring at me. those beautiful bright emerald eyes were narrowed and rageful as he stared at the Overlord.

Maybe he wasn't completely head over heels in love with me (thankfully) and maybe he could function around me. That would be nice.

"Commander Coleman, Jasmine, I presume you are both wondering why the City is so empty,"

"You threw them in the river?" I asked.

The Overlord wiped another stream of blood from his nose and smiled.

"Three thousand men. That is the number that is

heading for your Rebels,"

I wanted to smash his head in even more now. The Rebels couldn't defend against that number. Then a silly wave of emotion washed over me as I remembered why I was trapped here in this wooden hut, because I cared about them and their cause. I knew I was going to help them no matter what, I just had to get out of here first.

As the Overlord started to walk away, the Overlord said a final thing, I hated how cold and flat his voice was.

"And thank the traitor for me. I look forward to using your tunnels,"

I turned to Coleman and my eyebrows rose as I saw his face turn deadly white and cold, fearful sweat dropped down his face. (Not very sexy but this wasn't a sexy moment)

"What is it?" I asked.

"The tunnels lead them into the heart of the base. If they get to the tunnels, we'll lose before the battle begins,"

Listening to beautiful Coleman said that didn't make me nervous or scared, it made me excited. I always loved a challenge, and unlike Coleman, my bastard father and their little toy soldiers, I loved impossible odds and at the end of the day, war was a game.

So let the games begin and let the sword fall.

CHAPTER 12

Commander Coleman stared at the chunk of the Overlord's nose that laid on the cold, rocky ground as he tried not to panic. He couldn't believe there was a traitor in the Rebellion, he loved every one of those Rebels like they were his family. The idea of one of them being a traitor was disgraceful.

Looking over to his beautiful Assassin, Coleman knew for a fact that if she didn't get to the traitor before him, he would end the traitor. Hopefully, in a way that make Jasmine proud but as long as the traitor died Coleman didn't care.

As he stared at the Assassin's beautiful black leather trench coat and black cloak, Coleman couldn't understand her past. He never in a million years would have thought she was the Overlord's biological daughter, and that her name was Jasmine. It was a beautiful name perfect for the beautiful woman it belonged to, but Coleman wasn't sure it was the most Assassin-y name.

Taking a breath of the freezing cold air that reminded him of eating roasted hog in the snowy mountains a few years ago, Coleman looked around for a way to escape, they had to get out of here and warn the Rebellion and warn them about the tunnels.

Coleman frowned as all he saw were cold, unloved wooden walls and that ugly heavy iron door. They were unarmed and Coleman felt like an utter failure, he was a failure.

For his entire life since his father had passed on the cause to him (He didn't even know his father was alive until he rescued Coleman from the City of Pleasure), Coleman had fought the Overlord, killed his men and fought every ally the Overlord had. But as he stood in that cold wooden hut, a small part of him knew it was all for nothing. Coleman took a deep cold breath as he realised he was never going to escape and all his friends would die, even worse the Kingdom would never be free of the Overlord's taint. They would all be doomed.

Then Coleman's frowned deepened when he stared at the utterly stunning and beautiful Jasmine, who was looking at something near the door, if there were any gods or goddesses all Coleman would ask is if they would take him instead of her.

Coleman didn't want Jasmine to die.

The sounds of the wind howling across the City of Death made Coleman shiver a little. He stood up to go to the Assassin and-

A massive roar ripped through the City.

Three men screamed.

Coleman stopped and looked at the Assassin. As he saw she wasn't bothered, Coleman shrugged and went over to her.

"Are you done with your pity party?" Jasmine asked.

"Yes. But it wasn't a pity party I was planning our escape,"

She laughed. "Sure you were. Help me with the door,"

Coleman cocked his head as he saw the Assassin had cracked the wooden frame slightly. He smiled at her brilliance, he never would have thought of that. Why try and break through steel when you can break the frame instead?

The Assassin took a few steps back. Coleman joined her. She nodded.

They charged into the door.

It cracked.

They charged again.

It cracked louder.

They looked at each other.

They flew at the door.

The wood snapped.

The weight of the door did the rest.

The door smashed to the ground.

Coleman stormed out.

Checking the surroundings, but they stopped and Coleman's mouth dropped slightly when he saw two shredded bodies of guards. Their skulls were shattered. Their flesh flayed.

Coleman went over to them and picked up their swords and two for the Assassin. She nodded her thanks.

A roar ripped through the City.

More people screamed.

The Assassin ran up the slopes.

Coleman followed her.

A claw grabbed him.

He swung his sword.

Something shrieked.

Coleman looked.

A massive scaly bear stared at him.

The bear attacked.

It roared.

Coleman ran.

The bear whacked him to the ground.

Coleman swung.

Slashing the Bear.

Green blood splashed everywhere.

Covering Coleman's legs.

The Bear flew at him.

Slicing into him.

Rich red blood poured out.

The Bear rose up.

Exposing its underbelly.

Coleman slashed.

He rammed his sword into it.

Nothing happened.

The underbelly was armoured.

Coleman swore.

The bear stomped.

Coleman rolled.

The Bear slashed his back.

Destroying Coleman's armour.

Coleman spun.

Jumping up.

The Bear swung.

Coleman swung.

Slicing off the Bear's hand.

The Bear shrieked.

Green blood gushed out.

It fell to the ground.

Coleman thrusted his sword into the Bear's skull.

Twisting it.

Allowing the icy cold air to wrap around his body, he heard someone clapping at him and he looked at the smiling Assassin. Coleman gave her a bow and she smiled.

As he started to walk up the sharp, deadly slopes of the City of Death, at least he now knew why the City was called what it was, but most importantly he had made his beautiful Assassin smile. That was too precious for words.

Maybe there was a possible future, but first Coleman had to warn the Rebellion and defeat an army.

CHAPTER 13

After I whistled for my horse and we rode back to the rebels, and personally I was amazed at how slow the Overlord's army was but as I watched and remembered how strict they were on keeping their so-called perfect formations. I understood why they were so slow, if one person was slow then everyone else had to be slow to keep their *perfect* formation.

As I sat on a cold black leather chair I allowed it to mould to my body and relax a little, as I focused on the other people that were sat around the large wooden table in front of us.

I forget what Coleman had called this room we were in but I didn't like it. I hated the coldness and soullessness of it with its smooth yellow rock walls and white ceiling. It wasn't exactly what I expected from a group of Rebels that had lived here for over forty years.

Breathing in the smells of fake perfumes and sweat and body odour and listening to the sounds of the people talk, mutter and moan at each other, I knew straight away these other people sitting with me were true rebels, or at least Rebels that were high ranking.

I made sure I pulled my black leather trench coat tight and made sure my face was well and truly covered by my black hood, then I started to do what I did best.

Study people.

Looking at each of their faces, I guessed all I would have to do to kill each one would be a quick slice of my blades across their throats. It wouldn't take much and I was glad Coleman wasn't a mind reader, but these thoughts were necessary considering there's a traitor here.

My eyes narrowed on each of them and I made sure I studied their faces. I presume the first two mortals I looked at were sisters with their blond perfectly straight hair, I never liked people who tried too hard to look good.

When I turned to the other man at the table my eyes narrowed as much as they could as I noticed the man with his black beard and scars was staring at me. How dare someone stare at me, who does he think he is?

The sounds of their talking and annoying voices stopped as beautiful Commander Coleman with his amazing bright emerald eyes started catching them up on the situation.

I have to give him credit where it's due, it actually made the story sound gripping filled with slaughter and adventure. Of course the slaughter was all done by me, and with each detail of me ramming my sword into someone, the more concerned looks I got.

Normally I would growl or do something to make these fools scared of me but at that moment all I cared about was looking at Coleman. Admiring his smooth amazing face and trying to catch glimpses of those amazing emerald eyes.

"Coleman this assassin shouldn't be in here. She's a murderer, a threat to us, we need to stop her and-"

I raised a warning gloved finger to her. "I promised myself I wouldn't kill any Rebels. So don't tempt me,"

"Listen to her Barbic," Coleman said.

Barbic. Interesting name, I needed to remember that for later.

"Come on bossie what tha plan?"

"Abbic, it's simple. Gather the forces outside the mountain and we'll fight there. I don't want them anywhere near the base," Coleman said.

I nodded, I supposed it was a good plan but I needed to think of something. As much as I love these Rebels and Coleman (of course), my faith in their fighting abilities was limited to say the least, I just had to find a weakness in the enemy.

"That a good plan boss,"

"Thank you, Dragnist. Did you block the tunnels like I asked?"

Dragnist nodded but I hated how he kept staring at me, then as he licked his lips I knew exactly why he was staring at me. I don't know what it is with men with assassins. Half of them are turned off, half of them are very turned on.

They're a nightmare I swear.

"Bossie what ya gonna do about that campy," Abbic asked.

I leant forward. "What camp?"

Barbic rolled her eyes. "I told you she was useless,"

"Say that again and I'll prove how useless I am throwing a knife,"

Barbic rolled her eyes again. Part of me wondered if she was from a posh upper class family who thought everyone who wasn't upper class was trash, I certainly killed enough of those people before. It wouldn't surprise me if she thought like that.

"What camp?" I asked again.

"Well Missy whenever one of these armies pop along those bossies set up a massive campy like our base-y,"

My eyes narrowed on this Abbic character and I allowed my mouth to give a small smile.

"And if the Overlord was leading the attack he would be there right?"

"Course Missy. I bet ya money on it,"

My smile deepened as I imagined taking all her money because I knew for a fact the Overlord was long gone. I'm not sure how I know but leading an army to crush a little Rebel base, that didn't sound like a reason to leave the Capital for the first time in thirty years.

I truly think he left the Capital to trap me and see if this mysterious Assassin was his daughter. I… think that's why he did it.

Now I know the Overlord is my father (I always knew but it feels weird to have it confirmed), I don't know whether or not to hate myself. But whatever happens I will be the child that kills the father.

"Assassin something you want to share? Coleman asked with a massive beautiful smile.

"Will you all be able to draw up the battle plans with me?"

Coleman looked at the others. "Yes, but why?"

I looked at the ground then I managed to force myself to look at him.

"I have to go,"

"Typical, utterly useless. This almighty-"

I threw a knife at her.

The knife slammed just behind her ear.

Barbic went silent.

Turning my attention back to the beautiful Coleman, I had no idea it was going to be this difficult to say I wanted to leave and not see him for a day or two.

That's if I survived.

As much as I've hated his affection and how much he cares about me (I mean come on he's a bit possessive at times), I actually feel like I'm going to miss him.

Staring into those bright emerald eyes, I stepped

closer to him.

"I have to go to this camp. If there's someone in charge there. I have to assassinate him, it's the only way to keep you, the Rebels safe,"

I loved seeing Coleman smile at my words, his eyes softened and he looked like he wanted to kiss me. A small part of me wanted that too but I wouldn't kiss him in front of his... whatever these fools called themselves.

"Stay safe, Coleman. I need you when I return," I asked, not sure what I meant by that.

He smiled at me. "Stay safe yourself,"

Turning away and fighting away the urge to kiss him goodbye, I stormed out of the meeting and left those fools to plan their deaths.

Now I had to do my bit to make sure not all of them died.

CHAPTER 14

Commander Coleman's mouth dropped open as he felt the soft valley ground move under his feet and he looked straight ahead into the deadly jaws of the enemy.

He stared at three thousand angry, rageful soldiers march towards him, Coleman hated their cold black armour. The enemy wasn't moving slowly or quickly, they moved at a pace that allowed the Rebels' minds to lead them into a spiral of despair.

Coleman forced thoughts of his own death, the slaughter of his friends and the death of his Jasmine out of his mind.

He couldn't have those thoughts inside him, Coleman had to lead his people, even if it was to a mindless, pointless massacre.

Wearing his thick, perfectly shiny metal armour with his long sword and dagger, Coleman hoped he was ready for the fight of his lifetime. This wasn't a fight about freedom, their cause and defending the innocent.

It was a fight to stop their annihilation.

Breathing in a cold, icy breath of the piney valley air, Coleman took out his sword and pointed it into the sky. He didn't know why he did it, he just hoped it would inspire his Rebels.

The sounds of the enemy screaming and shouting filled the valley, Coleman could see his Rebels shake and shiver as they looked at the foe.

Coleman had no idea if they would win today but he had to try.

Looking at the surrounding sharp razor mountains lining the edges of the valley, Coleman hoped the enemy wasn't trying to outflank them, he had sent Rebels to guard the mountain passes but Coleman had a feeling their corpses were already being devoured by wolves and flies.

Staring dead ahead at the approaching army, Coleman felt his stomach twist as he worried about his friends but most of all Jasmine, he wouldn't have anything done against her.

But as Coleman stared with anger and rage at the enemy, he knew the only thing he could do to protect her, was to fight and try and buy her as much time as possible.

Coleman took a deep piney breath and he thrusted his sword into the air.

He charged.

A thousand rebels charged.

Rebel archers fired.

A storm of arrows rained down.
Stabbing into the foes.
Slashing at their flesh.
Lashing their armour.
Few corpses dropped.
Coleman kept charging.
A trumpet sounded.
The enemy charged.
Three thousand foes flew at them.
Coleman's heart thumped inside him.
He whipped out his dagger.
The two armies clashed.
They slaughtered each other.
Swords swung.
Cracking armour.
Cracking skulls.
Shattering bones.
Slicing into flesh.
Blood gushed out.
Limbs were severed.
Heads were chopped off.
Coleman charged forward.
Ramming his sword into a man.
Two foes swung at Coleman.
He ducked.
Jumping up.
Decapitating the two foes.
Coleman ducked again.
Three swords flew past.
Arrows flew down.

Stabbing the foes.

They fell.

Coleman jumped on their heads.

The enemy advanced.

Jumping into the air.

Firing crossbows.

Slaughtering Rebels.

Rebel chests exploded.

Coleman rolled his eyes.

The enemy landed.

Coleman rolled forward.

Thrusting the dagger into one chest.

He leapt up.

Swinging his sword in one bloody arc.

Slashed throats flooded out blood.

The corpses dropped.

Coleman looked around.

Hundreds of rebels were dead.

Their corpses smashed into the soil.

Rebels screamed.

Their blood turned the ground red.

Coleman ducked.

Slashing the chest of an enemy.

Enemy archers fired.

Coleman ran.

Arrows slammed around him.

He heard the arrows scream towards him.

Rebels screamed in agony.

Pain crippled them.

Coleman knew he had to go.

This battle was lost.

He had to retreat.

An arrow touched his ear.

Coleman spun.

An archer chased him.

Coleman stopped.

Throwing a dagger.

The archer's head split.

Coleman ran.

He ordered his forces back.

This was a stupid idea.

He had to fight the enemy inside the base.

More rebels screamed.

Their bodies ripped open.

Their guts pouring out.

Over five hundred Rebels laid dead at Coleman's feet.

CHAPTER 15

My feet silently moved over the hard rough black mountain as I advanced toward my target. I knew the enemy weren't going to set up camp nearby so I had to ride for another hour then I travelled the rest of the way on foot.

Stopping, I pulled my long black leather trench coat and black hood over myself as I smiled. I loved the pathetic look of their little military camp with their bright white and red canvas tents.

As I stared at it from the mountain top, the hot sun beamed down on me but the cold icy wind destroyed that heat quickly. I loved the cold.

My smile deepened as my eyes narrowed on my target, I couldn't believe how pathetic the enemy had been. It's one thing to send three thousand soldiers to destroy some (equally pathetic) Rebels but it's another thing to leave your main camp unprotected.

My eyes scanned the large white and red canvas tents with them neatly organised in neat rows upon rows. It was easily large enough for four thousand soldiers.

I wouldn't be surprised if the Overlord sent a thousand warriors to secure the mountain passages.

Listening to the screaming and shouting in the distance I knew the battle had begun but as silly as it sounded drops of sweat rolled down my spine.

Before this City of Death business, I would have called it a weakness or me being silly. But now I know it's because I care, not just about the so-called cause and my beautiful Coleman with his amazing emerald eyes, but because I feel like I have a… family there.

Discounting that Barbic woman, they like me and respect me, that's all I want. Maybe I could stay there when this is all over. Maybe.

Looking at the massive white and red tent in the middle of the camp, I silently leant forward as I tried to study it. It was some kind of major tent of course but I couldn't tell if the Overlord or anyone important was inside.

Then I remembered one simple fact. There were enough supplies here for four thousand soldiers, even if there wasn't a major pawn of the Overlord inside, that didn't matter.

If the camp was destroyed, let's say, by a horrific fire the enemy would be easy pickings. Especially without any sort of protection at night time.

I couldn't help but smile at the idea of slashing their throat as they slept. Oh yes, something was going to be done about these tents.

The sound of crackling fire made me turn my attention back to the military camp. My eyes narrowed as I saw those foul black armoured guards stand around little fire pits like they were perfectly safe and there were in no danger whatsoever.

A massive grin broke out on my face as I swore I was going to prove them very wrong indeed.

If they were going to slaughter the Rebels and turn the ground red with their blood. Then I suppose it's only fair if I do the same, right?

CHAPTER 16

Commander Coleman took a cold deep breath of the piney mountain air as he crouched waiting for the enemy to come.

He really hoped this wasn't going to be another silly choice on his part but he knew it had been right to fight the enemy in the open valley, this was the Rebel home base, Coleman wasn't going to let some ugly Overlord soldiers in there.

But now he had no choice.

His eyes narrowed on the cold hard black rocks below him as Coleman grabbed a rough rock in his hand. Looking at his friends around him, all in their leather and metal armour, Coleman prepared to smash the enemy with the rocks.

A small part of him knew this was useless but even if he only killed ten of the enemy then that was good. It meant ten less foes to kill his rebels. He didn't want any of them to die.

Coleman raised his head and nodded to the

rebels on the other side of the mini canyon that the enemy would have to walk through to get into the base. The other rebels smiled back, they were excited, Coleman was excited.

Remembering the other rebels boiling up some oil and other surprises to welcome the enemy, Coleman smile only deepened, victory was a certainty.

The strong smell of dry pine started to turn into the disgusting smell of sweat, blood and flesh. Coleman took a deep breath. The enemy were coming.

Listening to the sounds of excitement and hope of his friends all around him made Coleman hopeful of the battle ahead and-

Thick black armoured warriors stormed into the mini-canyon. Their swords and crossbows raised, ready to kill.

Coleman threw the stone.

It smashed into a head.

Crushing it.

Blood spattered up the rock.

The rebels attacked.

Launching rock after rock.

The enemy was slaughtered.

Their armour dented.

Their skulls smashed.

Their spirits melted.

Coleman smiled.

He picked up another rock.

He threw it.

The rock stopped.
It floated there.
It flew at Coleman.
He ducked.
His eyes widened.
Screams filled the air.
Coleman spun around.
Three black cloaked witches stormed at him.
Coleman whipped out his sword.
The witches laughed.
They shrieked.
Rebels charged at them.
Swinging their sword.
The witches twisted their hands.
Snapping the Rebels necks.
Coleman froze.
The witches gripped Coleman.
Coleman struggled.
He tried to scream.
He tried to warn the others.
All were useless.
The other rebels went to help.
The witches' eyes narrowed.
The rebels took out their swords.
Ramming them into their own chests.
The corpses smiled as they fell.
Coleman's blood boiled.
Rageful filled him.
How dare they!
Coleman roared.

Breaking free.

The witches' eyes widened.

Coleman charged.

The witches attacked.

Fireballs flew at Coleman.

Lightning shot at him.

Coleman kept charging.

He swung his sword.

Thrusting it into a witch.

The witch's corpse turned to smoke.

The other witches screamed in terror.

More rebels ran at the witches.

Coleman smiled.

Pots of boiling oil were coming.

The rebels threw the oil.

The witches thrusted out their hands.

Boiling oil stopped in the air.

Coleman ran over.

He knew what was going to happen.

The witches smiled.

Boiling hot oil splashed over the rebels.

Burning them.

They screamed in utter agony.

The witches waved their hands.

Throwing the rebels miles.

Shattering their bodies.

Coleman hated this.

He hated losing.

Coleman flew at the witches.

Torrents of fire licked his flesh.

Coleman kept charging.
The witches shot lightning at him.
He ducked.
The enemy were advancing.
Coleman heard their screams.
Coleman swung his sword.
A witch ducked.
The other didn't.
Slicing into her head.
The witch shrieked.
Coleman kicked her.
She fell to the ground.
Coleman slammed his sword into her throat.
Black blood gushed out.
An arm grabbed him.
Getting him into a headlock.
His neck burned.
The witch whispered ancient words.
Coleman hissed.
He whipped up his sword.
Slicing his own ear.
The witch gasped.
Her grip loosened.
Coleman whacked her.
Throwing her to the ground.
He charged over.
Stomping on her head.
Coleman ran towards the base.
It was filled with the enemy.
Rebel corpses laid everywhere.

The enemy hacked his friends apart.

Limbs littered the ground.

Coleman saw a mass of rebels tens of metres away.

They were protecting the door to the inner base.

He waved at them.

A sword swung at him.

Coleman ducked.

Slashing the throat of the enemy.

Coleman spun back.

The rebels had seen him.

They were retreating.

Rebels were pouring into the door of the base.

Coleman charged towards the rebels.

Every rebel was inside.

The door started to shut.

They wouldn't shut the door on him.

Coleman jumped over corpses.

He leapt over the enemy.

Swords swung at him.

Coleman dodged.

He kept running.

He didn't want to be trapped out here.

He had to go.

He had to survive.

He had to get inside.

CHAPTER 17

Making sure my entire body was covered in my long black leather trench coat and definitely making sure my black hood covered my face, I stepped into the main camp.

I made sure I looked confident and like I was meant to be here (that's the key with most infiltrations) as I slowly walked through the main camp.

Now I was here I didn't mine the large white and red canvas tents that were at least three metres tall, I wasn't expecting them to be that big. But I didn't see many soldiers thankfully.

Just in case, I placed my hands on the cold hilts of my swords to be on the safe side, as I continued to walk through the main camp I smelt warming hints of thick smoke and warn spices. Reminding me of the tastes of wild boar cooking over the flesh of some enemies I had years ago. That was a great night. (The guy made it even better)

Listening to the crackling of flames and distant talking of soldiers, I knew I wasn't alone but I never intended it to be. I was actually hoping this place would be crawling with ugly soldiers so I would have a worthy fight.

I stared ahead as I clocked the main tent tens of metres away, my eyes narrowed on its massive size as I focused on it. The size never truly bothered me but there being only one entrance, that did bother me.

A part of me wondered what if I slice into the canvas on the sides and walk in that way, but I forced that idea away as I realised that presented me with too many problems and unknowns.

Perhaps the only thing I hated more than the Overlord (my idiot of a father) was unknowns, in my line of work they were far, far too dangerous.

Which is another reason why I wanted to make sure this military camp was annihilated, with the camp destroyed the enemy wouldn't be able to ride back to the Overlord and by the time news of the mission had failed reached the Overlord, the rebels would have already moved their operations.

So I had, I absolutely had to find where they kept the explosives.

Out of the corner of my eye I noticed two black armoured guards walking towards me, they weren't looking at me but I knew the closer they got the more chance of them looking, and finding me suspicious,

If I was an amateur (which I am nowhere near) I probably would have changed course or run away, but that's so sloppy and to no surprise to me those assassins died far too quickly.

As I'm a professional I simply kept walking, standing straight and projecting my right to be here.

The guards passed and they saluted me, which I was a bit surprised at but if they want to salute the person who will ultimately hack them to pieces, more power to them.

Knowing I was getting closer to the main tent, I noted there was a crossroads of sorts up ahead and I rolled my eyes when I saw three squads of warriors marching towards the main tent. If that wasn't bad enough, I saw three Captains salute me.

What was with these people and saluting me!

Knowing I had to keep walking towards the main tent, I took a deep smoky breath and projected my confidence as I walked.

When I got in front of the main tent I slid into a squad as all three of them stood at attention outside. A small part of me wanted to whip out my swords and slaughter them all. I could easily kill most of them before they even reacted, but I had to behave.

The idea of behaving myself and not killing these horrific fools was very hard as every breath smelled of sweat, blood and rotten flesh. I wouldn't be surprised if one of these idiots had gangrene fever.

I smiled a little as I thought about offering them help with their condition by slicing off their arms and legs. That I could easily do.

The sound of rustling canvas made me look back

at the main tent as I noticed a large muscular man in heavy ornate armour march out. I suppose he's meant to be in charge. I frowned as four guards in thick golden armour joined him, they thrusted their staffs into the ground.

I like a challenge.

As much as I knew I shouldn't have been surprised at the Overlord not being here but my blood still boiled at that. I wanted to rip his throat out or ripped his guts out and make him watch.

"You all have new orders. I received a bird from our traitor. The tunnels will be secured for us shortly. Your mission is to storm them. Long Live The Overlord," the Ornate Armoured man said.

"Long Live The Overlord!" everyone said.

With everyone starting to move, I subtly moved myself to the back of the three squads as they marched towards their horses.

My mind spun a little at the idea of the traitor allowing the enemy to kill all the rebels, but what I was really horrified at was how stupid the traitor was. Did they really, really believe the Overlord wouldn't kill them afterwards?

I checked behind me to see the ornate armoured man and his guards had gotten back into the main tent, no one else was watching the main tent or me.

Sliding away I crouched into the rows upon rows of white and red canvas tents as I sneaked up to the main tent.

When I was there I found a little gap in the main

tent and I smiled as I saw the guards and the ornate armoured man left the tent once again.

Taking out my sword I sliced open the canvas and stepped inside.

I had to find something useful here. I had to find those explosives. Or at the very least I had to chop off the ornate armoured man's head.

Cut off the head and the body dies.

CHAPTER 18

Commander Coleman hated what was happening to his rebellion, he hated to think what his father would have thought about him. Coleman knew his father would never call him a failure but if his father wasn't disappointed with him then Coleman would have wondered what was wrong with his father.

Inside the dark cave tunnel with its smooth yellow curved walls, Coleman stood close to the heavy wooden door and hoped it would hold. But as he heard the enemy slam into it, shouting and screaming bloody murder outside.

He didn't know how much longer the door would last.

The sound thundered down the cave tunnel. Coleman hated all of this so he gripped the warm hilt of his sword and raised it.

If the enemy didn't storm in then Coleman was going to kill them.

The smell of fearful, cold sweat (that reminded

him of salty bacon) filled the tunnel as Coleman heard the mutters and shivering of his friends. They were all losing hope, they were all going to die, they were all going to blame Coleman.

Coleman didn't want to believe them but they were right, he had failed them all. His so-called master plans were failing one by one.

Looking around Coleman hoped, he really hoped this next stage wouldn't fail because if it did then there was only one place left to make a final stand. Coleman wouldn't allow these bastards to take his home.

This was his cause, his family, his life. The enemy were not taking it from him.

The sounds of slamming and shouting stopped for a moment. Coleman leant forward and pressed his ear against the heavy cold wood.

It sounded like the enemy were walking away and laughing. They were laughing! Cocking his head Coleman tried to understand why but he had no idea why the enemy would stop.

Rebels screamed.

Heads were smashed.

Necks were snapped.

Bodies were hacked apart.

Coleman looked at the door.

It was intact.

The enemy didn't come in.

The wall exploded.

Throwing Coleman into the air.

He slammed into the wall.

His ears rang.

Black armoured soldiers stormed out.

The tunnels!

The enemy must have dug through the tunnels.

Soldiers poured out.

Coleman jumped up.

His ears still rang.

A soldier grabbed Coleman.

Whacking him across the face.

The soldier picked him up by the throat.

Throwing him against the wall.

Coleman looked nearby.

Soldiers were stabbing Rebels.

Their knifes moving too quick to escape.

His hearing returned.

The hand around his throat squeezed.

Screaming filled the air.

The door exploded.

Shattering the wood.

Sending lethal shards into the rebels and enemy.

Coleman dropped.

The soldier's corpse on the ground.

Coleman whipped out his sword.

He charged.

The enemy poured in.

Coleman swung.

Slicing into flesh.

Slicing into armour.

Blood sprayed everywhere.

Covering Coleman's chest.

He smiled.

The enemy slaughtered the rebels.

The enemy didn't care.

Their swords chomped on their flesh.

Ripping it out.

Coleman fell back.

He swung his sword.

Again and again.

He kicked them.

Shattering their skulls.

Slicing into their chests.

Ripping open their throats.

Corpses fell.

It was useless.

This was utter slaughter.

The enemy advanced up the tunnel.

Pushing the Rebels back further.

Massacring the Rebels more.

Rebels died every second.

Coleman screamed in defiance.

He wasn't losing!

He charged forward.

Diving into the enemy swarm.

He swung.

In a bloody arc.

Again and again.

Corpses dropped.

Blood splashed up armour.

A fist slammed into him.

Coleman fell to the ground.

His vision blurred.

Fear gripped him.

Laughter filled the air.

He saw swords move.

Coleman tried to move.

He was too weak.

His vision twisted.

Hands grabbed him.

Screams of agony filled his ears.

Coleman let the hands take him.

He saw shadow after shadow jump over him.

His vision cleared.

Rebels flew at the enemy.

Swords hacked them apart.

Coleman jumped up.

He had to go.

It was time for a final stand.

CHAPTER 19

I silently stepped into the massive white and red canvas tent, my hands firmly on the warm hilts of my swords. If the enemy wanted to attack me, they were going to die.

Taking a shallow breath of the smoke filled air that reminded me of smoked apples over a roaring fire with my friends years ago, my eyes narrowed as I studied the main tent, there had to be something here.

In all my years of experience (and killing), everything precious to the enemy is always kept here. You just need to know how to find it.

Listening to the crackling of fire and quiet chatting of the guards outside, I rolled my eyes at the simplicity of the tent, I would have expected there to be golden decorates, grand icons of the foul Overlord and more horrors. But no.

For the tent's massive size the white and red canvas walls were plain and unloved with the only thing of note being a large brown desk with piles of documents on it. But I did like the large wooden crates nearby.

As I silently walked over to the desk, with a flickering candle on there, my eyes were fixed on the opening in the tent, which I presumed was the door, if I had known the desk was in direct line of sight from outside. I would have grabbed a bow and shot the ornate armour man in the head.

Running my fingers over the cold smooth wooden desk, I flicked through the piles of documents and I had no idea how many battle orders it took to get an army. Actually what I couldn't believe the amount of documents needed for the army to pass checkpoints every ten miles.

I rolled my eyes at the idea of the Overlord's security tightening, I didn't need to kill more soldiers just so I could move City to City. Well, I didn't need to but I wanted to, so it would hardly be a problem.

Knowing guards would back any minute, I pulled my long black leather trench coat and black hood over myself tightly. A part of me was hoping if an enemy walked passed they would think I was just another regular soldier in black armour. A bit insulting but that was my plan.

Turning my attention to the large wooden crates nearby, I ran my fingers over the rough wood and smiled as I popped one open.

My eyes widened and my smile deepened as I saw crates upon crates of black powder. My mind tried to understand how a military camp could have so much in one place.

It was like they were asking to be annihilated, and it's rude not to do what people ask!

My smile lessened when I looked at the large drag marks on the ground where other crates had been. I swore under my breath at the thought of the Rebels being exploded and ripped to shreds.

As much as I wanted to play here and let my blades swirl and twirl into the flesh of my enemy, I knew I had to go. I had to save them.

We all underestimated the Overlord and what he wanted.

I wanted to kick myself for this, if I had been better or worked harder or... I took a deep smoky breath as I remembered I was still here fighting for the Rebellion. I hadn't failed yet, the Rebels were bound to be alive, I just had to help them.

Picking up the flickering candle on the desk, I looked at the opened crate of gunpowder. This was crazy. This was wrong. I didn't even know how long I would have to escape.

Just to be on the safe(r) side, I walked over to the door, the flickering candle burning in my hand.

I heard the ornate armoured man coming.

His guards were charging.

I looked at the crate.

I looked at the candle.

What the heck?

I threw it.

The flame touched the candle.

I ran.

I RAN!

My feet pounded into the ground.

Guards flew at me.

Guards swung at me.

I jumped into the air.

I wasn't fighting.

I was running.

I whistled.

The main tent burned.

The guards shouted.

They moaned.

They threw things.

Arrows flew through the air.

I whistled again.

A guard tackled me.

My head hitting the ground.

This wasn't happening!

I grabbed his head.

Snapping his neck.

I jumped up.

I charged.

The black powder exploded.

Only one crate.

Flaming chunks of canvas rained down.

Engulfing more tents.

Guards screamed in rage.

More arrows flew at me.

I felt the flames lick my coat.

A horse passed me.

I jumped on.
The other crates exploded.
I kicked my horse.
It zoomed away.
The military camp was annihilated.
Now I had to save the Rebels.

CHAPTER 20

Commander Coleman felt drop after drop of cold fearful sweat pour off his forehead, he really hated how much of a failure he had become.

He looked around the Inner Keep, the most secure and innermost chamber in the Rebel base, he normally loved looking at its smooth dome yellow walls and those amazing little detailed carvings of warriors.

Coleman hated all of it all today, especially when as he looked into the cold wide eyes of the last hundred Rebels with their pale skin.

Breathing in the sweat filled air, Coleman wished he could comfort them but he couldn't even comfort himself. There was no hope.

The enemy had taken over the base and they were the final members of the Rebellion. The only hope for an entire nation, but they were all going to die. Coleman knew that, he just didn't want to admit it.

As he listened to mutters and talks of surrender, Coleman wanted to jump up and tell his people why they shouldn't surrender why he couldn't. He didn't have the energy or the conviction.

Maybe if he did surrender the Overlord would enslave his friends and work them to death. But at least his friends would be alive.

Coleman smiled as he remembered the Assassin's beautiful face and that amazing long black leather trench coat and that black hood, he loved it. Coleman hadn't seen a more beautiful woman in his life.

Shaking his head Coleman knew he wouldn't surrender, she would never forgive him for starts. And the idea of stunning Jasmine thinking less of Coleman made him frown and hate himself. How dare he even consider surrender and enslavement.

The sounds of thumping and slamming came from the thick red wooden door ahead of Coleman. He knew it would hold a lot longer than the last one but after this... it was do or die.

There was nowhere else to run or hide. If Coleman died here then he would be happy. Coleman smiled at the idea of being a martyr for the cause, a martyr for freedom, a martyr for a Kingdom with people being forced into a specific path in life.

Standing up, Coleman whipped out his sword and checked his dagger was still in his pocket. He wasn't going to give up. He smiled as he heard every other Rebel stand up and take out their weapons.

"We fight!" Coleman shouted.

"Death to the Overlord," everyone returned.

Coleman was about to say something when he felt an icy cold blade press against his throat.

A part of him thought if it was the Assassin but he knew it wouldn't be.

"Sis, what ya doing?" Abbic asked.

Coleman's eyes widened as he realised Barbic was the traitor all along. He wanted to channel his inner assassin but that wasn't going to happen. Not with a blade at his throat.

"Traitor. How long? Why do it?" Coleman asked.

Barbic moved Coleman closed to the door. "Three years to help my father,"

Coleman wanted to cock his head but the blade made it difficult.

"The Overlord ya father Sis. Can't be. Daddy's-"

"You always were stupid Abbic. I am not your sister, your mother and father adopted me you stupid girl,"

"Why Abbic's family?" Coleman asked.

"Because they were friends with your father. Now you will all die and the Rebellion will end,"

"Sis ya don't want this!"

The blade pressed harder against Coleman's throat.

"I am not your sister! I will kill him right now! Back off!"

Coleman held out his hand to tell his friends he was going to be okay. As much as his heart thumped in his chest he knew he had to buy the Assassin time to arrive.

"Your father will die,"

"Coleman, yes he will. I will kill him when the time is right, but you will die first,"

"Why kill your own father?"

"He is foul, dirt. I will rule the Kingdom,"

"You won't be better than him,"

"I will be. My Father is soft on these commoners,"

"Your father kills thousands each day,"

"Thousands must die. They must be tortured. Complete obedience must happen,"

Coleman rolled his eyes. Barbic was a great actor but Coleman knew she had lost the plot. She needed to die.

"I presume you want us to open the door and let your friends inside," Coleman asked.

"Of course idiot. Your Rebels friends will be enslaved and turned into mindless drones for the glorious Overlord!"

As much as Coleman hated that idea he had a feeling (A gut feeling? He didn't know) that the Assassin was close.

"What will happen to me?"

The blade cut slightly into his throat. Coleman gagged.

"You Traitor rebel, you will be sent to the Overlord and killed in the capital. All those glorious people must see the glory of their God,"

Coleman's eyes narrowed. He didn't know the

Capital people saw the Overlord as a god. Interesting.

"Open it!" Barbic shouted.

She forced Coleman over to the door and Coleman slowly opened it. The door creaked open and men hissed as they pulled it open from the other side.

Coleman felt his stomach twist into a tight knot as he saw tens upon tens of large black armoured warriors, their long swords shining with the dark rich blood of his friends.

The smell of the blood was overpowering and disgusting, Coleman hated this but he had what he wanted.

Coleman grabbed his pocket.

He whipped out a dagger.

Thrusting it into Barbic's leg.

She hissed.

The blade fell away.

He ripped out the dagger.

Coleman spun.

Thrusting it into her chest.

Again and again.

Blood poured out.

Coleman grabbed her head.

Pulling it back.

Exposing her throat.

He ripped into it.

Blood gushed out.

Covering him.

Coleman spun to the warriors.

They froze.

A warrior screamed.

Coleman looked at the cave entrance.

A woman was here.

Slashing and lashing.

Her long black leather trench coat flapping about.

Coleman smiled.

He charged.

This was now do or die.

A final stand.

A fight for survival.

CHAPTER 21

Utter lust filled me as I stepped into the cave entrance of the rebel base. I loved the beautiful splashes of wet dripping blood on the smooth rocky walls of the cave. This was going to be great!

Walking inside my smile deepened as I smelt the vapourised blood and the desperation in the air. It was cross between a fearful sweat and another smell I couldn't quite describe.

I admired the lumps and bumps on the rough cave floor as I kept walking, occasionally having to step over skulls and shattered bodies.

All this death and destruction was perfect, as an assassin this was wonderous for me. The sound of shouting and taunting in the distance echoed around the cave.

A small part of me hated the arrogance of those foul black armoured soldiers ahead. I hated them, everyone hated them.

But I couldn't be too mad at them, after all they

were kind enough to make themselves trapped so I can slaughter them all. My stomach filled with butterflies at the idea of ripping into their amazing flesh.

An assassin's dream.

To make sure nothing caught on any random rocks or edges, I pulled my long black leather trench coat and hood tight over me. Nothing was going to stop me doing this.

Taking a final few steps forward, I whipped out my swords and smiled at all the black armoured sacks of flesh and blood that were completely blind to my presence.

The sound of the heavy wooden door opening and the soldiers' laughter made me cock my head. What were the stupid rebels doing?

My eyes narrowed as I saw that Barbic woman was the traitor. Typical. I knew Coleman with those amazing emerald eyes needed a distraction. Who was I to refuse?

I charged.

Ramming my sword into a soldier.

He screamed.

Coleman killed Barbic.

Wonderful man.

I threw the corpse to the ground.

More guards moved.

They were too slow.

I flew at them.

My sword swirling in the air.

Slicing into their flesh.
Blood poured out.
Painting the ground red.
I smiled.
I charged.
Soldiers were alert.
They swung.
They ducked.
I slid on the ground.
Sliding forward.
Thrusting up my swords.
Slicing in between their legs.
Blood flooded out.
Corpses dropped.
I jumped up.
Arrows flew at me.
I dodged.
I saw archers.
They reloaded.
Too slow.
I charged.
Jumping into the air.
Landing on them.
Wrapping my legs around her neck.
I swung my weight.
Throwing her forward.
She smashed into the wall.
Cracking her skull open.
I landed.
Thrusting my swords into the archers.

Their bodies went limp.
Bodies littered the ground.
Rebels poured out.
Hacking the enemy to pieces.
Ripping into their flesh.
Fists slammed into me.
My head whacked the wall.
Blood splashed up it.
More fists whacked me.
I dropped my swords.
My nose cracked.
Someone grabbed my head.
Ripping off my hood.
Grabbing my hair.
No more.
I backflipped.
Ripping out my hair.
I landed.
Wrapping my legs around their neck.
Grabbing their face.
Pressing my fingers into their eyes.
They screamed.
I pressed harder.
Blood squirted out.
My fingers wet and warm.
The corpse dropped.
I picked up my swords.
More foes ahead.
Slicing through the Rebels.
Coleman staggered.

He was hurt.
Blood dripped from his stomach.
I had to help him.
Five soldiers surrounded him.
Rage filled me.
No one hurts Coleman.
I roared.
I flew.
The enemy turned.
It didn't matter.
I swung my swords.
Swords ripping into flesh.
Two dead.
A male slapped me.
He slapped me again.
I chopped off his hand.
He screamed.
I grabbed his cut-off hand.
Throwing it at him.
He screamed.
I dashed over.
Snapping his neck.
Three dead.
The last two fired arrows.
I jumped.
I landed.
I dropped to the ground.
Kicking them.
Knocking their feet out from under them.
They fell.

I leapt up.

Slashing their throats.

As I slowly got up I noticed rebel after rebel, in all their shapes and sizes with different amounts of blood covering them, run past me but I simply stood there amongst all the corpses.

The battle was won.

I turned to my beautiful Coleman he was alive and in that moment that's all I cared about, sure I knew there were other traitors in the base, but the other rebels could kill them.

I... I just wanted to make sure my Coleman was okay, because without him there was no rebellion, no hope, no nothing, and for me without him there was no... joy.

I needed him.

CHAPTER 22

Commander Coleman smiled as he stood firm, looking out over the amazing, stunning valley below him with the black dagger-like mountain range lining the edges of the valley. It was all so beautiful, so amazing, Coleman didn't want to lose it.

But times change.

Breathing in the sweet piney air of the mountains, Coleman embraced the cold chill as he savoured it and studied every little beautiful detail of the mountain range and valley.

Even now Coleman wasn't sure what his favourite part of the valley was, but he loved it all. He knew that, especially the little rabbits and deer running around on the valley ground.

As he listened to the cold air gently howl and the distance talking of rebels, Coleman knew he had done well today. He never ever expected today to be successful, he actually expected to die today.

Coleman gave a half smile as he wondered about the idea of dying as a martyr. A small part of him loved the idea of dying as a symbol of hope, justice and unity. A person who died so others may live in peace, that is what Coleman wanted to die for.

Feeling the soft fabric and bandages tied tightly around his stomach, Coleman brushed his fingers over the soft material. It was a reminder that anyone could die and that his days were numbered.

Coleman didn't have a problem with this, he loved the idea of it, but he had to complete his mission first, one day at a time.

As much as Coleman wanted today never to happen, he was proud of himself and his rebels. They were the real heroes, they were fighters who died, sacrificed and made sure the Rebellion fought another day.

Breathing in more of the refreshing piney air, Coleman nodded to himself as he realised that he had done right today. He had made sure people could live in peace and make their own choices in life.

His amazing, beautiful rebels had chosen to stay and fight for him, for the cause, for each other, and he rewarded them by fighting to make sure they could live in peace when it was all over.

Coleman smiled at that realisation, he hadn't thought of it like that before, he had always considered today to be a failure.

And it was.

Looking over the edge of the high mountain top he stood on, Coleman frowned as he saw the hundreds upon hundreds of rebel corpses that littered the ground and turned the black rock red.

None of this should have happened, that was a fact, but for Coleman there was a little bit of hope attached to the failure. Coleman noticed thousands of more Overlord corpses compared to the Rebels.

They had won.

Coleman shook his head about all the killing and executions him and the beautiful Jasmine had to do after the battle. There were so many traitors within their ranks that had to die, even more Overlord soldiers that were hiding in the corners of the base. They all had to die.

It was still a victory. The Rebellion was alive.

And that's what Coleman smiled about, he knew the next few months would be a nightmare, trying to find a new base and set up everyone, then try and find new rebels. It would be a challenge.

Coleman's eyes widened at the challenge, he loved it, a challenge is probably what kept him going. He wasn't fighting the Overlord because it was easy, he was fighting because he wanted people to live in peace and choose their own lives.

There's nothing easy about that!

Coleman wiped his soft cheeks with his rough hands as he remembered killing his friend, Barbic. The entire thing about her being a traitor was so... ridiculous but it had happened.

He didn't know how it happened, how he could let a traitor into their ranks but it wasn't the first, it wouldn't be the last, Coleman just had to be ready. He hoped a certain special Assassin would help him, but he wasn't sure.

Knowing there was a lot of planning to do and it was going to be interesting to get the Rebels ready to move, Coleman started to turn around.

As he looked at the piles of corpses and his Rebels picking through the bodies, taking armour and weapons (Coleman hated the necessary evil), Coleman saw a beautiful woman in her amazing long black leather trench coat and a little black hood.

If someone had asked him if the Assassin would have ever saved them before today, Coleman would have tried to deny it but he ultimately would have said no. He had no idea the Assassin even cared about the Rebellion, Coleman always thought it was the coin that kept her coming back.

It wasn't.

That fact was still mind blowing to Coleman, he didn't understand it, he loved her but she didn't love him. So why keep coming back?

Coleman smiled at the idea of the Assassin secretly liking him and just being too scared to admit it. He shook those thoughts away when he remembered how well she fought and killed. Jasmine wasn't afraid of anything.

Starting to walk down to the corpses below, Coleman just smiled at everything, him and his Rebellion were alive and thankfully so was Jasmine. That's all he wanted.

A part of him wondered if Jasmine would stay now the Rebellion was safe or if she would go again and make sure she was just another assassin, killing for coin and nothing more.

Coleman hoped not, he needed her. He was just afraid to ask.

As his mother used to say, don't ask questions, you don't want the answer to.

CHAPTER 23

Looking at a stunning corpse in front of me, I loved the way how the blood had pooled in the little cracks in the rocks, creating wonderfully dark rich blood pools.

Standing up, I stretched my back and smiled as I saw the thousands of enemy and Rebel corpses around me. I still love the massive streaks of dried blood on the black rocky slopes of the mountain. It was a great sight.

I didn't even care about the blood stains on my long black leather trench coat and I hoped no one was going to ask how I got blood on my black hood.

I took a deep bitter piney breath and licked my lips at the hints of vapourised blood in the air, this was a battle and a half. So many lives lost and so many corpses on the ground.

The damn Rebellion and them giving me a conscience felt a little sad at the sight, I normally never would have felt like this after a battle, but I did.

The idea of so many lives lost was staggering, that's why my father had to die. All those lives ruined and lives lost for his stupid ambitions.

Listening to the Rebels cry, talk and pull armour and weapons off the dead, I rolled my eyes as I wished they would stop crying. People were always going to die today but I hope, I really hope I lessened that number.

Feeling the cold mountain air wash over me, I cast my mind back to why I did all of this, I wanted to keep the Rebellion alive and protect that stunning Commander Coleman.

I had to smile as I stared at all the slaughtered, hacked up bodies of the enemy. Their corpses dripping blood and the Rebels walking around me, that made me smile.

Before today I would have smiled for the sole reason that there was lots and lots of beautiful blood on the ground (of course I still smile at that), but I smiled because my friends were alive too.

That's what the rebellion are to me, they aren't people who give me coins and I kill for them, they are people who love me, respect my work and want me for me. Most of them don't see a living weapon to use like a pet, they see me as a person.

So if someone asks me if I'm pleased that I saved them, I am. I really am. Now I have friends, a family and a hope for getting revenge.

I'm still not sure if that's what I want, I want (or think I do) Coleman, his beautiful body, face and those amazing emerald eyes. I might want him in the future but I don't want him just yet. I can't become involved with him in my state, I'm a killer, a cold calculating killer, I'm not made for relationships.

But I'll be lying if I said seeing him bleeding and hurt wasn't troubling, I wanted to lash out and kill everyone, ram by swords into every one, I had to protect him, and that's what I wanted to continue. No one hurts my Coleman, no matter how much I hate to admit it.

Taking another look around, I saw a group of Rebels laughing and smiling, truly smiling, they were having fun and enjoying life. That... made me feel something, pride? Joy? I don't know but I want more of that feeling, the feeling of what I do matters and it makes a difference.

For almost my entire life I've been taught to kill and do it for money and food and for survival, but now I want something different, I want a life worth living.

And because of that damn Rebellion with their kind words, warm hearts and their cause, I want them to succeed, I want them to kill the Overlord and free the Kingdom.

Smiling to myself I knew that was impossible without me, even I have to admit the Rebels were better than I thought, but I've killed, I've fought too many of the Overlord's soldiers to know the Rebels won't win. They don't have the armour, weapons or tactical intelligence to know how to beat the

Overlord.

So I will be with them for a little while, I'll fight and I'll protect them. Oh, I might be able to get a special title with that mission in mind, I like the sound of that.

Damn the Rebellion!

Knowing I was truly changing because of these people and their cause, I gave a little chuckle to myself at the oddity of it all. I never expected to be like this or have anything close to friends.

As I looked at the tall amazing man walking towards me with that smooth squarish face and those amazing green emerald eyes, I knew I was wrong, very wrong.

Walking over to handsome Coleman, I knew I had to help him move all the Rebels, find a new base and most importantly help them fight the Overlord and free the Kingdom.

Coleman gave me a stunning smile that made me want to hug him, and as I looked into those deep emerald eyes. I felt something special towards him, after all Coleman was one of the few living people who knew my name. A very dangerous thing, a thing of trust too.

Taking a step closer to him, I loved the feeling of his body warmth on my skin.

"I'll stay with you. I'll help you fight. But I need something in return," I said.

A small part of me wanted to say him so badly, I think I really wanted him in that moment, but I couldn't say it just yet.

"What?" he asked, smiling.

I hope he wasn't expecting me to say him too.

"I want to be known as the Protectorate of the Rebellion, Swore Protector and all that,"

To my surprise, Coleman smiled and I thought he was going to laugh.

"Sure, my Lord Protectorate,"

I don't know why but having my own little title made me feel special and important, something I've never felt before, I've never truly mattered to anyone, but things were changing.

I was about to start walking but Coleman gently grabbed my shoulder and smiled at me.

"Barbic, she said something that I didn't like?"

I smiled. "What?"

"She said the Overlord was her Father. Making her your-"

"Sister or half-sister," I said, slowly. I had no idea about a sister, it was always just me and my little perfect brother before…he died.

I just nodded. There was nothing I could say to that. I hated the idea of having other family out there but after seeing the treachery Barbic had committed, I wasn't sure I wanted to meet these other family members.

"What ever happened to those Hunters I thought they'll be here?" Coleman asked.

I cocked my head and thought for a moment.

"We didn't see them after the Overlord trapped

us so I fear I was right all along. The Overlord was after me, he sent the Hunters to hunt me and that's it,"

"Think they'll return,"

I smiled at that and placed my hands on the hilts of my swords.

"I hope so,"

He nodded at that.

As me and Coleman walked over to the Rebel base to finish the move before we headed out, I knew fighting the Overlord, Hunters and my family were all tomorrow's problems, and I had found my true family, not of blood but of friendship (or something very close to that).

A family I was going to protect to the end.

AUTHOR'S NOTE

I really hope you enjoyed that story, I know for me I had a blast writing it.

The entire story behind the story was really strange for me and it was a first. Because I've done City of Assassins short stories for a little while.

The first one (*City of Fire*) was done in January 2021 as an assignment on a writing course I was doing, then the second one (Awaiting Death) was a story I wrote after my Great Uncle died in March 2021.

Then I let the series until August 2021 and I was writing along then I got to the end of City of Vengeance (I really encourage you to read it) and I realised there was a massive event coming.

No short story was going to cover the invasion of the rebel base, so I decided to write a novella. And before you ask there will definitely be a series out of this because I really want to know:

- How will the Rebels defeat the Overlord?

- Will the Assassin kill her father?
- Will Coleman and the Assassin ever get together?

But I'm also interested in how will the Assassin change over the course of the series. Because from the beginning of the book to the end, there's a lot of change in her and we learn a lot more about her.

This will be interesting!

So I really hoped you enjoyed this little behind the scenes Author's Note and I look forward to seeing you in another book.

Have a great day!

CITY OF MARTYRS

CONNOR WHITELEY

CHAPTER 1

My rebellion cannot die.

As much as I love to think that, I know at some point all my friends, rebels and everyone I love will die or be killed. My job is to make sure that happens as far into the future as I can, which is why I'm in this godforsaken place.

The sound of peasants walking in the mud, talking and laughing with the other peasants filled the air as I looked down at them from the high window that I carefully hid behind.

As a female assassin I don't have anything against peasants and everyday people, I was once one of them, and some peasants did look after me time from time after the Overlord killed my Assassin siblings and forced me to go on the run.

But I have never understood how they can find live quietly at peace whilst the Overlord and its servants make their lives a living hell. I don't understand why these people don't stand up and fight for their freedom.

For example there's a woman down there who is being shouted at by some Overlord Guards in their horrid black armour that I would happily slice through, but is she saying anything? Is she defending herself? Is she doing anything that would make these men think twice?

No.

And that is why I do what I do, I want to defend the innocent, protect them and make sure my life is worth living. Yet I also suppose that's why I joined the silly rebellion with their damn values, cause and heroics.

I saved them once, they loved them and gave me a family of sorts, so now I feel like I have to protect them.

The horrible smell of poo, urine and rotten food fills the air as I realise what one of the nearby buildings below was used for, I didn't want to be here any longer than necessary.

If I wasn't on official business then I would never have stayed here for as long as I have (four hours), but if I was ever going to free the Kingdom, kill my father the Overlord (don't judge) and protect the rebellion, then I needed to do something here first.

I went away from the window and went over to the large wooden door that was the only entrance to this place. I hated the formal hard wood floors and walls to this office and its small official desk that was far too grand for purpose.

How I didn't smash it up the moment I got here I didn't know. But soon everything would be destroyed because I needed to kill this Governor.

Lord Governor Marisia of Outpost Ova was nice my favourite of people, if you asked anyone (including the Rebellion who meant to know all these things) they would have told you she was a rich woman who donated thousands to the poor each week, and she was one of the best Governors in the Kingdom, ruling over her district with fairness, justice and righteousness.

Rubbish!

Whereas if you were an Assassin (like wonderful old me), then you knew her as a cold, calculating, cunning killer. I first heard of her when I was a contract killer and she hired me to kill a hundred peasants because... I quote... *I don't want to feed those extra mouths*.

Not exactly the worse reason I've ever been hired but it does come close.

Anyway I'm going to stab her with my two long swords, and she needed to die now because apparently she had learnt the location of the rebellion, and I wasn't going to allow her to kill my friends for love, money or spite.

The sound of footsteps came from the hallway behind the door and I pulled my black leather cloak and hood tighter as I prepared to strike.

The door opened.

Lord Governor Marisia walked in with a massive smile on her face. I hated her straight away with her long pompous robes, her stunning jewel and her perfectly done hair.

This was the image of a woman who didn't care about anyone else, if she had then she would have focused more on her people and not herself.

The door shut. I heard the guards walk away.

I went up to her. Placing my blades firmly against her throat.

"I wasn't expecting the Assassin Protectorate of The Rebellion," she said.

I know I got that title a month ago, being the Protectorate of the Rebellion, but I really don't like it. It sounds pompous, arrogant and like I'm far superior to my station. I so wasn't going to let her say that again.

"You know Assassin, your friends have made a lot of progress along the St Julian's Way,"

As much as I needed to spill her blood now, I felt as if I had to know how much she knew, the Rebellion had mentioned taking that path towards the so-called Holy Sections of the Kingdom, but that was silly. The Overlord ruled those lands directly, no one would help them there.

"Relax Assassin, I haven't sent the orders yet and I presume I never will now. But there is something far better waiting for you," she said with a smile.

I pressed my swords harder into her throat.

"The Overlord has activated them again. The

Hunters will come for you and the Rebellion. They will find you, kill you and deliver you to the Glorious Overlord,"

Damn!

That is not what I wanted. I couldn't have those silly, stupid half-human, half-demon shadowy monsters after me. I had enough trouble with them last night.

Damn it!

I needed more time. I needed to meet up with the Rebellion, plan our next moves, we were ruined after the Overlord attacked us, slaughtered our forces and forced us to move bases.

We didn't have any fighting power left, we couldn't fight back, we were barely surviving. And that is what I wanted to change.

"Don't worry *Lord* Governor, I will kill you. I will make sure you're found. Then I will save the Rebellion, find a City and we will kill the Overlord,"

Marisia shook her head. "The Hunters will stop you. You won't get far,"

I moved closer to her ear. "Then we'll go to the one place they would never dare step foot inside,"

Marisia gasped. "The City of Martyrs?"

I had no idea that was where they couldn't go. I was making it up based on some stories I'd heard years ago but at least I knew where the Hunters would come for me now. Hopefully that City would help me and my friends rebuild, regroup and take the fight to the Overlord.

I didn't want any more unneeded deaths.

"Yes," I said.

Marisia struggled. "That is Holy ground. That is outrageous. That-"

I slit her throat, threw her body out the window and escaped to meet up with the Rebellion. I had to warn them about the Hunters.

CHAPTER 2

Commander Coleman stared at the two rows of the bloodied injured men and women that laid before him as the carriage rode along the long twisting road ahead.

Coleman had hated leaving their base over a month ago but there was no other choice. The Overlord knew where they were and unlike the Rebellion's forces, the Overlord had unlimited numbers of soldiers at his disposal.

It was only because of the Assassin's quick thinking that had bought them enough time to escape.

The Assassin was stunning with her amazing body, long black hair and her deep dark eyes that Coleman wished he could stare into every day.

He didn't want to keep thinking like this but he had to. Coleman loved the Assassins that much was fact, but he didn't know how to talk to her, show her his affection and develop whatever was between them into a relationship.

But it didn't take a genius to know that the Assassin probably wasn't into a relationship, especially with Coleman. Especially after Coleman had apparently tried to control her or be overprotective, he still hated himself a little for even trying such a thing. But love definitely made him do stupid things.

Especially towards one of the most beautiful, kick-ass women he had ever met.

The quiet sounds of moaning, coughing and hissing reminded Coleman of the horrific losses the Rebellion had suffered and it wasn't like most of these injured soldiers would heal or survive. The Rebellion didn't have those sorts of supplies.

Coleman had tried to reach out to allies but none of them were interested. As far as those so-called allies were concerned, the Rebellion was dead, long live the Overlord.

That sentence alone was disgusting and Coleman didn't understand how these people could so easily live under that foul Overlord's tyrannic rule.

Coleman was more than glad that his father had rescued him from the City of Pleasure as a teenager. He didn't want to become a sex slave for some Noble or Monarch, he wanted to be free.

But now he was, he had to free others.

The smell of blood, disease and damp filled the air and Coleman didn't like any of it. He wanted better for his people, he wanted to show leadership, courage and that he had a master plan. But he didn't. Coleman had failed as a leader, a fighter and now he was leading his friends on the run.

That was no way for a Rebellion to fight, too weak to defend themselves, much less attack the Overlord.

But at least Coleman had one weapon. He didn't like to think of his beautiful Assassin as a weapon, but at this point he didn't have a choice, the Assassin was the only advantage the Rebellion had.

If anything happened to her, then the Rebellion was truly dead (and so was Coleman's heart).

A man with a blood spattered face and covered in bandages weakly raised his arms towards Coleman, he went over to the man. He smelt awful with hints of sweat, blood and sick assaulting Coleman's nose.

"Closer," the man said weakly.

Coleman knelt on the ground and put his ear close to the man's mouth.

The man's arm moved.

A blade sliced through the air.

Coleman shot back.

The man jumped up.

Ran at Coleman with the blade.

A gunshot went off.

The man dropped down.

Coleman looked to see who the shooter was and Coleman was relieved to see it was a tall woman with her wonderfully smooth face, long blond hair with a smile that always lit up the room.

It was one of the few people in the entire world that Coleman trusted automatically. It was Abbic. And considering that her sister had betrayed the Rebellion a month ago and almost killed them all, Abbic was doing rather well.

"Alright their Bossie?" Abbic asked.

Coleman looked at the corpse. "I am now, thank you. Tell security to double check everyone again. That's the ninth attempt this month. There can't be that many traitors still here,"

Abbic's smile melted away. "Ma sis was traitor enough so anything possible me Lord,"

Coleman gave her a nod of respect and wished he could do or say more to her. He didn't want anyone to be in pain but clearly her sister's betrayal had scarred her. Coleman couldn't blame her really, they were close and as much as Coleman didn't want to admit it, her sister was a close friend.

Abbic started to walk away but stopped. "Me Lordie, tha Assassin's back,"

Coleman couldn't believe his luck and for the first time in a month, he smiled. He truly smiled. Coleman felt as if the tides were turning in his favour, but most of all he was just looking forward to seeing the woman he loved.

CHAPTER 3

I wasn't impressed in the slightest as I felt the horrible carriage jerk, bump and jump in the air as the entire Rebellion travelled along the massive long road ahead of them.

All I wanted was a good gently ride to our destination, which I don't think even the Rebellion knew where they were going. That alone was why I had returned, to warn them and hopefully give them some kind of direction.

I stood in front of a silly little wooden table with some maps, documents and unlit candles covering it. I presume this table had once been used as a way to plot their course and note down the various intelligence reports me and my "agents" (if you can call them that) had sent the Rebellion over the past month.

But now like the rest of the Rebellion, the table had been reduced to scraps and eroded by the constant grind of the journey.

The sounds of people talking, coughing and splattering wasn't the best of sounds to hear considering what was coming. These Rebels would last five minutes against the Hunters or any sort of major attack by the Overlord.

There were few options left for us, but I had to leave them for a time. That was the clearest one. My blood Father The Overlord would always focus on hunting me over the Rebellion, so if I went, it would at least buy them a few more days.

The smell of mould, damp and spoiled ale filled my senses as I looked up at the man standing opposite me.

Coleman's right hand man Dragnist kept staring at me and smiling. It wasn't creepy or anything but it was like he was obsessed with me. Granted his long black beard, killer smile and scar covering his face had a certain attractive quality to them. I wasn't interested in him.

I did like Coleman though.

I wanted Coleman to get here so I could tell him my news and hopefully help him lead.

The entire reason why I had left for the past month was simple, I didn't want to see him in his crippling pain of self-perceived failure, hate and disappointment.

The door opened behind Dragnist and Abbic with her perfectly long straight blond hair walked in and stood next to me. Then I saw my beautiful Coleman with his amazing dark emerald eyes, fit body and… his stunning smile was gone.

A small smile formed on his lips when he saw me but it was nothing compared to the smiles I got before the Overlord attacked, slaughtered and almost ruined the Rebellion.

I had to change that.

I pulled my black leather cloak and hood tightly over myself and nodded at Coleman.

"Come on Assassin, what ya gone for us?" Abbic asked.

Under my hood I smiled. "Where are we heading?"

Coleman tried to smile but he couldn't. "Holy Section of the Kingdom. We have-"

"Turn back Coleman. Everyone in those lands will kill us. Everyone serves the Overlord. We have no allies there,"

Coleman shrugged. I hated seeing him like this.

"Ha. Assassin, we don't have any allies. The Rebellion is defeated, dead, useless," Coleman said.

I shook my head. "Dragnist, report,"

Dragnist physically shivered as I said his name.

"Yo girl, ten percent of surviving Rebs are fighting strength. Rest are injured,"

The problem with being the cold calculating assassin I'm known of is it makes me very glad to have my hood hiding my face, as I know for a fact that my face was horrified at that number.

But that's the problem. Because I'm the Rebellion's and the entire Kingdom's only hope for survival, freedom and peace, I can't show my horror. I have to be strong or everything is lost.

"I killed the Lord Governor," I said.

Coleman let out a breath.

"Thank ya!" Abbic said jumping in the air.

"That might have bought you a week at least. But the Hunters are returning for us. Their mission apparently is to kill me, you and the Rebellion," I said to Coleman.

He didn't even react.

I really didn't like how bad he had gotten. I wanted to support him, lead with him and show… and show how much he meant to me. But I couldn't love anyone in this much self-hatred.

"What do you all know about the City of Martyrs?" I asked.

Coleman, Dragnist and Abbic just stared at each other. Then looked back at me.

"Yo Assassin, we ain't going there,"

"Na to that," Abbic said.

I looked at Coleman.

He looked at me. "The City of Martyrs is one of the most fortified Cities outside the Capital. No one goes there. No one lives there, not really. No one… survives going there,"

"What is it?" I asked.

Abbic came over to me and placed a hand on my shoulder. I forced myself not to react.

"Ta City of Martyrs is a church City. The High Priestesses and Priests and Synagogue live there. The entire City is dedicated to ta Overlord,"

I smiled at the sound of that. I do love killing, I love killing Religious figures even more.

"Ta City isn't friendly. Religious rules over tha people-"

Coleman tapped the table. "Wait! But no one likes the Religious leaders. The Leaders keep such an iron grip on the City that the people are terrified of them. They want the Rebellion there. I received message after message years ago from them. Then nothing,"

I leant over the table. "Why?"

Coleman shrugged. "Unknown,"

I stood up straight and turned to leave. "Ready me a horse. I'm going to the City of Martyrs. We're going to free it, kill the Religious Leaders and save the Rebellion,"

Coleman gave me a mocking laugh. I just glared at him.

"Assassin you can't do that. The Rebellion-"

"Be silent Coleman! The Rebellion isn't dead. The City of Martyrs is filled with people who hate the Overlord. People that want to be free. People that can heal, feed and fight for us!"

His eyes lit up at that.

I went over to him. "Please, Coleman come with me,"

He smiled. "Fine. You, me and Abbic can go. Dragnist you're in charge. Abbic knows the City well from her... what do call it,"

"I call it ya studies. I studied that City like I did my magic area when I was 16. I know everything about it,"

That was just disturbing.

I smiled at all of them under my hood. "We leave in half an hour. We ride to the City of Martyrs, free it, kill the leaders and claim it for the Rebellion,"

Everyone nodded.

I pointed a finger at Dragnist. "Be at the City in six days,"

I didn't want to put a countdown on my mission, but I had to make sure the Rebels were safe, secure and alive.

Everyone nervously nodded.

And with that, I realised we only had six days to loosen the Overlord's iron grip on a City or the Rebellion would truly die.

That scared me more than anything.

CHAPTER 4

Commander Coleman was relieved to know the Rebellion still had some friends left in the Kingdom as he sat on the bow of a small fishing ship that was heading for the City of Martyrs.

There was always something breathtakingly magical about sailing in the dead of night with the bright stars shining in the cloudless sky and the full moon guiding their way.

Coleman had always loved sailing, boats and the sea ever since his father had rescued him from the City of Pleasure all those decades ago, and despite the freezing cold night Coleman still loved the sea just as much.

Coleman ran his fingers along the smooth cold wood of the bow and stared at the beautiful glassy sea below as the ship surged towards their destination.

The City of Martyrs could be the true death of the Rebellion, but at this point Coleman didn't care. There were no more options left, regardless of what the beautiful, stunning Assassin said.

If anything this pointless attempt to invade, capture and free the City was just an excuse so Coleman could die meaningfully. He didn't want to think like this but that was the cold, hard truth of the Rebellion.

And the sooner the Assassin learnt that the better.

Coleman didn't even understand why she was still here. The Assassin could go on with her life, live happily and free in the Kingdom. But instead she chose to die with the Rebellion.

Whether that was brave, stupid or a mixture of the two Coleman hadn't decided yet, but he wanted to protect her as much as he could.

The sounds of the waves crashing against the ship, the creeping of the ship and the muttering of crew members reminded Coleman how alone the Rebellion truly was.

Once the Rebellion travelled on loud noisy warships filled with thousands of angry people shouting, screaming and demanding their revenge against the Overlord. Now there were basically none.

Coleman wanted the old times to return.

The sound of someone sitting next to him made Coleman look up and stare into those perfect dark eyes and imagine that perfect body under the long black cloak and hood of the Assassin.

He wasn't sure if he wanted to talk to her, he already knew she thought of him as pathetic, weak and not a leader. So should he make his situation worse in her eyes?

"I have missed you Coleman,"

Coleman's mouth dropped. He hadn't been expecting that. He was expecting some demanding pet talk but in front of him was a kind, gentle woman that actually wanted to support him.

"I missed you too," Coleman said, knowing how lame it sounded.

"I had heard reports but I didn't know the Rebellion was this bad,"

Coleman wanted to shout some dramatic defence about how grand and valour the Rebels had fought. But he never ever wanted to lie to the Assassin, so he realised he could only tell her the truth.

"A few days after you left they found us. They kept coming wave after wave after wave. We... we were almost slaughtered again,"

The Assassin looked out to the sea. "I'm sorry for leaving,"

Coleman cocked his head. "It wasn't your fault. I charged you with being our Protectorate and you did that. You went after threats that could have ended us,"

The Assassin still didn't look at Coleman. He was starting to wonder if there was something she wasn't telling him.

"What's the plan?" the Assassin asked.

Coleman checked if they were alone and leant closer. He savoured the smell of her delicious coconut scented hair.

"There was an old friend of my fathers who ran a pub in the City. We head there. Investigate it. Hopefully he will still be alive,"

"If not?"

Coleman shrugged. "Then we find a new base and go from there,"

The Assassin laughed. "Okay, you do that. I've got another thing I want to look into,"

Coleman felt the hairs on his arms stand up. Had he disappointed her? Coleman hated the idea of being weak or not doing the right thing in her eyes, but this was what he knew to be right.

If he could just find his father's friend then they would be safe to conduct their business in the City without any risk of discovery.

"You do that. I know what I'm doing. You can meet us at the pub," Coleman said before realising how demanding he was being.

The Assassin nodded, pointed behind him and walked away.

Coleman felt the sweat roll down his spine as he looked behind him, he hoped he hadn't annoyed her.

But when he looked behind himself, his eyes widened as the stunningly beautiful City of Martyrs. For miles upon miles up and down the coastline stretched thousands upon thousands of little candles stretching as far back as they did long.

It was like hundreds of thousands of people were standing their perfectly still with a candle to light the way for any ships coming.

It was stunning.

Coleman didn't know how to describe but his eyes narrowed on the true marvel of the entire City. All the hundreds of thousand of lights were designed in such a way that the massive golden dome in the centre of the City was lit bright.

It must have been a cathedral or important place because it was the focal for the entire thing and Coleman loved it.

Except for how terrifying the entire effect was, in a way Coleman supposed it looked like a massive army with their impressive command station standing firm against all passing invaders.

But unlike those perceived passing invaders, Coleman and his friends weren't passing. They were invading and Coleman swore he was going to invade, conquer and free the City no matter the cost.

CHAPTER 5

This is far from the best killing ground I've visited.

This is utterly ridiculous because how the hell am I meant to kill people without others seeing me!

Take this long cobblestone road up the hill me, Coleman and Abbic are walking up, there are so many candles lighting up the cobblestone that it might as well be daylight.

And these little white stone houses are just silly, their white paint is perfect for reflecting the light and lighting up the road even more. This is not good. This is far, far from good.

If I was to kill someone now then I could almost certainly be seen, the guards would be summoned and I risk getting captured. This is not good at all!

The sound of the fishing ship unloading behind us is comforting as none of those creepy fishermen are chasing me, calling the guards or trying to flirt with me. That was why I talked to Coleman earlier, I was done with the fishermen flirting with me.

One of them even wanted me to sword fight with him. If you catch my drift.

And as for Coleman, I understand he is sad, depressed and a so-called failed leader but I wish you wouldn't worry so much about what I think of him. I know he wants to look strong for me, but I.. like him anyway.

If I wanted a cocky, strong man who would deal with whatever the world threw at him then I could have sex and love a noble man or one of the Overlord's puppet monarchs. But I don't want them. I want, I truly want Coleman (Not that I'll ever admit it to him, at least not yet).

But thankfully his cockiness gave me the excuse I needed to leave him and Abbic for a while, I wanted to explore the City myself and find an answer to why the Hunters can't come here. If I could find that out then maybe I could create a weapon, charm or something that would make them never want to find me.

A girl can hope!

The smell of sweet oranges, cake and honey filled my senses as we kept walking up the cobblestone road and I pulled my long black cloak and hood tightly and placed my hands on my swords.

I loved the cold feeling of their hilts.

"This is beautiful, don't ya think?" Abbic asked.

"I suppose it. It's a rubbish killing ground," I said coldly.

"Come on Assassin, there is some kind of romance here, isn't there?" Coleman said.

As much as I love his dark emerald eyes, fit body and movie star smile, I wasn't going to flirt with him in the open. That was never going to happen.

"Romance isn't what Assassins do. And where should I meet you both later?"

I heard something behind us but I couldn't subtly check yet.

"Ya not coming with us bud?" Abbic asked.

I smiled at her. "No. I have some exploring and investigating to do. But I'll be back in a few hours,"

We turned a corner and I saw Coleman look behind us, he shook his head at me. There were people behind us and Coleman clearly didn't want me to react but I wasn't good at doing what I was told.

"Okay Bud, look forward to ya returning to us,"

"Me too," I said to her.

The footsteps behind us were getting louder. Coleman looked at me, shaking his head.

I didn't listen.

I spun around.

There were five men.

Heavy.

Muscular.

Possibly armed.

Coleman dived for me.

I went to whip out my swords.

Coleman grabbed my hands.

He kissed me.

The five men simply walked past us, laughing, joking and enjoying their evening. They were simply five friends returning from a pub or something and I had almost attacked them, blowing our entire operation.

Coleman released his lips from mine and I realised I had completely forgotten that he was kissing me. Something I had longed for, for so long was now over, and I hadn't even tried to enjoy it.

Coleman walked away from me and his eyes were hollow like he was filled with the most disappointment he had ever felt. He probably thought I was going to enjoy it, savour it, want more. But I hadn't focused and he probably thought I was rejecting him completely.

I grabbed his hand but he shook me free and walked quickly over to Abbic and I just stood there.

Abbic looked at me but her and Coleman, my beautiful Coleman just kept walking on to complete their mission, like I was just another member of their Rebel team that was about to go on a solo mission.

Because in a way that was all I was now, just another Rebel, not Coleman's stunning love interest, I was just the woman who had shattered handsome Coleman's dreams of being with me.

I feared that I had just lost the only man that had ever loved me.

And that killed me inside.

CHAPTER 6
3 Days Left

As some strange kind of bells rang all over the City to mark the passing of the night and into a new day, Commander Coleman was furious at the Assassin. After everything they had been through together she didn't love him, like him or anything. She was simply manipulating him to get to her own goals.

No longer.

Coleman was never going to allow her back into the Rebellion, she was dead to him. How dare she not even pretend to respond to his kiss. He loved her. He wanted her. He gave her a chance when no one else would.

Damn her!

Coleman and Abbic went into a large wooden pub filled with rough wooden walls, plenty of drunk men and women and even a stray cat that hopped along the rows upon rows of tables.

There was something rather comforting about the normality of it all, Coleman would have imagined all their alcohol could have been sieged or destroyed by the Overlord, but here it all was accompanied with people who were happy, drunk and laughing with each other.

But Coleman didn't need a witch, wizard or warlock to know that these people were only drinking to mask their pain. It was the only bit of advice he had received as a young teenager in the City of Pleasure, *make sure you're drunk for when they come, it makes the Act a lot more bearable.*

Coleman had little doubt these people were doing the same.

The smell of urine, alcohol and grains filled Coleman's nose as he and Abbic went towards the massive bar on the far side of the pub. Coleman had to admit it was well stocked but the three barmen had already seen them and they didn't look happy.

Maybe it would have been a good idea to wear masks, cloaks or even hoods but Coleman wasn't going to look like the Assassin for anyone's love, money or respect. He was his own man, a great leader and he was here for a purpose.

Abbic marched over to the bar and sat up and smiled at a tall slightly muscular young barman who was carefully checking that the other barmen weren't within earshot.

The young barman's eyes were fixed on Abbic's long perfectly straight blond hair, and Coleman couldn't blame him. But as much as Coleman wanted this young man to be a friend, in this City he didn't have high hopes.

Coleman sat next to Abbic. "Two ales please,"

The barmen looked at Abbic and she shook her head.

The man went away.

"What was that about?" Coleman asked.

Abbic smiled. "Come on Bossie, I told tha man ya my husband, an alcoholic spiritualist,"

Coleman placed his face in his hands. "Really?"

"Ya, I had to give him something. We new, ya know? We need peeps to think we're normal,"

That wasn't the worse idea she had ever come up with, maybe the Assassin could have created something better... but he had to stop thinking like this. The Assassin was stunning, beautiful with her amazing body, black hair and eyes. But she was dead to him.

And that was final.

"Did ya say finding ya friend involved some code word?" Abbic said.

Coleman realised there was a reason why he always bought her along, he had completely forgotten about the so-called code word that the letters had told him about to find his friends in the City of Martyrs.

The only problem was the letters were sent years ago and maybe the sender was killed, exiled or simply left the City after the Overlord's grip tightened.

The young barman came over again. "Here you

go sir and beautiful Madame, our finest river water with a hint of lemon from the capital,"

Coleman smiled and nodded. "Tank you, do you know where one would find a *beautiful woman to be my guiding light to salvation?*"

He hoped he had the code right. He would seem pretty stupid without it.

The young barman shrugged and went away.

"What tha about?"

"That was the code. He doesn't know it. We need to ask around, try and find out if anyone here is a regular,"

Abbic leant forward. "Or ya just find out who owned the place when the letters were sent?"

Coleman shook his head. "Of course there is the simple option,"

Abbic finished her own river water and clicked the young barman back over.

"Yes Madame,"

Coleman could see if Abbic's eyes that she wanted to ask what time he got off shift so he could show her the sites and… that wouldn't be the worse idea. Maybe Coleman could encourage that.

Coleman leant closer to the man. "My friend is too shy to ask but what time do you get off shift?"

The barman smiled at Coleman. "Sorry but I don't swing that way and I'm more one on one,"

Coleman shook his head and smiled. Not exactly what he meant.

Abbic laughed hard. "Soz mate, he was asking

for me,"

The young barman stopped and went straight over to Abbic with a massive smile.

"I get off in a few minutes. My house isn't too far away?"

The entire house idea was interesting, if this man had a house to himself then maybe the barman could be recruited, trained and that could be their base of operations. It would be easier than trying to find the letter sender.

Abbic looked at Coleman. Coleman nodded.

"Um, ya that would be good," Abbic said clearly unsure of it all.

The barman smiled as he left to serve more people.

"What tha about Bossie?"

Coleman finished his river water, he wasn't keen on the strange sour taste it left on his tongue, but at least it was a good drink.

"You need to go with him. Convince him to join the Rebellion. Remember we need a base of operations,"

Abbic cocked her head. "Tha man hot though, what if he dies?"

Coleman threw his arms in the air. "He won't we'll protect him,"

The young barman went to Abbic wearing a long brown leather cloak that perfectly matched his dark brown eyes and smooth cheekbones, and Coleman supposed he understood why Abbic was attracted to him.

But Coleman still wanted his Assassin back, he wanted to run his fingers across her smooth skin, hair and body. He wanted her, needed her.

Yet the Assassin had made her choice.

Abbic wrapped her arm around the young barman's waist and they started to walk away.

The young barman stopped and turned towards Coleman. "Commander Coleman, I see you got my letters,"

CHAPTER 7
3 Days Left

I still wasn't impressed with myself for how I handled Coleman earlier. I did, do love him, he's great, funny and has everything I want in a man. But he thought I had rejected him. I had to prove him otherwise.

And what better way to prove I cared about him than to learn something critical about the City and its leader?

I knelt down on a flat slate rood overlooking a so-called grand entrance to a cathedral near the heart of the City. I wasn't impressed with its grand golden statues of gods know what, the jewels that encrusted it and even the little offering outside made by the other people.

It was silly how so many people would give away vital food, money and even body parts to an organisation like the Church that clearly didn't need it. The people inside this cathedral had to have millions of coins stacked neatly inside whilst there are people all throughout the Kingdom that barely had ten coins to their name.

It was disgraceful!

The smell of sweet oranges, overpriced perfumes and scented oils only added to my annoyance as I knelt here waiting for the leaders of the Cathedral to leave. There was no need to pump the air full of all these chemicals that quite frankly smelt wrong!

And the taste of mouldy oranges they left in my mouth was disgusting!

The sooner the City of Martyrs died the better.

The sound of soft voices came from below as I saw three figures in long white robes walk proudly out of the cathedral. I instantly didn't like that because they were all holding pots, boxes and clay containers full of coins and gold. They were probably taking it to their Masters, the bank or the most likely explanation as they were simply taking it home to add to their collections.

I had never understood why worshippers want to line the pockets of already-rich men. It wasn't going to make them rich in return, it wasn't going to gift them magical powers and it wasn't going to protect them.

But I couldn't help but feel like I had to do something to these men. These men were smiling, joking and mocking the poor souls that came here each day to worship and try to better their lives. That was wrong. These people had to understand that

173

these so-called pointless peasants wanted their money to matter.

So perhaps I needed to help that money find its way back to more deserving owners.

I pulled my long black cloak and hood tightly over my body and face, and placed my hands on the cold hilts of my swords. These men were going to pay dearly.

"Did you see that pig face woman today?" the tallest man said.

"Ya with her pig face daughter. She gave me two hundred coins. I told her the Gods will need a lot more to transform her piggy little face," another one said.

I was so going to kill these so-called priests.

"I know! Those piggy people keep coming here. Giving us money. Long may they live!" the shortest man said.

"Long may they live and may they keep giving us their money!" another one said.

"Here, here!" they all shouted.

I had had enough.

I jumped down.

Whipping out my swords.

Slashed the throats of two men.

Blood spattering everywhere.

Blood painted the entrance.

Two corpses dropped.

I spun around.

Slicing off the hands of the tallest man.

Of course someone would have probably heard the banging, smashing and screams of the men and the gold, but I was hoping to be long gone before anyone came to check.

And the tens of candles that lit up this cobblestone street and cathedral entrance alone wasn't good. I had to be quick.

I pointed my swords at the man's chest and throat.

"I need information," I said coldly.

"You have failed Assassin. Your Father sees you here. He will come. He will kill you. You won't win,"

"How do you know about my father?"

"The Overlord is divine. He will lead us into the heavens so we shall all dine with the Gods and Goddesses at their diamond table,"

Wow! He was a real nutter.

"Why can't the hunters come here?" I asked.

The man smiled. "Because they are demons. Monsters. Witches. Wizards! They cannot step onto this holy ground. They will burn, die, slaughtered by its majesty,"

I was so going to take some gold for myself as a fee for listening to this nutter.

"Who controls the City?" I asked.

"The Gods and Goddesses rule here. The Overlord is a puppet to them. The Hand of Divinity rule on the Gods' behalf. They will smite you for your unholiness taint upon-"

I slit his throat.

I wasn't going to listen to his pointless words anymore. There were no gods, goddesses or any divine in the Kingdom. Sure there was magic from the witches, wizards and warlocks but they weren't pretending to rule in the name of False Gods.

Who ever the Hand of Divinity was, I had to find them, kill them and hopefully free the City in the process.

But first I had to make these corpses look a bit more... presentable.

So I went over to each corpse, sliced open their stomachs and heads and pulled out their guts, organs and brains for all to see and admire.

Of course almost no one would actually admire my work because they're all philistines, but I think my point would be clear enough.

I was here and I was ready to play.

CHAPTER 8
3 Days Left

Commander Coleman was livered with the Assassin, this is getting beyond a joke. This was outrageous!

Coleman stood on a long wooden balcony that overlooked thousands of little white houses with their hundred of thousands of candles lighting everything up. It was beautiful in a way but Coleman hated the large tide of torches walking through the streets.

He could taste the foul black smoke on his tongue as it filled his lungs. It was disgusting and all because presumably guards were walking around with torches looking for someone.

It had to be the Assassin.

It might have been pitch black but against the candles and burning torches of the guards, the City looked as if the sun was dimly rising.

Coleman didn't know how long they had before the Guards would knock on the young Barman's door, so they needed to be quick. All because of the Assassin. He might have once loved her but she was out of control, she was going to damn him, his friends and the Rebellion.

He couldn't allow that.

The sounds of muttering, wood creaking and torches burning made Coleman go back into the Barman's drawing room that had an impressive array of art on the walls with an immense black table in the middle surrounded by chairs.

It reminded Coleman of his war room back in the Rebellion's old headquarters but that was long gone.

Abbic and the Barman were kissing when Coleman went over to them and looked at the maps, documents and letters on the table in front of them. Then Coleman tapped on the table and they realised he was there.

"What are the torches in the streets? And who are you?" Coleman asked.

The Barman frowned. "There were whispers you carry an Assassin around. It seems they've killed someone and the guards are performing door to door searches,"

For Gods sake! This was not what Coleman needed.

"When the Guards search my house, I have somewhere for you to hide. I have alerted my friends to look for an Assassin and guide them here,"

Coleman stepped forward. "Who are you? Why

should we trust you?"

The Barman smiled. "Isn't that a question you should have asked earlier? You are in my house now,"

Coleman ignored him. "You're clearly no barman. No barman could ever afford this place,"

"Come on Bossie give tha man some slack," Abbic said.

"This art alone is worth a few hundred thousand," Coleman said gesturing to the stunning art on the walls.

"Fine. Your father knew my father. I met you once when our fathers met but you never looked at me,"

Coleman shrugged.

"My father was the Lord Castellan of this City," the Barman said. "My name should be Lord Castellan Richard of the House of Martyrdom,"

Coleman sunk to his knees as did Abbic at the sound of his name. The Lord Castellans were masterful people before the Overlord rose up 50 years ago. The people gifted that title were some of the kindness, most generous and master craftsmen in the Kingdom.

To hear of one alone was a rarity but to actually meet one in the flesh. Coleman had never met another soul who had been blessed by the presence of such a being.

But Coleman supposed the true reason why Lord Castellans were so graceful, respected and powerful were because they were apparently magic users in all but name. They were meant to be some of the most powerful witches, wizards and warlocks in the Kingdom, but Coleman didn't want to spoil this moment with the idea of magic.

"My Lord-" Coleman said.

Richard pointed at Coleman. "I do not have that title. My family ruled this City fairly, justly and everyone and I do mean everyone was happy here once. Now look at my City,"

"So ya wrote," Abbic said.

Richard nodded. "I did. My father died and I was... angry at the Overlord. I was hoping for aid but it never came,"

Coleman looked at the floor. "I... I am sorry,"

Richard placed a warm finger under Coleman's chin and raised it so Coleman looked into Richard's eyes.

"There will be time for sorrow but that time is not now. There are people to free, save and protect. That is our mission. I will tell you all I know but your friend is in great danger,"

"Let her rot," Coleman said, automatically.

Coleman heard a blade drop on the floor behind him.

"Is that how you feel about me?" the Assassin asked.

CHAPTER 9
3 Days Left

That bastard Coleman!

I had given him everything! I had fought for him! I was willing to die for him! And now he wants me to rot, die and leave him alone.

Well then maybe I should. Maybe I should just leave him. Let that stupid bunch of Rebels die. Let the Kingdom suffer.

Hell I might even join the Overlord and personally hunt down each and every Rebel til they are all dead!

Of course until Coleman, that annoying, sexy man with those deep emerald eyes, I can actually keep my emotions in check and I don't insulate every single bit of hope I have. Because whether he likes it or not he is stuck with me, as without me the Overlord will quickly and easily kill the Rebellion in one surgical strike.

And as for this drawing room, it is not the nicest

one I have seen. It's small filled with horrible tacky art that I suppose Coleman would find stunning, and even the black table in the middle. Come on, seriously?

A corpse would find a better table than that in a graveyard. I'm not even going to start on the chairs. All in all I am not impressed one bit.

I saw Coleman, Abbic and a rather hot barman staring at me, I just wanted to be human for a few seconds. Not a cold blooded, calculating assassin, just a woman who could love a man if she wanted.

I went over to Coleman and gestured that I wanted to hold his hands.

"Do you want me gone?" I asked, forcing some emotion into my voice.

"No," he said automatically.

"I didn't reject your kiss earlier. I honestly didn't realise it was happening. I was too focused on those… young men that could… that could have hurt you," I said, very proud of the emotion in my voice,

"You mean it?"

I nodded.

"Who is this woman?" the hot man asked with such arrogance I wanted to stab him right there and then.

"Richard, this is our Assassin. Assassin this is Richard, rightfully Lord Castellan of the House of Martyrdom,"

Now I know I was meant to act so surprised, shocked and in awe of this god amongst man, but seriously? This man wasn't going to beat me in a fight, he wasn't going to fight an army a thousand strong with a sword or do anything else that the stories apparently said he could do.

He was just a man. A hot but weak man at that.

"Ever fought before?" I asked.

Richard shook his head.

"Thought so. Your power might be in your blood. But it isn't activated until you rule the City, is it?" I asked.

"She's right," Richard said. "That's why I need your help,"

I pulled my long black cloak and hood slightly loose as I realised I had him exactly where I wanted him.

"You need us as much as we need you. Well, we don't need you too much, but the Rebellion will strike a deal," I said.

"What deal?"

Abbic wrapped her arms around him. "When we take ta City for ya, ya becoming an ally, give us a home, soldiers and food,"

Richard kissed Abbic and looked at me. "I agree but it can't happen. I have no idea how to take the City,"

And people honestly wonder why I worked alone for decades before I had to save the Rebellion, people are useless!

"What is the Hand of Divinity?" I asked.

Everyone looked blank at me. Typical.

"I killed three Priests-"

"You did not!" Richard shouted.

I gave him an evil smile.

"No wonder they're hunting you. Knocking down doors. Priests, Priestesses and all religious figures are seen as living Gods here. You don't kill them!"

I waved him silent. "Anyway the last one mentioned the City is ruled over by the Gods. But in reality the Hand of Divinity acts in their name,"

Still everyone looked at me blankly.

This was going well.

I heard something outside. It sounded like tens of voices walking up and down the street.

"I know somewhere we could find out. Your killing might be good for us actually," Richard said.

"How?" Coleman asked.

"Three Priests never get killed here so the Maiden of Light will call a summons in a few hours at nine O'clock. The last time a summons was called I was a boy and I remember seeing six people at the front,"

"Hands don't have six fingers, ya know?"

I smiled at Abbic. "They don't. But a hand has five fingers coming from a palm that is attached to the rest of the body, or in our case the rest of the Overlord's network,"

Oohs and aahs filled the drawing room as everyone else realised we had to go to that summons tomorrow (whatever a summons was!)

Someone thundered on the door.
They were smashing it down.
People were shouting outside.
"Quickly hide," Richard said.
The door shattered.
Guards poured in.

CHAPTER 10

2.75 Days Left

Commander Coleman hated being stuffed into a tiny wooden closet with the Assassin and Abbic next to him. Their weapons were jabbing into his back. Their hot breath was awful on the back of his neck.

He hated all of this.

The sound of the guards in their black armour made Coleman place his hand tightly on the hilt of his blade. If the enemy found them then he was going to fight, the enemy were not taking him and his friends alive.

That was a promise.

The disgusting smell of rot, sweat and death attacked Coleman's senses as the guards' footsteps got louder and louder and louder. Even Richard's voice was only a mutter compared to the heavy footsteps of the guards.

Richard could be trying to hint where the Rebels were hiding, but Coleman doubted it. He truly believed that Richard wanted their help.

The footsteps stopped in front of the closet.

Coleman prepared himself.

The closet door shattered.
Coleman stormed out.
Whipping out his sword.
The Guards were everywhere.
The Assassin jumped over him.
She attacked.
Coleman joined her.
His sword swung.
Shattering metal armour.
Slicing off heads.
Smashing bones.
Crunching arms.
The guards screamed.
They tried to fight.
Coleman and the Assassin didn't give them a take.
Abbic stabbed them.
She thrusted her knife into their chests.
Blood painted the walls.
Covered the art.
The floor flooded with blood.
The Guards screamed.
One tried to escape.
The Assassin rushed over.
Snapping his neck.
More Guards poured in.
They whacked the Assassin to one side.
They swarmed her.
Coleman dashed over.
Someone tackled him.
Slamming their fists into him.
Abbic grabbed the Guard's neck.
Snapping it off.
Coleman jumped up.

Raised his sword.

The Assassin was standing in a sea of corpses.

Richard ran over to them. Passing Coleman and Abbic cloaks.

They had to leave.

Coleman heard more guards coming.

Coleman realised the enemy knew they were here and that terrified him more than anything.

No backup. No support. Just four people against an army.

CHAPTER 11

2.75 Days Left

I barely managed to clean all the blood off my cloak but that's great fun. There is nothing like killing a bunch of foul ugly guards to get the heart pumping. I love it!

In my long black cloak and hood me, Richard, Coleman and Abbic went into a massive Cathedral filled with tens of thousands of sweaty, dirty poor people who attempted to wear their best for such an occasion, but in all honesty they were just wearing scraps of cloth.

I wanted to help them and I really hoped that the gold I gave to random houses helped some people, but I doubted they had kept it, probably gave it back to the Church for *safe keeping*.

Fools!

The Cathedral was rather beautiful with its massive gold domed roof that looked so perfect, so angelic and stunning in the way that it reflected the light from thousands of candles that floated in the air.

If anything I was stunned at the amazing scale of the Cathedral, I saw this earlier when we were coming into the docks and sure the golden dome was massive, but the Cathedral was immense. It easily went on for a good few miles in all directions. No wonder it could fit tens of thousands of people at any one time.

Actually I was even more surprised that we might have been a few hundred metres away from the main raised platform that surprise, surprise was solid gold and covered in jewels. But it wasn't packed. Everyone had some kind of personal space regardless of how many people were packed in here.

Behind me I heard some people in utter awe of the Cathedral's smooth dark blue walls with thousands of little images of saints, the Overlord and heroes painted in gold, jade and even bronze. The Overlord had really gone all out with this place with his Hand of Divinity and that was what I wanted to find out about.

The Hand had to be discovered but this wasn't a good killing ground. There were far too many people, it smelt and I was too far away from the raised platform where the Hand of Divinity would be. And as much as I wanted to stalk the crowd and edge closer to the target platform, there were still too many people.

"Look behind you," Coleman whispered.

I did and I was more than pleased to see there was an immense balcony built into the Cathedral covered in nothing except a golden star with rays of white light coming out of it in the centre. But I focused on the claw marks on the balcony around that star.

My thinking was someone important stood there so they could worship without any interference or having to deal with all these sweaty smelly people. I really wanted some of them to have a bath!

The entire cathedral went quiet as five people went up onto the raised platform and I checked behind me, and as I guessed there was a woman standing on the balcony.

But she troubled me. She was covered completely in thin sterile white armour, even her face was faceless with a thin plate of white armour covering it. She didn't look real at all, it was almost like she was beyond human and looking down at her mortal slaves.

"Turn around," Richard said firmly. "You'll draw attention,"

I turned my focus back on the five people on the raised platform. There was nothing too remarkable about three of them as they just wore plain black face masks made from iron and horrible long white robes. I couldn't imagine it would be too difficult to kill them but it all depended on what they had underneath.

Speaking of which I wouldn't mind seeing what Coleman had underneath.

"People of Martyrs!" a tall elegant woman said.

I hated her pompous voice as she sounded so arrogant, so superior to these people and she sounded like she was a Goddess.

"We are under attack," the woman said.

Everyone gasped in horror.

"It seems that there is a killer on the loose. They murdered in cold blood three of our most Holiest Priests. By attacking them. They attack our gods and you!"

I was expecting another gasp from everyone but only a quarter of the room gasped. Maybe these people weren't as religious as I believed. Maybe they did want their rulers dead after all.

"We tracked the killer down to the House of Former Lord Castellan Richard and I am sad to hear he is dead,"

Wow their information was awful.

"Now we will continue to hunt down the killer but our Honourable Maiden of Light would like to say a few words," the tall woman said, gesturing for everyone to turn around.

We did and I stared at the cold faceless mask of the woman on the balcony.

"My subjects. The Gods have spoken. You have all failed in your dedication. There were witnesses last night. None of you stepped forward to protect your Hand. So Hand judges you. Arrest a thousand people and the Gods will judge them,"

As the people at the very back of the Cathedral screamed in terror as the guards grabbed them, beat them and dragged them away. I focused on the coldness of her words. I couldn't imagine a human being so cold with such disregard for the life of others, but here this woman was.

Coleman grabbed my hand. I loved the sexy hot electricity that flowed between us but I squeezed it and released his hand.

"Richard, who is she?" I asked.

"The Maiden of Light is um... the true Ruler of the City. No one has ever seen her face but she is apparently the avatar of the Gods. They speak through her,"

"What happens if she dies?" I asked.

The Maiden just looked at me and I felt her borrowing into my mind.

I grabbed Coleman's arm. "We-"

"Rebels!" the Maiden shouted.

I hadn't even realised there were hundreds of guards lining the edges of the cathedral. They were storming towards us.

People screamed.

They ran.

They didn't care about their Hand.

The Hand flew off the raised platform.

They whipped out their white swords.

They were ready to fight.

So was I.

CHAPTER 12
2.66 Days Left

Commander Coleman was going to gut these bastards for daring to attack him and his friends.

He stood back to back with Richard and Abbic, each with their swords at the ready to chomp, slaughter and kill these guards and even the Hand.

The Hand with their black masks looked stupid anyway as they marched towards Coleman surrounded by the majesty and stunning beauty of the cathedral. Coleman loved the blue walls with their images of heroes.

Now it was his turn to be the hero.

The sounds of screaming, panic and pain filled the air as the tens of thousands of worshippers rushed out of the cathedral and some people fell and were crushed.

People were dying all because of the Maiden of Light.

She was staring at them and the Assassin was

staring at her.

"Kill her!" Coleman shouted.

The Assassin nodded and ran off into the crowd. Coleman had to protect her. Coleman couldn't let the Assassin face her alone there was something off about the Maiden.

Coleman raised his sword and prepared to attack.

The Guards flew at them.

Coleman swung his sword.

Sparks flew everywhere.

The Guards kept charging.

He felt Richard and Abbic press against his back.

They were being forced back.

Guards were everywhere.

The Guards swung their swords at Coleman.

He blocked.

Coleman screamed as the force of the impact whacked his sword away.

He didn't have a weapon.

He had to break formation.

Everyone broke it as one.

They all rolled away.

The Guards swung.

They missed.

They slashed their own chests.

Coleman kept rolling.

He grabbed his sword.

Jumped up.

Thrusted it into someone's chest.

The Guards kept coming.

Coleman needed a new plan.

They were outnumbered.

Abbic was being overwhelmed.

Coleman couldn't let her die.

He dashed over.

Ramming his sword into a Guards' back.

Then all the Guards simply took a few steps back and Coleman felt his stomach churn as he saw the three members of the Hand of Divinity with their black iron masks hold their swords at Coleman's, Abbic's and Richard's chest.

Coleman wanted to attack them all now but he noticed a strange white energy crackling around them. He didn't know what weapons they were holding but nothing good was ever going to happen by attacking them head on.

He needed a new plan.

"You dare attack the Maiden," someone said but it was clearly a man.

"What it to ya?" Abbic asked. "We gonna gut ya all,"

One of the Hand swung their sword in the air and Abbic screamed in crippling pain as white crackling energy wrapped around her.

"Stop that!" Coleman shouted.

Another of the Hand gestured they would do the same to Coleman.

"You can't do this. Our friend will find you and kill you," Coleman said.

The three members of the Hand exchanged

looks with each other and made a series of clicks. Coleman wished the Assassin had taught him the clicking language like she had offered because it sure would have been useful about now.

"You will not do that to us!" Richard shouted, clearly knowing the language.

One of them swung their sword in the air and the white energy crackled around Richard.

"We will imprison, kill you and send a direct message to the Assassin. Her father wants her back,"

Coleman wanted to explain how that message would only end in their deaths but he just stayed silent. Nothing good was going to happen if he spoke. He fully planned on just leaving these deluded Holy figures to their delusions that would certainly come back to kill them in the end.

"Commander Coleman, I trust we will not have any problems with you," another asked gesturing that they would swing their sword.

"Of course not, *my Lords and Ladies*," Coleman said, mockingly but seriously enough.

The woman in the long white robes who spoke to the masses earlier stepped forward.

"Good, Guards take him and the other two away," the woman said before she looked at the three in the masks. "You three, kill the Assassin. Kill her,"

Coleman's stomach churned and churned and churned as he forced himself not to lash out. He had to be taken away and not end up like Abbic and Richard, who were still screaming, if he was free to move about then maybe he could help her in the long term.

But now he was captured Coleman had a very bad feeling about the mission.

Especially with the entire remains of the Rebellion coming here in a few days.

CHAPTER 13
2.5 Days Left

I hated this Maiden of Light for daring to kill me and my friends. Who the hell does she think she is? No one and I mean no one attacks us and gets to live! This is beyond outrageous!

I pulled my long black cloak and hood tightly over myself as I stepped onto the horrible massive stone balcony where the Maiden of Light was when I last saw her. I hated everything about this balcony from its foul blue walls to utterly arrogant scripture saying how amazing she was.

I wasn't to gut her.

Even the horrid smell of burning incense was nothing to make me furious at her, and the sounds of my friends in trouble made me want to burn this entire Cathedral to the ground...

Oh. Now that's an idea!

The sound of three heavy footsteps came from behind me and when I looked at them I was hardly surprised to see the three members of the Hands with their black iron masks. Two men, one woman.

They all had their long white swords with magical energy crackling around them. I knew what they did but I hoped they wouldn't affect me.

They all swung their swords in the air.

The magic energy crackled around me.

It was closing in.

I wasn't scared.

I wanted the pain.

I wanted to feel.

I wanted to kill the magic.

The magic energy diffused away from me. Coward!

With the three iron mask wearers exchanging glances with each other, I took my chance.

I flew at them.

Jumping into the air.

Whipping out my swords.

I landed on one of their necks.

I pulled my momentum to throw the Hand Member to the ground.

Ramming my swords into his head.

The other two swung at me.

I ducked.

They lost their balance.

I kicked one.

The woman grabbed my head.

I backflipped.

Making her fall.

I stomped on her face.
Something cracked.
She didn't die.
The last man charged at me.
I jumped.
Not in time.
He caught me.
Ramming me into the stone of the balcony.
It started cracking.
I went to scream.
I looked below.
One of my friends might help me.
They were gone.
They were in danger.
They could be dead.
The man grabbed my throat.
He squeezed.
My friends were in danger!
I kicked him in-between the legs.
He fell to the ground.
He moaned.
I stomped on his manly goods.
He screamed.
I whacked his head.
I kicked him again and again.
His blood splattered everywhere.
He tried to stand up.
I grabbed the mask.
Ripping it off.
It was melted into his face.

I threw the mask at the woman.

She ducked.

She wasn't attacking me.

I jumped on the barely living man.

Grabbing his head.

I smashed his head on the floor.

Over and over.

And over.

All until there was nothing left in my hands and there was only the shattered corpse of a man in front of me.

I stood up and stared at the woman who was impressively holding a shaky sword at me like she would actually kill me. I always admire ambition so I had to give her her due.

But my friends were in danger and I don't stop for anyone when that happens.

So I simply walked to her, gently took the sword of her hand and wrapped my hands around her throat.

"Where are my friends?" I asked coldly.

The woman didn't answer so I snapped her neck.

I went over to the spot on the balcony where the Maiden of Light stood each service and I understood why she stood here. It felt as if this spot had power, purpose and the admiration of hundreds of thousands locked into the very stone. Which was off considering there were no markings on the stone ground.

Yet as beautiful as this all looked it was a symbol of the Overlord's power, influence and corruption in the City so it had to be annihilated.

I just didn't know how but I would find a way.

Just like I always do.

CHAPTER 14
2.25 Days Left

Commander Coleman sat in a large metal cage with Abbic and Richard hissing, screaming and moaning as the white energy crackling them kept torturing them.

Coleman felt the cold metal cage vibrate and bang as it was pulled through the streets of the City of Martyrs with its little white houses and the thousands of candles lighting the way.

It was strange that there were so many candles lit even though it was only early evening with the sun brightly lighting the evening sky, Coleman had bigger problems so he didn't care too much about the ways of the City.

He had to figure out a way to escape, the guards had escorted him, Abbic and Richard to various cells, transports and now they were meant to be taking them to some advanced interrogation centre, but Coleman wasn't going to let that happen.

The sounds of pain from his friends grew more intense and Coleman hoped the so-called Maiden of Light was going to get an agonising death. She was in charge. She gave the orders. It was her that was going to die.

Pulling the metal cage along were two large black horses and one of the Hand were guiding them. Coleman wished he could reach that idiot Hand driving the cage and kill them but he couldn't reach.

From what he could see of the Hand member, it wasn't the tall woman with white robes that spoke to the masses nor was it the three members with their black iron masks. It looked to be a man wearing long white robes with red crosses and golden jewellery covering the robes.

It was clear that he was important so Coleman hoped he wasn't that good at combat.

The sound of people singing, chanting and shouting came from ahead and Coleman raised his head to see a massive mob of people with knives, pitchforks and spades standing there.

They blocked the street completely.

The metal cage came to a stop and Coleman went over to the cage's door at the back and inspected it. He had hoped for screws or something easy to break open.

But the door disappeared.

"Move!" the Hand Member said. "I am Lord Bishop Anchor, I demand you to move!"

No one moved. Everyone smiled.

"What say you Rebels?" the man at the very front of the mob said.

Coleman stood up. "I say we can help each other,"

The mob nodded. "What say you Commander, can you free us?"

"Yes," Coleman said.

"What say you Lord Bishop, do you want to live?"

"Ha! You cannot hurt me. I am-"

The mob flew forward.

They raised their pitchforks.

They raised their spirits.

They raised everything.

The Lord Bishop whipped out his sword.

Magical energy crackled around them.

Coleman shook Abbic.

She hissed louder.

He had to help.

The mob started screaming.

Abbic moved her arms.

Coleman realised something. The more the mob screamed. The freer Abbic was.

Coleman shook her head more and more.

The Lord Bishop screamed.

The mob were stabbing him with their pitchforks, spades and knives.

The Lord Bishop screamed.

Then all went silent.

The man who presumably led the mob walked up

to the metal cage, and Coleman had a good long look at him. He was clearly a skilled worker with his smoother-than-most hands and his well maintained features. But there was something strange about him, he didn't seem bothered that he had just killed a member of the Hand of Divinity, he must have known the consequences. The man didn't seem bothered.

To Coleman that normally meant one of two things. One, the man was somewhere on the crazy scale, or two, he had killed so many times it didn't affect him more.

Coleman didn't know what one he hoped for.

"Grab his sword," Coleman said.

The man clicked his fingers and the Lord Bishop's sword flew over to him. He passed it to Coleman.

He had no idea how it worked but it was clearly some kind of magic, and normally magic worked by a power, a focus and an effect. Coleman hoped he was right about the focus being the sword and the effect (he really hoped) would be the unlocking of the cage and freeing of his friends.

The power? He had no clue but it could be something as simple as his Will.

Coleman closed his eyes and imagined Abbic and Richard being free from the magical energy that trapped him. He swung the sword.

Nothing happened.

Coleman focused on the love, respect and

admiration he had for them. He didn't want them trapped, he wanted them free to live, love and fight against the Overlord. He swung the sword again.

Nothing.

Coleman swore as he tried a final time. This time Coleman really, really focused on his feelings for both Abbic and Richard, then he focused extremely hard on imagining them being free.

Two bodies hit the ground.

Coleman opened his eyes and went over to them both, he helped them up and gave Abbic a massive hug and Richard a hard handshake.

The mob clapped.

"Impressive Commander. Not seen that for decades," the Mob Leader said.

Horns, marching and flames roaring echoed around the street as everyone saw a stream of black armoured guards marching from the Cathedral down to them. Coleman had to be quick.

He went to the "walls" of the metal cage, closed his eyes and focused. He wanted to slaughter the cage, destroyed it and most importantly be free.

He swung the sword.

The metal cage turned to ash.

Arrows pounded the ground.

Guards fired.

Guards charged at them.

The mob fled.

Coleman grabbed Abbic and Richard.

Dragging them away.

They were free and ready to bring the Maiden of Light's rule crashing down!

CHAPTER 15
2 Days Left

Something I absolutely love about the religious folks of the world is their ability to find the most amazing places to hide their alcohol. It has taken me over three hours, a lot of killing and sighting for me to finally find enough alcohol to blow this Cathedral up.

I couldn't help but smile at my impressive pile of hundreds of wine, brandy and ale bottles and even more crates of Gods know what alcohol that was all piled perfectly in the middle of the Cathedral.

Blowing this place up was definitely going to be a highlight of my life. Getting rid of those horrible blue walls with their silly images, blowing up that stupid balcony and turning this symbol of my father's corruption, power and influence to ash.

That was going to make me extremely happy.

Sure I really, really wanted my beautiful Coleman to be here with me, I would love to stare into his stunning dark emerald eyes in the dancing light of the flame, but I sadly had to do this alone.

I do love burning things down though.

But all the alcohol made the cathedral sink of wine, bad ale and sick. I was starting to question if everything in that pile was alcohol.

Loosening my long black cloak and hood, I held out my flaming torch and prepared to throw it at the pile. Sure it would take a few seconds to light, blow and burn but I'll be lying if I said I wasn't concerned.

Two arrows shot at me.

I threw the torch at the pile.

More arrows fired.

It knocked the torch off course.

It landed far away from the pile.

I spun around.

Instantly raising my arms as the Maiden of Light with her horrid white faceless mask and white robes walked towards me with four guards carrying crossbows.

"I admit your arrival was a surprise, Jasper," the Maiden of Light said.

How the hell did she know my true name? Besides my dickhead of a father only Coleman knows it and I doubted either of them would tell her my name.

"It was fun watching you run about like the little mortal fool you are," she said.

I watched the guards walk around me. I couldn't let them near that flaming torch.

"What is your aim here Jasper? You cannot win. The Gods and Goddesses have foreseen your death here,"

I have never quite understood why people use that as a fear tactic. I have never feared death and now… now I actually think I am living a life worth living and I have a purpose.

And right now that meant my purpose was destroying the Hand of Divinity, including her.

I whipped out my two swords.

"Oh Jasper, I was hoping we could have avoided all this. Your Father will be most disappointed,"

She waved a hand and the torch went out.

Rage filled me.

I flew at her.

I swung.

She ducked.

She whipped out her own swords.

We clashed.

Sparkes flew.

Sparkes flew!

I kicked her.

She dodged.

She punched me.

Throwing me across the cathedral.

I slammed into a wall.

She disappeared.

She punched me from behind.

Throwing me forward.

She kicked me.

I jumped up.

Swinging my swords.

We clashed.

I punched.

I kicked.

I headbutted.

She dodged them all.

Our swords clashed against.

I pressed all my weight on her.

She jumped away.

I fell forward.

She rammed her swords into my back.

I screamed.

I wasn't dead yet!

I rolled over.

Raised my swords.

She bought her swords down.

We clashed.

Sparkes flew everywhere.

Whooshing filled the cathedral.

And I could never not smile as I watched her eyes widen in utter horror as she realised I had made her fight in such a way that she would be closer to the pile of alcohol.

She kicked me in the stomach as we both watched the massive pile of alcohol light up and become a flaming inferno.

The Maiden of Light and her guards simply walked away.

I tried to stand up but I couldn't. My back was

hurting too much. I felt blood run down my back.

I couldn't escape. I was going to die here.

More and more alcohol started to light up. It wouldn't be long until the bottles exploded.

My swords started to heat up and I knew what I had to do.

I rolled over and rammed my swords into the alcohol fuelled flames. Then I forced myself to sit down and took off my long black cloak and my leather armour beneath.

Exposing my bare bleeding flesh.

My swords were starting to glow now.

I took out the red hot swords and pressed them against my wounds.

I screamed in agony.

Crippling plain filled me.

But my wounds were healed.

A bottle exploded.

Splashing flaming alcohol everywhere.

Adrenaline flooded me.

More bottles exploded.

I jumped up.

And ran.

More bottles exploded.

The entire cathedral burnt.

Toxic smoke filled the Cathedral.

I kept running.

A deafening whoosh came from behind.

I saw the door outside.

I ran as fast as I could.

I jumped through the door.

The explosion rushed past me.

My ears rang.

But my eyes focused on the twenty guards aiming their crossbows at me.

CHAPTER 16
2 Days Left

Commander Coleman sat with Abbic and Richard at a massive oak table inside a wonderfully dark room with tens, maybe even hundreds of peasants around the table, waiting for their leader to return.

Besides from the honestly horrible smell of sweat, dirt and urine coming from the peasants, Coleman loved the atmosphere at it felt as if everyone was here illegally and this was all one big conspiracy against the Rulers of the City of Martyrs.

Coleman had to convince them to fight, kill and slaughter the enemy and hopefully make sure they wanted to join the Rebellion. He wasn't sure who these people were but after travelling around with them for six hours now, he was at least fairly sure he could trust them. But the sounds of their talking, muttering and laughing didn't exactly comfort Coleman.

At the very end of the table a large old man sat down wearing a dirty cloth, a belt and a sword at his waist. Out of everyone he had seen, this was the first person who screamed leader to Coleman.

The man just stared at them for a few moments before he waved his friends away and everyone took a few steps back.

"Ya father would be eased Commander," the man said.

Coleman leant forward. "You knew my father?"

"Yea, we were once rebels like yourself us lot. Your father sent us here to die, become a distant memory and let me run *his* Rebellion as he wished,"

There were plenty of rumours about the Rebellion's twisted history that Coleman had heard of over the years, including something about a legion of troublemakers sent to a forgotten City to fight, kill and hopefully die themselves.

"You kept fighting all this time?" Coleman asked.

Richard placed a gentle hand on Coleman's arm.

"What my friend means-"

"We know what he means. He didn't keep fighting. We failed. We ran away and didn't die here like we were meanna," the man said.

Coleman stood up. "My father might of had his reasons. But I am not my father, the Rebellion needs you again,"

All Coleman could hope for at that moment was not to get attacked, sworn at or reported to the Overlord's puppets.

The man stood up too. "My name is Justicus Pilon... but my friends call me Justin,"

Justin bowed to Coleman as did every single man and woman under his command.

"Tonight we do not fight for the Rebellion, the people who hated us. Tonight we fight for Coleman, for blood and for Freedom," Justin said.

Everyone cheered.

"And when we claim this City, you will have your freedom," Coleman said.

Justin smiled.

"Then everyone, prepare ya weapons, ya food and ya loved ones. We march on the City at dawn,"

Everyone walked away so only Justin, Abbic and Richard were in the room with Coleman.

Justin walked over to them.

"What ya mean boyo marching at dawn?" Abbic asked.

"Ya didn't tell 'em did ya?" Justin said to Richard.

Coleman frowned at Richard. "What aren't you telling us *Lord Castellan*?"

"The Cathedral might have burned but that isn't the Hand's main base of operations," Richard said.

That was ridiculous, how the hell was Coleman meant to lead, make a plan and defeat the enemy if everyone was only telling him half the information!

"Where is ta Assassin?"

Coleman felt his body warm and sweat roll down his back as he realised that his beautiful Assassin was missing. She had destroyed the main cathedral hours ago and now it was completely ash.

That alone would trouble him but she always found him somehow and she hasn't yet. That wasn't like her.

Coleman wanted to shout, scream and demand some kind of search party or form some kind of plan to save her, but he had no idea where to look.

He had to save her by any means.

"Where is their main base then?" Coleman asked firmly.

Richard exchanged glances with Justin. "There's a temple underground. Simple layout. Simple defences. Simple to attack. But the Maiden defends it herself. Going inside is a death sentence,"

Coleman laughed. "Oh Richard, Justin, you clearly have no idea what lengths I'll go to to rescue the Assassin. We need her,"

Justin slammed his fist on the table. "Or do *ya* need her?"

Coleman said nothing.

"I will not send my forces back for ya to rescue ya girl," Justin said walking away.

Coleman looked at Richard and Abbic. "I will save her,"

Abbic jumped off her chair and smiled. "Course ya will, I gonna help ya too Bossie. Assassin my friend and friends protect each other,"

Both Coleman and Abbic looked at Richard. He rolled his eyes.

"Fine, I'll help you save your Assassin,"

CHAPTER 17
1 Day Left

I was not happy!

These idiot guards dared to capture me, lock me up and dump me in some fucking cell! The cheek!

I can promise them that the second I get out of this cell I am going to gut them so much that the Overlord can see their mutilated corpses from his palace!

I honestly wouldn't mind being trapped in a wet dirty box room made of horrible stone, but the smell is awful. Some overweight prisoner must have taken an almighty poo in the corner and the guards haven't cleared it up yet.

Even the coldness of the cell isn't making me any happier, I love the cold of metal bars but as I ran my fingers across them icy coldness isn't shot into me. It was a pathetic kind of coldness.

I had had enough! I was getting out of here!

Of course the idiot guards hadn't given me any

weapons and it was only because I snapped a neck of a guard that I had been allowed to keep my long black cloak and hood. Thankfully I always keep a small blade in there.

I slipped it out of a pocket but judging by the bar metals and tough stone walls I wasn't going to be able to escape that way, but on second thought I could have sworn these stone walls were made of flint.

And flint can light.

Granted I honestly can't remember the last time I lit poo up, but I know it burns well and guards don't like fires. Especially when the Maiden of Light gives them specific orders to keep me alive whilst she arranges transport to the Capital (and my dick of a father) for me.

I went over to one of the flint walls, chipped away at it and managed to break off a piece of flint.

Then I looked at the massive pile of poo and realised I had to do the most disgusting job in my assassin career, I had to move it around the cell. Believe me, this sounds unneeded and I wished it was, but if I just lit up a pile in the corner then the guards wouldn't care.

I needed to make them care.

I went over to the pile (and really held my breath) as I gently kicked it to different areas in the cell, giving me six perfectly small piles of poos.

I lit each one up.

Black smoke filled the cell and filtered into the stone corridor beyond where I hoped the guards.

Then the piles started popping.

Little fires started elsewhere.

The fire spread.

I pressed my back against the metal bars. I didn't want a raging fire. The flames consumed the rest of the cell.

The flint started exploding.

Shit!

I pulled my hood over my face. Shards of flint hit me. Slicing my cloak.

The Guards shouted.

They ran towards me.

The flames got closer.

They licked my flesh.

I felt hands grab me.

Massive shards of flint exploded.

Deadly shards flew towards us.

I jumped back.

The guards screamed.

Their blood ran down their faces.

They were crying on the ground.

More flint exploded.

Shredding them to pieces.

And there I had it, I snapped the neck of one guard, took his weapons and simply left the exploding flint to do my job for me.

Now I was free, armed and more than ready to kill every single enemy in this place.

CHAPTER 18
1 Day Left

Commander Coleman stood with his sword drawn as he peeked around a corner of a little white house and looked at a heavily guarded cobblestone street.

Abbic and Richard were behind Coleman and everyone was ready to move. There was a small manhole cover in the middle of the street that was the entrance to the underground temple dedicated to the Maiden of Light.

And that was where his Assassin was.

Coleman had to save her, he loved her, he wasn't going to let her die. But there were so many silly guards here that needed to die.

It was annoying as hell that the exiled Rebels had abandoned Coleman, but he didn't need them. He was a leader and an amazing fighter and he was going to do whatever it took to save the woman he loved.

Richard had tried to warn him earlier about the

maze the temple was and how it could take them hours just to enter the main temple complex, but Coleman did not care. This was the Assassin he was going to save.

Coleman looked at Abbic and Richard were climbing on the white rooftops of the houses, they nodded at him. They were ready.

Coleman raised his swords.

He charged.

The guards didn't see him.

Coleman jumped on them.

Ramming his sword into their chests.

Ribs cracked.

Blood flooded on the ground.

Coleman hacked his way through them.

Armour smashed.

Bones shattered.

Coleman stomped on their skulls.

The Guards knew he was there.

They charged at him.

They swung.

Coleman ducked.

They all kicked him.

Coleman felt the impacts.

He hissed.

Pain flooded through him.

He wasn't stopping.

Coleman ran.

Jumping into the air.

He swirled his swords.

Becoming a hurricane of death.

The guards tried to block him.

They couldn't.

Coleman's swords ripped into their armour.

Slicing into their warm flesh.

Abbic and Richard jumped down.

Thrusting their swords into the Guards.

It was a slaughter.

And within a few minutes Coleman, Abbic and Richard had massacred all the guards, but the problem with these sorts of places where there were always more guards just round the corner, Coleman had to be quick.

They all went over to the manhole cover that was nothing more than a little black iron circle in the ground, but Coleman instantly spotted a problem.

It was magically sealed.

"Anyone know how to break a magic seal?" Coleman asked.

Abbic shrugged, so did Richard.

Coleman pointed a finger at Richard. "Wait a minute, you're a Lord Castellan. You can break it,"

Richard frowned. "I am not a Lord Castellan yet,"

Coleman stood up. "Maybe you don't need to rule to be a Lord Castellan. The power is in your blood. You just need to believe in yourself,"

Coleman had no idea if it was true but they didn't have a lot of other options at this point.

"Don't be-" Richard said.

"Don't ya dare call my Bossie silly. Ya need to take responsibility for life!"

Richard stared at Coleman. "I don't know how to be a Lord Castellan,"

The sound of guards from streets away made Coleman's stomach tense.

"Say it with me, *you are a Lord Castellan. You are powerful. You are a Leader. You are magical*,"

Richard repeated it but he didn't sound convinced.

"For Gods and Goddesses sake, Richard focus. You are a born leader. You secretly fought against the Overlord for years. You survived. I saw your schemes in your house. You funded, supported and loved those exiled Rebels," Coleman said.

Richard nodded.

"You have an amazing mind. You are willing to die to save someone you hardly know. That makes you a born leader to me. And Leaders are what Lord Castellans are!"

Richard smiled. "I am Lord Castellan,"

It was really starting to annoy Coleman that he wasn't saying it convincingly enough.

The guards were getting closer.

Coleman grabbed Richard's arm. "Who are you?"

Richard looked to the ground but Coleman grabbed his face and made him look him in the eye.

"Who are you!" Coleman shouted.

"I am Lord Castellan Richard of the House of the Martyrdom and I demand you to release me!"

The air crackled with magical energy as Coleman released him and the very air hummed, popped and banged as something was happening.

Richard was engulfed in bright white fire but he did not scream. He laughed, smiled and wanted this to happen.

Coleman watched the lightning shoot around them all as Richard presumably became and took up his birthright.

When the white fire got absorbed into Richard, he fell to his knees and Coleman noticed that Richard was stronger, tougher and every single part of him had changed slightly. His skin was thick, his jawline stronger and his hair thicker.

Coleman realised he was looking at the peak of human attractiveness and physique. (He just hoped the Assassin still had eyes for him after this battle)

"Guards! Flamethrowers!" Abbic shouted.

Coleman just looked at Richard.

Richard went over to the manhole cover.

He extended his arms.

Flamethrowers screamed through the air.

Coleman grabbed Abbic.

He pulled her to safety.

They rushed over to Richard.

The air crackled.

The manhole exploded into shards.

Richard threw the shards of the guards.

All three of them jumped down into the temple below and Coleman was ready to save the woman he loved and kill anyone who tried to stop him.

CHAPTER 19
0.75 Days left

Whoever created this stupid underground temple was going to die!

It was ridiculous that I had just spent six hours (including a quick power nap) searching, running and killing my way through its twisted network of horrible black stone tunnels.

I had had enough and I was going to find the Maiden of Light and slaughter her for ever trapping me here in the first place!

Raising my swords as I went along another awful stone tunnel, I prepared myself for whatever horror or silly guard was going to try and stop me.

But to my surprise, I saw a large door ahead of me made from solid gold with tens of candles lighting it up. Someone clearly wanted any onlookers to see its amazingly smooth golden surface, sparkling jewels and even the little pieces of scripture in the door that praised the Gods and Goddesses.

It was clear who was behind there and a wave of pure excitement filled me as I relaxed my body, loosened my shoulders and prepared to storm in there and kill the Maiden of Light.

She had to be in there.

But I felt my stomach tighten, relax then tighten again as I realised that I was alone down here. My beautiful Coleman wasn't here to protect (and fail) me, he wasn't here to jump in front of a sword or try to die for me. Like I found that attractive anyway (I didn't).

If I went into that room then I was truly alone, no one would be there to support me, protect me or do anything. If I got into trouble then I was dead.

I kept walking towards the massive golden door, all I had ever wanted from life was to live a life beyond killing, I wanted a life worth living. And Coleman had given me that, if I died today then I would have died sacrificing myself for something greater than I ever could have imagined.

I was going to die so millions of people could have a shot at freedom.

As I walked past the tens of candles they started to go out one by one, then two by two and they all went out and I was alone in the darkness.

The freezing cold darkness surrounded me and I couldn't tell where the stone tunnel walls began and my body ended. It was pitch dark.

Then the golden door started glowing. First it was bright gold, then red, then white, and with each colour change I realised my long leather cloak and hood were getting hotter and hotter and hotter.

Shoot!

I ran away as quickly I could before the door exploded. Sending me flying.

Boiling hot gold splashed all over the tunnel and a tiny amount splashed against my long black cloak.

I forced myself back up and to my utter amazement that arrogant Maiden of Light with her long white robes and white faceless mask was just standing there where the door once was.

The dark stone walls of the tunnel were now covered in bright shiny gold allowing me to see everything because of the horrible white light the Maiden was projecting.

Of course she didn't have any facial expression but I could have sworn I felt her smiling or just curious about what I would do next. I wanted to run, fight and kill her, but I felt like that was what she wanted. I supposed she had to wait to find out.

Fat chance!

I charged at her.

She flicked her hand and I froze. I really, really hate witches!

"Relax now Jasper. My spell will wear off in a few moments. But we have time my darling,"

I wanted to rip her throat out for saying that.

"Do not struggle my darling Jasper, your mother made me promise never to hurt you but I never did like her. The Overlord was a fool for choosing her,"

My eyes narrowed. "What do you know about my mother?"

"Jasper, you and your brother, were failures as far as the Overlord was concerned. Deficit stock from a defected woman,"

I forced myself not to scream or lash out. I had to keep her talking but I would end her painfully for mentioning my brother as deficit. The Overlord never should have killed him.

"So that is why Jasper, The Overlord moved onto more correct women with your mother's weaknesses, problems and... well, abnormalities,"

I felt my fingers move and the Maiden stared at me.

"We can fight in a moment and I will kill you, but I think I have time to answer one more question on your behalf,"

I rolled my eyes and noticed my swords were on the ground a few metres from me. When it was time I had to be quick.

"Your father had so many women lined up to bed. So many women to give him rightfully children but he chose your mother. A weak, pathetic abnormal woman and look where that got him. So that is why I came to the City of Martyrs,"

I laughed hard. "Seriously? You ruled over the City just because you were heartbroken. Just because the tyrant you loved, didn't choose you?"

The Maiden shook her head. "You silly little girl. I was never heartbroken. Who did you think birthed the Hunters?"

My eyes widened.

The Maiden flew at me.
The final battle begins now!

CHAPTER 20
0.75 Days left

Commander Coleman was fuming at this Gods forsaken place, who would create such a pointless maze of dark stone tunnels? It was silly, pointless and Coleman was going to kill all the Guards that dared to stop him getting to the woman he loved.

Coleman slashed the throat of another guard as the corpse fell onto the cold stone tunnel floor. He looked around seeing Abbic and Richard standing their swords drawn.

They were all ready to act, kill and protect Coleman. But he needed a direction, he needed something to tell him where his beautiful Assassin was.

Heavy footsteps ran towards them.

Coleman spun.

More horrible black armoured guards charged at them.

Coleman raised his sword.

More and more guards were coming.

Far too many for them to kill.

Coleman didn't care. He was going to fight. He was going to kill for what he believed in.

Richard flew forward.

Magical energy crackling around him.

Coleman joined him.

Both him and Abbic charged.

Roaring as loud as they could.

Richard shot out his hand.

Magical pink lightning shot out.

Disorienting the guards.

Coleman swung his sword.

Hacking the guards to death.

The guards recovered.

They ran at Coleman.

Swinging their swords.

Firing their crossbows.

Firing their arrows.

Richard thrusted out his hands.

Magical energy crackled.

It hissed, popped and exploded.

Richard screamed.

His hands burnt.

Coleman smashed the head of a guard into a wall.

Richard was out.

He was useless.

Coleman dashed over to him.

The guards kept coming.

Hints of smoke filled the tunnel. Coleman hated

the smell.

Abbic shrieked.

She was thrown against a wall.

She fell to the ground.

The Guards raised their swords.

Coleman rushed over there.

Hands grabbed him.

Forcing him to the ground.

The cold steel of a sword kissed his neck and Coleman stopped moving, struggling and trying to escape as he realised that the guards were holding him too tight.

"Stop," a young female voice echoed around the tunnel.

Whilst Coleman had heard more than enough voices in his time, he would never forget the voice of the Maiden of Light. Especially as she walked past her guards with her wonderful white robes and interesting faceless mask.

But Coleman couldn't understand why she appeared ghostly, none of her looked solid or of this world.

"Commander, I must admit I would have loved to have seen you die in person. But alas I am killing your Assassin, this is the day the Rebellion dies truly,"

Coleman felt rage fill him. This Maiden of false gods and goddesses was attacking his stunning Assassin. He wasn't having any of that!

"Kill the girl," the Maiden ordered.

The entire tunnel lit up.

Flames rushed down the tunnel.

The guards loosened their grip.

Coleman ducked.

Flames roared through the tunnel.

Coleman felt his body warm.

Sweat dripped down his face.

When the flames were gone and Coleman stood up, flaming, smouldering corpses were all around him. Richard and Abbic stood up with their eyes wide in confusion.

Coleman couldn't blame them. The entire tunnel had just been attacked with some kind of flame weapon. Yet he and his friends had survived.

And there was only one group of people he knew that would try to save them.

"Turns out ma peeps like ya?" Justin said as he walked down the tunnel holding some kind of flamer weapon.

But what impressed Coleman ever more was the massive long line of exiled Rebels behind Justin that looked like they wanted a fight.

Justin knelt.

All the exiled Rebels knelt to Coleman.

"Well Commander, ya wanted us to fight. We're ya army,"

Coleman smiled. "Get-"

Deafening chances of blood, murder and slaughter echoed around the tunnel from behind Coleman.

He saw little flickering torches. There were

hundreds. The Maiden of Light appeared in front of Coleman.

"Enjoy every single last one of my Guard," she said.

Coleman thrusted his sword through the ghostly woman and to his surprise tears formed in her eyes and she bleed.

Then disappeared.

Justin grabbed Coleman.

"Go! Find ya woman. We'll hold 'em back!"

Justin and the Exiled Rebels pushed past Coleman. They wanted to fight. They wanted Coleman to succeed.

Abbic grabbed him. "Bossie, ya know we lost without her. Get her back,"

Coleman was never going to argue with his closest friend. He had to go. He had to leave them.

This wasn't about being a leader, helping the Rebellion survive or anything like that. Coleman had to do this for him. He had to save the Assassin or die trying.

The entire tunnel filled with the sounds of screaming, clashing swords and limbs being hacked off.

Coleman hugged Abbic and ran.

He had to find the Assassin.

He just hoped she was still alive.

CHAPTER 21

0.75 Days Left

I'm going to kill her so bad! I'm going to rip her stupid white faceless mask off!

I flew at her.

She whipped out her swords.

Our swords clashed.

Sparkes flew everywhere.

Lighting up the tunnel.

I kicked her.

She dodged.

The Maiden headbutted me.

Pain shot through me.

She jumped into the air.

Spinning and swirling.

Becoming a hurricane of death.

I couldn't block her attacks.

Her swords went wild.

Slicing through the air.

She sliced my black cloak and hood.

I rolled back.

She kept swirling.

I rolled back.

Again and again.

She landed.

Swinging her swords.

I raised mine.

Our swords clashed.

The impact jerked my hands.

My hands ached.

My bones cracked a little.

She didn't stop.

She kept swinging.

Swing after swing.

Unleashing rapid attack after attack.

I wasn't fast enough.

Her attacks were too quick.

Her swords whacked into mine.

My hands screamed in pain.

She kicked me.

I fell back.

She kicked again.

And again.

And again.

The Maiden leapt into the air.

Spinning around.

Kicking me in the head.

As I fell to the ground utter agony pulsed through my entire body. I had never fought someone as good as that before. I couldn't see any openings in her attacks.

She was masterful. She was a Goddess of fighting. She was unbeatable.

But I was an Assassin. I could and would find a way to kill her.

The Maiden of Light walked over to me pointing her swords at my chest. I raised my swords and weakly met hers.

My body ached with every breath, movement and thought. I needed help. I wished my Coleman was coming.

She smiled at me. "I did expect better from the great Assassin, First Daughter of the Overlord,"

The Maiden pressed her swords harder against mine. Making me hiss.

"Don't worry Assassin. You won't be alone with the Gods and Goddesses, a form of myself is killing Coleman as we speak. He will join you in the Afterlife,"

I surged forward.

Collapsing back down in agony. My body was never going to allow me to attack her like that again.

I forced my swords to press harder against hers as I stood up. My posture weak and pathetic but I was standing.

I could kill her still.

"Your Coleman will never win against me. Do you have a final message I could say to him?"

I swung her swords.

She dodged.

Disappearing.

She reappeared behind me. Slamming her fists into my back.

I fell to the ground as crippling pain filled me.

"Coleman won't die today," I said.

The Maiden of Light walked in front of me and grabbed me by the throat. Pulling me up to her level.

"I have sent my entire-"

The Maiden hissed, moaned and blood poured from her stomach.

I didn't care what did it.

I kicked her in the stomach.

She dropped me.

I jumped up.

Unleashing rapid of swings my swords.

She couldn't dodge them.

She was in too much pain.

My swords chomped onto her flesh.

Hacking lumps off.

Her blood painted the tunnel walls.

She moaned louder.

I jumped into the air.

Swirling.

Becoming my own hurricane of death.

My swirling swords sliced her throat.

I landed.

But as I landed I didn't see a dying body on the ground, the Maiden of Light was still like she had just completed some kind of glorious task. She seemed happy and her faceless mask just looked at me.

Her blood poured down her long white robes. Then it started to travel back into her wounds as they all healed themselves.

"That was a good try Jasper, The Masterful Assassin. But the only way to kill me is to break my mask. You can't do that,"

She punched me in the face.

Breaking my nose.

The bitch!

She swung her swords.

Slicing deep into my arms.

As I dropped my swords and placed my hands around myself to stop the bleeding, I could only stare up at the imposing white robed woman in front of me.

I was defeated. A living dead woman. A female assassin who was about to lose everything.

The Maiden placed both her swords on each side of my neck. Ready to slice it clear off.

You know my only regret is not telling Coleman I did love him. I actually did love that crazy strange man who seriously thought he could take on the Overlord with his friends.

I closed my eyes for the final blow.

Crippling pain faded into numbness as I had clearly lost too much blood and even my vision was starting to become black at the very edges.

The Maiden raised her swords. I prepared for the end.

Someone shouted something behind me.

I didn't know the words.

But the voice I knew that.

It was Coleman.

He had come for me!

My Coleman was alive!

I opened my eyes.

The Maiden raised her swords.

I wasn't going to die.

Coleman jumped over me.

Tackling the Maiden.

I grabbed my swords.

Screaming in pain.

I jumped up.

The Maiden whacked Coleman off her.

I thrusted my swords into her mask.

Shattering it.

As the Maiden of Light glowed bright for a final time, her white faceless mask shattered into millions of pieces and as they fell to the ground so did her long white robes.

But I wasn't shocked to see that there was not a body of flesh, blood or anything inside the robes. The robes fell just only air filled them because I knew that was what she was.

The Maiden of Light might have once been a person but that was a long time ago. Now she was ash, dust and air.

Purely magic for a soulless monster.

I felt more and more blood drip down my arms.

And as I collapsed into unconsciousness, there

was one thing that echoed in my mind from the Maiden.

The Hunters will come now.

CHAPTER 22
0 Days left

Commander Coleman stood on the cobblestone path in front of a long wooden jetty where in a few minutes his entire Rebellion would be stopping, unloading and joining him in their new home.

The air smelt amazing of sweet treats, caramels and cakes that the citizens of the City of Martyrs were baking as quickly as they could. Not because they needed to be made quickly but because the people here wanted to officially celebrate their new found freedom as soon as possible.

Even with the amazing warm air blowing past Coleman making a piece of his hair go crazy, he still loved every single little thing about the City now. This City was no longer a symbol of the Overlord's power, influence and corruption. For now it was a symbol of hope.

That is what Coleman had wanted.

As he watched the tens of massive wooden ships

that carried his Rebels towards the City come ever closer, wave after wave of excitement filled him. Because he could finally show them that he was their rightful leader.

He hadn't truly realised it before now but Coleman didn't feel like the Rebellion deserved him as leader, they deserved someone stronger, diplomatic and capable. And now Coleman could finally prove to himself and his Rebels that he was a mighty leader.

For whilst Coleman might have come here in doubt as a failed leader who wanted to show leadership and rebuild the Rebellion.

Now Coleman stood on the wonderful cobblestone path that would take his Rebels to their new home, base of operations and into the arms of their brothers and sisters in arms.

Coleman still didn't know how the Exiled Rebels had convinced Justin to aid Coleman in one of his darkest hours, but they had and to Coleman that was all that mattered. He had now had a real chance of fighting against the Overlord with new troopers and once again the Rebellion could and would grow into a force to be reckoned with.

Yet that was truly a problem for another day, Coleman had new things to do, explore and be happy about. He had to get to know the new Ruler of the City, Lord Castellan Richard. Coleman even offered to serve as an advisor as he tightened his kind grip on the City.

Then there were the matters of formulating a

plan against the Overlord now the Rebellion had a City under their control that they could use as a base to launch their attacks from.

In all honesty Coleman had no idea what message this would send to the Overlord, but he hoped, he really hoped that the fall of the City of Martyrs would send shockwaves through the Kingdom and inspire others to join Coleman and his Rebels.

It might have been a long chance but Coleman still had to have hope in these dark times. And it was they were, Coleman had no delusions that the Overlord wouldn't allow him to rule over one of his Cities for too long.

The Overlord would send an army to reclaim the City of Martyrs that was true, a certainty, an absolute. But that wouldn't be for days, weeks or months so Coleman just wanted to enjoy the next few days with his friends.

Coleman briefly looked towards the City with its thousands of burning candles, little white houses and now the amazing wreckage of the burnt out Cathedral for Coleman knew there was someone in the City he wanted to spend all his time with.

His beautiful Assassin with her amazing body, long black cloak and her deep eyes had almost died on this mission. She had been stolen from him and that had almost killed him inside.

Coleman never wanted to risk anything happening to her again without him telling the

Assassin how he felt.

Coleman took another amazing breath of the sweet scented air and promised himself that the moment that he could escape from his duties as a leader who had showed leadership to his people, freed a City and given his Rebels a home once more. Coleman was going to find the Assassin and confessed his love for her.

He just hoped that she felt the same way.

CHAPTER 23
0 Days Left

Sitting on a little window ledge belonging to a large brown office with its horrible little desk, chairs and some impressive art on the walls. I watched all the ships carrying the Rebels unload their passengers, cargo and even some animals into the City as the entire world seemed to become calm for a moment.

I might not have been entirely impressed by the sweet smells of treats, cakes and maybe even some liquorices (something I hated), I actually stood why everyone was baking so quickly.

After talking to some of the newly freed people as I made my way up here, I learnt that everyone had suffered for so long that they had actually given up hope believing that life could be different. And now their life was different, it seemed like some weird dream that they would wake up from soon.

I supposed I could understand that, I often get the feeling after a mission or a kill, those precious few seconds where the world seemed to slow down, focus and quieten down for a few moments so I can actually enjoy it all, before the next kill.

Of course I miss those moments which was I why I was sitting here, watching the peace flowing past me for as long as the world allowed.

The warm ocean breeze felt amazing against my long black cloak and hood and my swords were carefully placed behind me because I knew I wasn't in any danger, for now.

I'd be lying if I said the final words for the Maiden hadn't scared me. I didn't want the Hunters to come here, I had only come here to escape them because this was the only place in the Kingdom the Hunters did not dare come to.

Sliding my hand into my pocket my fingers tightened against a cold shard of the Maiden's mask, I supposed I was hoping that there was something in the mask that could help me against them when the time came.

I doubted it, but I needed anything.

At the end of the day, I was the Protectorate of the Rebellion and whilst I couldn't be happier I had helped to protect them by giving them a home and a new stream of recruits for their doomed mission. I was terrified of what was to come.

My father would never let me live inside a fallen City, you never know he might actually come for me himself. I wouldn't mind that. I had questions and I wanted, so badly, to ram my swords into him.

But that was definitely something to think about tomorrow.

My current theory why the Hunters couldn't come here is the Maiden of Light projected some kind of "holy" energy that was absorbed by the walls, roads and everything else in the City. So with her dead the energy would slowly start to disappear and only then would the Hunters come for me.

As the Overlord's puppets could say the Hunters, soldiers and other puppets were coming for the Rebellion all they wanted, but I knew the truth. My father was hunting me down for some reason I don't understand.

And that I feared was the key to stopping him.

The sound of gentle footsteps coming up behind me made me force those ideas away because they were problems for the future, right now I needed to just enjoy these few moments of precious silence before the world turned crazy again.

I hopped off the ledge into the office and saw a stunning man in front of me. I loved Coleman's dark emerald eyes, wonderful body and that killer smile that was far too seductive for its own good.

I grabbed my arms and pulled him closer. So close that I could feel his warm breath that smelt of sweets on my mouth. He wanted, longed to kiss me and I wanted him to, hard!

Coleman looked into my eyes. "When you were taken, it killed me. I couldn't handle it if anything happened to you. I don't know what I would do without you,"

He took a deep breath.

"I know you're an assassin, an amazing one, and you probably think it's a weakness and I'm pathetic but"-

I kissed him.

My lips softly pressed against his, I savoured the feeling of those soft sweet lips and now I knew what I had missed earlier. And I never ever wanted to miss him again.

I broke the kiss.

"I... I love you too,"

As Coleman pulled me closer and we continued kissing, letting our soft lips do the talking. I knew everything was complete and these precious moments of silence were going to last a lot longer than usual.

I had protected the Rebellion, freed an entire City and now I had the love of my life in my arms (and lips). That was the perfect ending to a great mission by my standards.

And now I was going to make these moments of silence count.

AUTHOR'S NOTE

Thanks for reading and I really hope you enjoyed the book. There will definitely be more books in the series so please check out City of Assassins Fantasy Stories at your favourite book retailer to find them.

For the people who like to know a bit about the creation of this novella, the entire idea for the book came from a history programme presented by Bettany Hughes, an amazing Historian. As well as on this programme they were exploring the history of Istanbul or better known as (at least in the history books) as Constantinople.

Therefore, I was watching the programme and Istanbul is a beautiful City with a massive golden dome in the centre which is a cathedral and inside it (I think) there was a special balcony for one of the Queens of Constantinople to pray away from the masses.

I'm not a 100% sure if that history stuff is correct but you get the general idea. The setting of this book was drawn from Istanbul and then I build the story on top of it.

Because the Rebellion was in tatters, Coleman felt useless and I wanted to explore the wider world of the City of Assassins Universe. So we explored some beliefs, power structures and even some magic within the world. As well as at least we got to explore the Assassin's past before and I'm really excited about exploring the world more.

So please check out the rest of the books at your favourite booksellers.

Thank you for reading and I'll see you in another book soon!

CITY OF PLEASURE

CONNOR WHITELEY

CHAPTER 1

Sitting on a wonderfully soft metal chair on a stone balcony that looked out over the City of Martyrs, even I have to admit this is actually a rather beautiful morning.

Normally I never ever would have considered a morning beautiful, bad or something, because after years of being a female assassin, life was just... well life. There wasn't anything good or bad about it, it was just something lived and enjoyed along the way towards my own inevitable death.

As I stared out over the City with miles upon miles of little white houses, thousands of lit candles burning and the amazing glassy ocean on the horizon, I knew being here was starting to benefit me. For the first time in my life, I felt whole, loving and I was really enjoying life.

From the table I picked up my large mug of coffee that filled the air with amazing hints of bitter coffee, hazelnuts and almonds. But when I took a warm sip of it, I wanted to gag at my entire mouth burnt of the strong almond syrup that people in the City used.

I have no idea why these people don't like to drink their coffee normally, but every single person here has to pour a liberal amount of almond syrup in their coffee. Apparently it's just part of the culture here, yet it's a part I would happily stamp out. I just needed to remember to ask for coffee without syrup in the future.

The sounds of people laughing, talking and joking about made a sense of calm wash over me as that was the reason I was still here. After me and the Rebellion freed the City of Martyrs a month ago everyone had been constantly having fun and enjoying their freedom.

Of course I had tried to enjoy this month of peace but I had pulled my weight too. For I knew my idiot of a father, the Overlord who ruled the Kingdom cruelly, would send an army to invade and retake the City after a while.

That and my favourite supernatural demons would return at some point too, surprisingly enough I was actually looking forward to fighting those three supernatural Hunters again. I wanted to beat them, but even I doubted I could.

The sound of someone walking up behind me made me smile as I knew exactly who it was. It was the real reason I was still here and I hadn't travelled the Kingdom to do some more killing, my beautiful

Coleman with his amazing fit body, wonderful hair and those dark emerald eyes pulled out a chair to sit next to me.

Of course dating the leader of the Rebellion had its advantages and disadvantages, but being an assassin and separate from the rest of the Rebellion meant I didn't get bullied, picked on or accused of manipulating Coleman for my father.

The last person to accuse me of that lie had choked on his own blood.

For a few precious moments we just sat in silence, stared out over the City and admired our handy work. But I knew Coleman was here on official business, he knew not to disturb me (regardless of how handsome he was) during my morning coffee break.

Loosening my long black cloak and hood, I turned to him and blew him a kiss. It was still hard to imagine I had almost died without telling him how I felt but here we were together, a couple and the fate of the Kingdom rested on our shoulders.

And now we were together, the idea of losing Coleman was even harder for me to bear.

"You look beautiful this morning," Coleman said.

I was immediately suspicious.

"Not so bad yourself but why you here?" I asked.

He smiled. "Because I got an intelligence report,"

Bless him, as much as I love Coleman, what he classes as an intelligence report is simply a few men running away from the City, scouting the local area and reporting what they thought they saw to him. Some of it was lies, some of it was useful, most of it was useless.

I took another sip of my coffee to stop myself smiling.

"There are ten thousand Overlord Soldiers heading our way,"

I spat out my coffee. "What! How far away?"

"Two days march away. They'll be here no matter what and they seek to kill us all,"

Go figure! I always believed the Overlord's soldiers wanted a tea party with us.

I put my coffee down on the table. "Can the City hold?"

Coleman shrugged.

"Come on Coleman, I thought the Ruler Lord Castellan Richard was organising the defence,"

Coleman gestured if he could have some of my coffee. I shook my head.

"Fine, Lord Richard is busy. He oversaw most of the defence building but we left the final stage to Dragnist and Abbic,"

Don't get me wrong I love those two senior Rebels, they're great fighters and I love them to death. But I would not put them in charge of something that would decide the fate of hundreds of thousands and possibly the entire Kingdom.

"I see." I said. "What about a sea invasion?"

Coleman leant closer to me, as if there was a

chance of getting overheard on a completely silent balcony.

"Three ships have disappeared in the past few days. There's a chance the Overlord has sent an armada,"

This was getting serious. I had watched the defence plans get written up and build, I had ever suggested a few improvements from my decades of being an assassin. We had all focused on a massive wall that protected the City from an inland army.

We never considered a sea-based army to attack.

"So we're going to be facing an attack on two fronts," I said.

Coleman was silent.

"What?" I asked.

Coleman went to grab my hand but I gestured him to just drink my coffee.

"It turns out there was a spy for the Overlord and he knows about the temple under the City,"

Just great!

When we liberated the City from the Overlord's control I had the wonderful experience of being trapped, imprisoned and almost dying in a massive temple underneath the City. But since that delightful experience, I had found two other entrances to the Temple from beyond the City limits. And of course, to make matters even worse I had discovered that these entrances were countless.

Meaning it was damn well impossible to seal them all up.

"Please tell me you ordered for all the known entrances to be sealed," I said firmly.

"Yes, and all the known entrances into the City have been sealed. The soldiers will be able to get into the temple but not into the City,"

I blew him a kiss.

It turned out he wasn't as useless at preparing for a siege as I thought but none of this was good in the slightest. We were all going to be attacked without a proper army and without reinforcements.

Unless I changed that.

"How long do you think you peeps you hold out for?" I asked.

"Lord Castellan has good tactics, we have the Rebels and new recruits. Maybe a two days,"

Wow I loved Coleman but surviving a siege for two days was both impressive, and a tat pathetic considering I had been fighting full blown invasions for decades.

I stood up and gently rubbed his shoulder. "I need you to take control here, be at Richard's side and make sure he doesn't do anything stupid,"

Coleman just looked at me.

"Cole, you have experience in surviving sieges. You kept the Rebellion alive long enough for me to do my part, I need you to do it again,"

Coleman stood up and wrapped his wonderfully strong arms around me. "What are you going to do?"

"I... I'm going to find us allies and I know where to start but you aren't coming,"

Coleman looked to the ground as he knew exactly where I was heading. The City of Pleasure was one of the Overlord's strongholds where unless you were rich, powerful and noble, you were born into slavery and once you reached the age of 18 you were used as a sex toy for the rich.

It was where my beautiful Coleman had been held for so long before he was rescued and now I had to go there, get his revenge but most importantly find us allies.

"You know who to find?" Coleman asked, not looking me in the eye.

"Yea, there are a few Lords there that hate the Overlord. They have their own armies and I think I can get them to help us,"

Coleman looked at me and kissed me. I savoured those amazingly soft lips.

"Please don't get caught. Please don't become one of the slaves. I... I couldn't live with myself if-"

I kissed him again. "I'll be fine and I'll be back for you. I promise,"

Coleman's eyes turn wet and I knew exactly why. This wasn't a good place to go to especially as a woman and if I got caught then my life would be over, and the fate of the Kingdom would die too.

But most importantly, if I got caught then my beautiful, sexy Coleman would die.

And I couldn't allow that.

CHAPTER 2

Commander Coleman sat on a hard wooden chair around a grand oak table surrounded by tall men and women that were supposedly meant to be commanders, captains and generals.

Coleman had never met any of them before and he would have liked to believe some of them had combat experience and knew what it was like to fight against the Overlord. But that was beyond a joke now as he watched their elegant posh movements and he knew that they were all Richard's friends. Friends that had no idea what it was like to see your friends die on the battlefield.

The sound of their posh snobby laughter, talking about the weather and latest fashion and even their light breathing was starting to get Coleman angry. He had never minded the posh except when they started to abuse him as a child in the City of Pleasure.

But Coleman needed, wanted them to take this seriously. The entire City was about to be attacked on

three fronts by the Overlord and the Overlord was
not going to send amateurs here. The Overlord would
want to send a clear message to any person who even
considered for a second about joining the Rebellion.

Rebelling against him had consequences.

The idea of the Assassin running off to the City
of Pleasure made Coleman's stomach twist, churn and
tighten as he couldn't handle facing his childhood
again. That City was full of predators, monsters and
pure evil that no one should ever see.

But the Assassin was doing the right thing, she
would find the support and get them to come,
Coleman just hoped it would be in time to save
himself.

Because these posh elegant faces that clearly had
never seen real work or labour belonged to the people
who Coleman doubted would ever save anyone but
themselves.

The smell of their earthy, flowery and chemically
perfumes assaulted Coleman's senses as he stood a
tall man in shiny silver armour walk in and sat next to
him at the head of the table.

Everyone fell silent as they looked upon the Lord
Castellan Richard, Coleman still couldn't believe the
amazing sights he had seen in the past month because
of Richard's power. Richard had created armour from
air, food from rock and water from wine.

And many more amazing things.

Coleman just hoped Richard was a good leader
under the threat of annihilation.

Richard clicked his fingers and blue lightning shot across the room and everyone focused on him.

"Commander Coleman wishes to update us on the situation," Richard said.

Coleman's eyes widened at the unexpectedness of it. He had expected to be ignored throughout the entire thing.

"Thank you my Lord Castellan," Coleman said, looking at the other people. "The situation is dire,"

None of them seemed to be interested.

"Unless we act we will be slaughtered by the sea, underneath and land armies that are converging on our position. There are tens of thousands of soldiers coming here,"

The others were starting to look a bit more interested.

"We need to formulate a plan. Conscript all able-bodied men and women into the army. We need to fight, build our defences and ensure we can survive,"

One man stood up. Coleman hated his long blue silk robes and golden teeth.

"Why bother? If these so-called tens of thousands are coming here, we will die. We should spend our final days doing what we love and allow the Overlord to kill us,"

Coleman shot up. "No! There is one hope we have,"

The golden teeth man mockingly threw his arms up in the air.

"Oh yes, your girlfriend. Isn't she Overlord's

daughter?"

Everyone gasped.

Coleman hadn't been expecting that attack. He didn't even know how this man knew about the beautiful Assassin's past.

"Just admit it, Commander. The Assassin has gone off, you're safe. Is she threatening to kill you? Is that why you are creating these stories in some attempt to weaken ourselves?"

Coleman had no idea what to say to something like that, the Assassin hated her father, she was going to kill him that was a fact, and now Coleman was really starting to understand why she hated the politics of leadership so much.

"She is loyal to me. She will kill the Overlord and she has left to help us," Coleman said.

The Golden Teeth man smiled. "Where is she going?"

Coleman looked at Richard and he was frowning and gesturing him to tell everyone.

"Fine, she is going to head to the City of Pleasure,"

The golden teeth man started clapping. The air around him started to buzz.

"Thank you stupid Rebels, that is exactly what my Master wished to know,"

Coleman whipped out his sword.

Throwing it at the man.

The man disappeared in a puff of smoke.

Coleman just looked at Richard. "I presume he

279

was one of yours. And now I fear he has just teleported off to the Overlord and told him exactly where his... prey will be,"

Richard frowned.

"And on top of that, he now knows about our last-ditch attempt to ensure our survival,"

CHAPTER 3
49 Hours Until the Rebellion Falls

As I passed under the massive iron gates into the City of Pleasure I completely understand why it gets its name. All around me as I rode in on my horse were so-called beautiful women walking all over the muddy ground flirting and throwing themselves at whoever passed through the gate.

There was another woman on horseback in front of me, clearly a stuck-up noblewoman, and her horse was carefully guided by guards over to a group of young (and very attractive) young men. They must have only have been twenty or so, but they were attractive I'll give them that.

The air stunk of hormones, sweat and damp as I forced my horse to travel through the crowd of young women, guards and young men. I was hoping beyond hope that with my long black cloak and hood I would be mistaken for one of the Overlord's covert agents and allowed to pass without having to hire a young man.

But I feared I was sadly mistaken.

As I looked past all the young women that were trying to flirt with me, touch my legs and ask about my business, I stared at the massive spires of the City of Pleasure.

From what little I actually knew about the City, I saw there were thousands of little wooden houses where the slaves were chained and lived. Then there were the massive iron spires where the most precious slaves were kept for the on-demand use by their masters.

And that was what I was interested in. I once ran into (well my sword did) one of these Masters and he ever so kindly explained how these ten Masters ruled over the City in the Overlord's name and every so often they sent beautiful young women to the capital for the Overlord to use.

If I had told Coleman that little detail, or at least reminded him, then he never would have let me come, because there's a chance someone here knew about my mother. She was apparently the Overlord's true love then he slipped into madness, tyranny and had sex with hundreds of women in order to create my half-brothers and sisters.

I wasn't even sure I completely understood it all yet, but I was hoping that this City (or sex prison) would give me some answers.

Yet I had to go to these spires.

"You there,"

I rolled my eyes as a tall rather young and handsome guard in their horrible black armour walked up to my horse. I was interested in how he was looking at me because he clearly had no idea what to do with me.

He probably knew I was strange with my long black cloak and hood, and I clearly wasn't a Lord, Lady or an obvious member of the Overlord's inner circle. So unlike most people he didn't know where to send me.

"What is your business here?" he asked.

I playfully stroked his cheeks. "Well darling, I do what one must in the City of Pleasure. Now darling can I hire you?"

As the guard's cheeks lit up like a fire, I forced myself not to laugh. Now he really didn't know what to do with me.

"If you want young men, my Lady, I suggest you go to Lord Master Gillman. He has a plentiful supply of young men for your entertainment. There is even a rumour that he enhances his boys,"

"Thank you darling, I hope we meet again," I said, blowing him a kiss.

"Wait Miss, you need this," the guard said fluttered as he passed me a sheet of parchment saying I was allowed into the City.

That's something else I loved about this job, sure sometimes you need to sneak about, kill a bunch of people and do mass damage. But other times you simply need to let laypeople do their jobs and they make your job ten times easier.

I stroked my horse and we started to move through the crowd until a bunch of young women started dancing in front of me.

I knew these dances only lasted a minute or two or three but behind me I heard a number of horses stop and talk to the guards.

"My Lord Hunters," the guard said.

Shit! Shit! Shit!

I couldn't have those supernatural Hunters here yet. I didn't think they could find me so easily. I didn't even know they would be normal, I thought the guard would have fled at the sight of them.

"There is an assassin here. A best of the Rebellion. We must hunt her. Hunt her soul. Have you seen her? One of the Rebels told us she was here before we killed him,"

Damn it!

Now the Overlord and Hunters clearly knew exactly what I was up to. There must have been some kind of spy in the Rebellion and my beautiful but far too trusting boyfriend, clearly told others about my mission.

I hated it when this happened.

Logically it might have been an idea to run off, escape and try and kill the Hunters, but I was hoping they weren't going to see me.

"My Lords, what does she look like? We must stop her,"

I didn't need to look behind me to know the

Hunters were looking and breathing in my direction.

"We agree. Do you know where she is?"

"No, my Lords,"

I tensed as I heard this neck snap.

"He lies. She is within the City. He saw her. He loved her. She... is there!"

I jumped off my horse.

The Hunters screamed.

My ears bleed.

I ran deeper into the City.

I had to survive.

CHAPTER 4
48 Hours Until The Rebellion Falls

Commander Coleman wanted to destroy the entire damn Overlord army as he stood on top of the massive yellow stone wall that was meant to be their bulwark against the attack.

For the past two days everyone in the City had been helping to finish the wall, it completely ringed around the land facing parts of the City making it impossible for the Overlord's army to go around the wall.

The enemy would have to go through the wall.

That was meant to give Coleman some comfort yet it really didn't. He wanted a sure-fire way to keep the enemy out of the City but after watching people finish off the wall for the past few days, he wasn't sure if the wall couldn't withstand an assault.

It might last twelve hours but much of the wall hadn't been made out of granite and Coleman hated that. He had commanded Richard to build the wall out of granite but that was never going to happen.

Coleman understood that partly, granite did take a while to mine, cut and lift into place but it was just infuriating that the wall wasn't going to be as strong as it needed to be.

The entire wall was a beautiful marvel of engineering and determination on the people's part to stay alive, Coleman couldn't have been prouder of these people.

Especially with the grand solid granite towers that ran along the wall like imposing giants.

The sound of marching made from the distance and Coleman knew this was just the calm before the storm. All around him stood rows upon rows of archers armed with bows and crossbows. As soon as the enemy were in range they needed to fire, the archers had to buy the rest of them as much time as possible.

But Coleman still couldn't forgive himself for telling that enemy spy the plans, he didn't want to imagine he had put his stunning Assassin with that amazing body, hair and cloak in danger. But he knew he had.

He couldn't afford to make that mistake again. He just hoped this top secret backup plan he had made with Abbic, his closest friend, was going to work. Coleman hoped that if nothing else, Abbic could get the chemicals, potions and powder she found in a vault to work once more. Coleman didn't have high hopes for Abbic's chemical abilities.

The smell of horrid rotten meat filled the air as pink lumps were flying through the air towards the City. Thankfully the lumps of meat hit the wall and bounced off outside the City.

If they were as disease filled as Coleman feared he didn't want anyone touching them, he made a mental note to inform everyone of disease protocols. But that meant something else too, the enemy had catapults or something that could throw projectiles grand distances. And it was only a matter of time before those lumps of meat became something far more destructive.

Lumps of rock.

Coleman felt his stomach tighten as he imagined all the bloodshed, death and destruction this attack was going to bring down on the City. It wasn't fair, it wasn't right, it wasn't just.

It was life.

Ever since his father had gifted him control of the Rebellion, Coleman knew one day he would fight not for the survival of the Rebellion, he had done that before, but for the very survival of the idea of freedom.

If the City of Martyrs fell then it would send a shockwave through the entire Kingdom telling them that no one ever sides with the Rebellion and gets to live.

Coleman felt his skin turn white as he realised that this wasn't a mission for the enemy to retake the City. This was a mission to annihilate them all.

The enemy was never going to allow anyone to survive. The Overlord probably wanted to carry their bodies through each of the other Cities as proof of his supremacy.

Coleman wasn't going to allow that. He was going to deny the enemy that message and he was going to send out a message about the Overlord's weakness throughout the Kingdom, even if it meant sacrificing himself in the process.

Actually that wasn't a bad idea. Coleman started walking along the massive wall, passing each of the archers that were preparing themselves and went over to one of the towers in the wall.

Coleman loved this tower the best because unlike the others that had massive braziers, with their towering piles of wood inside an immense metal pan, this tower had crates upon crates of birds.

The three women who stood there aiming their crossbows at the incoming enemy were definitely Rebels at heart. Their posture was perfect, their rage was controlled and these three wanted to slaughter the enemy. That bought Coleman some level of peace at least.

"Excuse me?" Coleman said.

The three women turned and spoke as one.

"Commander Coleman," they greeted.

"I need you all to help me with a massive favour,"

They nodded.

"Do you have a pack of parchment, ink and

string up here?" Coleman asked.

The women looked at each other like Coleman was clueless before they bend down and picked up the supplies.

"Great. We need to send out a message to all settlements in the Kingdom,"

"What?" the women asked.

"I know there are a lot of settlements but the birds can fly to them all. I just need a simple message sent,"

The women looked at each other and nodded.

"Fine, what do ya wanted Commander?"

"We need to tell every single settlement that the City of Martyrs stands with everyone,"

The women were about to start writing but they stopped.

"Is that it?" they asked.

It was really creepy now how they spoke.

Coleman looked out over the wall and saw the ten thousand soldiers and their catapults marching at full speed towards them.

The Catapults fired.

The battle had started.

"It's all we have time for,"

CHAPTER 5

47.5 Hours Until The Rebellion Falls

After I barely managed to escape those idiot Hunters, I sold my horse to some young men and hoped that they would escape in time and get away from this sex-focused hell hole.

As I knelt on a cold wooden roof that was attached to one of the endless wooden houses that homed the sex slaves for the Masters of the City of Pleasure, I made sure my long black cloak and hood were tightly covering me as I stared down on the street below. I was a little concerned at first that I might be seen but the more time passed, the more I was starting to understand how the City worked.

The entire City was basically built upon the idea that no Master, noble or anyone with any power walked the streets, and those that did only went onto these streets for one purpose.

To get beautiful fit young men and women to bring back to their spires so they would do the deed and then dump them back out onto the streets. And judging by the conversations I've overheard if the sex slave does a good job at the pleasing the Master (which I learnt was the title for both men and women with powers here) then the slave might get a bowl of food, or even a bit of money.

Apparently the slaves could buy their freedom but as an assassin who's been killing for a good two decades, I know that was an absolute lie. People born in the City of Pleasure would only ever be used for one purpose- sex slavery.

It was disgusting, outrageous and it made my blood boil. This was stupid on so many levels and the Overlord would know my feelings on the topic sooner or later.

The smell of hormones, sweat and perfume filled the air to create a horrid concoction that I really didn't want to smell anymore so I started to move across the rooftops. Jumping from one wooden house to another.

Well, I say jump, it's more like hop because all these houses are so close together if there was a fire, it would only take a few minutes for the entire street to be alight.

As I hopped across the rooftops, I focused on the massive iron spires that rose high into the sky in the distance. The sheer scale of the City of Pleasure was starting to strike me as it must have taken years if not decades to build all these miles upon miles of wooden houses only for the iron Spires to be perfectly centred in the middle.

I suppose in a way the spires had to be in the dead centre of the City, because those poor sex Masters wouldn't want to have to go too far, or further than another Master, to get their prey.

As much as I wanted, needed to free these people and kill all their Masters, I needed to remind myself that I wasn't here for them directly. I was here to find the Lords that hated the Overlord, had their private armies and were willing to help the Rebellion against the Overlord's invasion.

My stomach tightened as I imagined what was happening in the City of Martyrs. I didn't even know if the City still stood, I didn't know if my beautiful Coleman was alive and I most certainly didn't know if our 48 hour window was still that long.

The sound of whispering followed by deadly silence filled the street below me as I knew the Hunters were riding along looking for me.

This wasn't good. I didn't need them here, not right now. I needed them to leave me alone, carry out my work but after I killed the woman who apparently birthed them on my last mission, I highly doubt they were ever going to leave me alone.

"Have you seen her?" one of the Hunters asked a young woman on the street.

I instantly stopped moving and knelt closer to the edge of the rooftop. Of course it was an amateur mistake but I couldn't leave unless I knew there was nothing, absolutely nothing I could have done to save the young woman.

Then one by one each of the young men and women in the street started to look around. Some were even looking up and I realised something in that moment, all these sex slaves were interested in keeping each other safe. They didn't want to live like this, they wanted to be safe, free and protected.

That's something I could definitely use.

Young men and women started to jump out the way as a horse-drawn carriage threatened towards the Hunters.

But they didn't seem concerned, threatened or nothing.

They just stood there in their long shadowy cloaks and faces made from shadow stared coldly at the carriage.

After a few seconds, the carriage stopped and out stepped a short man wearing long golden robes that were covered in jewels, fine silks and even packs of food were hanging from his waist.

And as the man looked at each of the young people in the street, he didn't look menacing, happy or like a predator, he actually looked sad for each of them.

After killing for as long as I have, I like to believe I can read people well and this man was far from the evil, predator that this City bred into the rich and powerful. I truly believe if this man could, he would happily take over the City and free everyone.

That was definitely something to take note of.

"Leave this City!" the man shouted.

The Hunters stared at him. "We are the Hunters. We never leave. Our prey is here. We-"

"Are leaving. I know the Overlord has you under this control. But if you leave I can promise you your day of freedom will get closer,"

Now that was interesting.

Even the Hunters seemed to look at each other and they even took a step away from the man.

"The Day of Freedom is a myth. Only the Overlord can free us. He will never free us,"

The man smiled. "I promise you if you live the Assassin and me live in peace for six hours. Your freedom day will get closer,"

The Hunters hissed, shrieked and moaned with each other. It was awful to listen to, it sounded like dying animals but they were clearly considering the offer.

What I wanted to know was how the man knew I was here in the first place, and it wouldn't have surprised me if he knew I was in earshot.

"Six hours then we execute the Overlord's command," the Hunters said as one as they all disappeared in the wind.

I jumped off the rooftop and landed on the top of the carriage.

The man turned around and smiled. He was actually glad to see me.

"Assassin, it has been a long time. I have waited for this day for even longer. Come, we have much to discuss," the man said.

The only problem was, I had never met this man before in my life and he clearly knew about me.

And that unnerved me more than I wanted to admit.

CHAPTER 6

47.5 Hours Until The Rebellion Falls

Commander Coleman stared with utter horror as the disgraceful Overlord's army in their ten thousand marched towards the Wall. Coleman had never imagined he would have to face this many foes, he never wanted to.

But now the entire fate of the City of Martyrs rested on his shoulders.

Coleman had to lead the Wall's defence, he had to marshal the strength of the brave men and women that stood by him properly, he had to be brave. Because he knew with all certainty that if he failed then the Rebellion would be slaughtered and Coleman could never allow that to happen.

All around Coleman on the massive Wall stood archers aiming their bows and on his command they would fire, unleashing extreme amounts of fury at the Overlord.

The sounds of massive chunks of rock smashing

in front of the wall filled the air as the enemy's catapult tried to stop it. As much as Coleman wanted to believe the Wall would always stand, that was a lie and he knew it.

Sooner or later that catapult would be within range and the Wall's time would be limited. If that was Coleman's only problem then he might not have cared, but considering there could be an army coming up under the City would the underground Temple and a sea invasion.

Coleman wasn't impressed.

Then he noticed every single man and woman on the Wall was staring at Coleman waiting for his command.

Coleman took out his swords and took a deep breath of the sandy air. This was where history would define Coleman, so he wanted to make it memorable.

"Fire!" Coleman shouted.

As soon as Coleman gave the order hundreds of arrows fired into the air, screaming towards the Overlord's men and then it had truly begun.

The battle for the City of Martyrs had started and now Coleman's entire fate rested in the hands of his beautiful Assassin.

The arrows slaughtered the enemy.

They screamed.

The Archers fired again.

More arrows flew through the air.

Hammering into the enemy.

Peppering bodies with holes.

The catapults were getting closer.

The Archers fired again.

More enemies screamed in agony.

Coleman pointed his sword at the Catapults.

He could see them now.

The enemy was loading rocks into them.

They were flaming rocks.

The enemy was turning them.

Coleman's stomach tightened.

The Catapults fired.

Flaming rocks screamed towards Coleman.

They were dropping.

Dropping fast.

Coleman didn't order anyone to move.

The rocks smashed into the base of the wall.

Coleman felt a vibration.

No damage done.

The Wall stood.

Coleman ordered the Archers again.

They fired.

The enemy stopped marching. They stood still. They were waiting.

Coleman went to say something.

The enemy charged.

They broke formation.

The archers fired.

Arrows flew high into the sky.

They slammed into the enemy.

The enemy kept moving.

They were quick.

They were getting closer to the Wall.

Closer and closer.

Coleman needed to do something.

He had to act.

The catapults were moving fast.

Coleman focused on them. The enemy were pushing them. The Catapults were within range.

The catapults fired.

Flaming rocks flew towards the Wall.

Coleman shouted a warning.

But by the time the warning left his mouth it was too late. The massive flaming rocks slammed into the Wall.

Coleman grabbed onto anything as he struggled to remain standing. Shockwave after shockwave ripped through his body.

People were thrown off the wall. Slamming onto the ground below.

Coleman forced himself up. The Archers were in chaos. The enemy was almost at the Wall. All ten thousand of them.

The Catapults were getting nearer and nearer. Soon they'll be able to attack the City. Burning it to the ground.

Coleman ordered the archers to never stop firing. And he started to walk away. He had to get rid of those catapults even if it killed him.

Screams echoed all around the City of Martyrs. Coleman looked over the edge of the Wall inside the City.

His eyes widened as he saw black armoured soldiers walking around his City killing his people and defenders.

He was right. The Overlord's army had come through the underground temple. They were now being attacked on two fronts. This wasn't good. Coleman needed help. He needed to fight.

He needed his Assassin.

Coleman grabbed onto the Wall as more flaming rocks slammed into it.

Time was running out fast and scared Coleman more than anything!

CHAPTER 7

47 Hours Until The Rebellion Falls

Well I have to say that carriage ride through the City was awful, simply awful. My long black cloak and hood kept getting caught on the fixtures, and I have never experienced such a slow and bumpy ride through streets. Yes I know there were tons of people, young beautiful men and women, but they need to learn to get out of the way.

I am trying to save them after all!

Anyway I am more than happy that the carriage is over, as I went into a small office filled with walls lined with bookcases, a small brown desk in the centre with no chairs. But I did have a soft spot for the massive golden bed tucked away in the corner.

Now I will not have sex with this man whatsoever, I only have sex with my Coleman with those amazing dark emerald eyes, but I can appreciate the man's preparedness at least.

The air smelt of utter awful hints of jasmine, rose

and chocolate that was clearly designed to bring young women (or men) back here and seduce completely into the man's grip.

But what I did find strange about it all was the office (and this was presumably his living quarters too) was on the lowest level of the Spires. I would have thought that a man who acted like this would be more powerful, and my opinion it was the more powerful people lived at the top of the spires.

Then of course I remembered that I was in the City of Pleasure and nothing was ever it seemed. And in all honesty, the most powerful people probably lived at the bottom so they didn't need to carry their slaves too far and waste precious time where they could be shagging them instead of carrying them.

The sound of the wooden door closing made me really focus on the man with his long expensive robes, jewels and fine silks. All the food packs that hung from his waist were now gone as he threw them out of the window as we rode.

I even threw the money I got from selling my horse out too. I had to give these poor slaves something to make their lives better.

The man made sure the door was locked and went over to his desk sat on it. Then it twigged how clear the desk was and I instantly knew that was the desk was a nice hard surface for a rougher time for the slaves.

"Tell me why I shouldn't kill you now for using sex slaves?" I asked.

CONNOR WHITELEY

The man cocked his head. "Because Assassin you know I don't support their slavery and look at my desk. Is there a drop of sweat, cum or blood on it?"

I didn't need to check it to know he was telling the truth.

"Fine, what is the Day of Freedom to the Hunters?" I asked, going over to inspect the bed.

"The Day of Freedom is a prophecy that spells the end of the Overlord's enslavement of the Hunters and there are two ways to free the Hunters,"

"And if we free the Hunters they will leave the Kingdom?"

"Assassin, they will leave this world forever,"

I went over to him. "How do we free them?"

Of course I could have been a bit eager but I didn't want to spend the rest of my life running, fighting and risking Coleman's life with the Hunters' threat.

"I have a map in my possession that details the location of an Oath rod that if broken can free the Hunters,"

It was interesting enough that there was a map for an Oath Rod. They were funny creations because they were only a long rod with detailed carvings of ivory, but when two (or more) people held them and made an oath. It made the oath unbreakable.

Yet if the oath rod was damaged enough or outright destroyed then the oath never existed in magical law. And I fully believe the Hunters wanted that more than anything else in the world.

"Give me the map," I said firmly.

The man opened his desk and took out a tiny

308

piece of parchment.

"The City of Martyrs stands with everyone," he said.

I instantly knew it was from Coleman and my stomach tightened more and more as I feared the worse. I forced myself to stay put and not run off towards the City to save him.

The man smiled. "I am Lord Gillman. I met you once when you were a baby and your mother was shipped off to the Capital. I was her best friend and I... I really tried to keep her hidden, but she loved the Overlord too much,"

I bit my lip.

"I know you want me to tell you everything and I promise you I will. I will give you the map, your history, everything. Just help me please," Gillman said.

Normally I might have been cocky, arrogant or just and horrible person but today I wanted to be kind. I took Gillman's hand and rubbed it gently.

"What do I need to do?" I asked.

He beamed at that. "As you can probably guess, the powerful, most richest members of the City live on the bottom of the Spires,"

I knew it!"

"My money, possession and supplies are safely stored away, so I want you to do what you're best at,"

I just looked at him.

"News of your destroying the Grand Cathedral in the City of Martyrs reached me. Think you could destroy the Spires?" he asked.

I shook my head. "I could easily but the shockwave and damage caused by the four spires falling would kill more slaves than save,"

Gillman nodded. "Fine. I will arrange a meeting of the Masters and you will be there. Kill them all and I will gather you an army,"

I cocked my head at that. "But with the Masters' dead, the City would be free anyway right?"

"Oh Assassin, no. There are stories that the Masters bring certain slaves into the Spires not for their own pleasure but the pleasure of a True Master. They aren't stories,"

CHAPTER 8
46.5 Hours Until The Rebellion Falls

Coleman slashed the throat of another horrible black armoured soldier and as the corpse fell to the ground, covering the yellow cobblestones in deep red blood, he couldn't believe how bold and stupid the Overlord's soldiers were being.

It was bad enough they were attacking the City with Catapults that smashed flaming rocks into the Wall every few minutes but now they were infiltrating the City.

That was outrageous.

It wasn't a gentleman tactic, it wasn't honourable and it certainly wasn't going to help Coleman save his people. And to make matters worse, Coleman hadn't seen, hear and smelt any allies nearby for half an hour.

Coleman looked around at the little white houses that all stood around him like some judgemental parents who were going to tell him off for not doing his best. Coleman had to find allies, friends and anyone who was still alive.

Because that was his greatest fear, not only could he be the last man in the City standing with only those on the Wall left, but he could be the last man to be hunted down and slaughtered of by the Overlord's soldiers.

The sound of sword clashing and smashing and lashing in the distance made Coleman breathe a sigh of relief as at least he knew he wasn't alone. But if he didn't help, he didn't know how much that still rang true.

Coleman ran through the streets.

Passing white house after house. The cobblestone streets were wet with blood. Corpses littered the ground.

Coleman turned a corner.

Ten enemy soldiers stood there. Smashing down the door of a house. They were going to attack innocent people.

Coleman flew at them.

Slashing his sword.

Slicing into their armour.

Their armour shattered.

Breaking off.

Coleman didn't stop.

He kicked them.

Punched them.

Slashed.

Blood spattered up white walls.

Coleman rammed his sword into their chests.

The soldiers were too slow.

The door opened.

Rebels poured out.

Lashing the enemy's chest.

Blood poured out.

Screams echoed all around.

Coleman charged again.

His sword swinging madly.

Hacking the enemies to pieces.

With ten corpses hacked to multiple pieces lying at their feet, Coleman took a deep breath of the cold air that was filled with plenty of vapourised blood. He looked at the Rebels and nodded his thanks.

"Good job everyone," Coleman said, looking around for any more foes.

One of the Rebels, a wall woman with short hair, leather armour and two swords, stepped forward.

"Thank you ma Lord. We saw 'em coming out of the main sewage tunnels near the old Grand Cathedral,"

If Coleman wasn't focused on staying alive, he would have kissed her for that information. At last he knew exactly where the enemy were coming from. It made perfect sense, all the other known entrances were sealed and that sewage entrance was definitely not known about.

Coleman had to seal it now. But he had to give the Overlord's soldiers credit, he wouldn't want to crawl through thousands of litres of raw sewage just to kill some people.

"Thank you. With me," Coleman said, firmly.

Coleman and his newfound Rebels went to start running but twenty black armoured soldiers stood there pointing their crossbows at them.

Aiming at their chests.

A tall man wearing spiked armour walked to the front of his men and sneered at Coleman.

"I look forward to delivering your head to the Overlord," he said to Coleman.

Coleman pointed his sword at him. "That will never happen,"

"Fire!" the man shouted.

Crossbows fired.

The Rebels ducked.

Coleman was too slow.

The arrows screamed towards them.

An arrow ripped into Coleman's flesh.

Coleman hit the ground.

He hissed.

The enemy reloaded.

The Rebels charged.

Whipping out their swords.

They hacked the enemy to pieces.

Coleman heard something.

More soldiers were coming behind them.

Coleman forced himself up. He grabbed his sword. He went to swing it at them.

Another arrow rammed itself into his back.

Coleman collapsed to the ground.

He felt the blood oozing out of him. The Rebels

were surrounded. Both sets of soldiers got closer.

They were doomed.

White magical lightning shot through the air.

Turning the soldiers to ash.

Archers flooded the streets.

Slaughtering the soldiers.

Corpses slammed to the ground.

Coleman hissed. He forced himself up to see one of the few people he actually wanted to see at a time like this. Lord Castellan Richard swirled and twirled and whirled his magical energy at the enemy reducing them to ash.

As Richard's Archers secured the street, Richard marched over to Coleman and covered Coleman's face with his hands.

Coleman didn't like it at first but as he felt magical energy seep into his flesh and his wounds heal themselves, he started to learn to like it.

Richard took away his hand and Coleman nodded his thanks to him.

"These are dark times to travel alone Commander," Richard said.

"Agreed my Lord. We must go to the main sewage tunnels, the enemy are coming from there,"

Richard frowned. "My powers are needed at the Wall. But take my personal archers,"

The entire City shook as more flaming rocks slammed into the Wall. But to Coleman's utter horror massive chunks of stone fell off the Wall.

And now it had truly begun. The Wall's time was

running out as Coleman knew each and every hit would weaken it more and more and more until the Wall collapsed entirely.

Then ten thousand soldiers would swarm the City of Martyrs and kill everyone.

Coleman couldn't let that happen. He just didn't know how to stop it.

Yet.

CHAPTER 9
44 Hours Until the Rebellion Falls

When Lord Gillman said he was going to call a Meeting of the Masters, I was expecting something rather evil, posh and very, very condensing. I did not expect to be hiding in what could easily be mistaken for a sex shop.

With my long black cloak and hood tightly wrapped around me, I hung onto an extremely disturbing chandelier. Normally chandeliers are made from wonderful gold, jewels and silver.

Oh no, this one was made from gold mixed with blood, skulls with the candles sitting in the mouths and another one of my favourites, human hair was the only thing holding it all up.

Seriously!

I mean how stupid, perverse and just utter wrong can you yet. If I had actually come here today not knowing why I was going to kill all these Masters, I certainly knew why now.

As the smell of roasted meat, manly sweat and semen filled the air, I looked down onto the massive feast table below. Considering the slaves didn't get much food (they only got enough of the right food to keep their muscles big and their bodies slim), this must have a punch in the stomach to the slaves attending.

There were ten people (five women, five men) sitting at the table wearing long sexualised leather pants and tops. Each one held a leash for their slave in one hand and in the other they held a fine glass of red wine. But to only add to the disturbing nature of the meeting, on the table in front of them were what only be described as... sex instruments.

There were whips, chains, gags and plenty more things I had never seen or wanted to use in my life. I almost feel sorry for the slaves but that's when I realised they wanted to be here more than their Masters.

Of course, don't get me wrong, I could "understand" the possible thrill they might get from a group session. But clearly these slaves were not in the right mindset considering some of those so-called sex instruments, I could easily use to kill people.

So as harsh as it sounded, I was far from concerned if I killed a few slaves in the process. Especially as these slaves would probably come to the aid of their Masters.

A tall man in shiny leather stood up at the head of the table and raised his glass to everyone.

"Today we dine for the Glory of the True Master. May he give us as much as pleasure as we give him,"

Wow!

I had to kill these people now before I vowed never to have sex again!

I jumped down.

Landing on the table.

Whipping out my swords.

I swirled on the table.

Slashing four throats.

Their slaves jumped up.

Running at me.

I kicked them.

I slashed them.

I killed them.

The other Masters grabbed a weapon.

I kicked food at them.

Some food whacked them.

I flew over.

Ramming my swords into their chests.

Three more died that way.

A Master whipped me.

I spun around.

Jumping on her.

I snapped her neck.

Slaves pounced on me.

Punching me.

Smashing their fists into me.

Enough was enough.

I jumped into the air.

Spinning out.

Extending my swords.

My swords slit their throats.

Blood poured all over the food.

Three Masters left.

But as I stood up on the table to prepare to strike, I saw all three of them (Three women) were clapping at me. They were smiling, but it was an erotic smile. These women enjoyed the killing.

In fact, I'm sure all of them properly thought this was part of the Lord Gillman's plan at calling the meeting. They probably all got off on violence.

I threw my swords at them.

The swords skewered two of the women.

Now she was the only one left, the last woman in her dull leather suit looked so helpless and pathetic as the enjoyment drained from her face.

"You… you aren't friend, are you?" she asked.

I went over to her and ripped my swords out of her friends.

"You go… going to kill me?"

I looked at her undecided, I knew I was going to kill her but I at least could have given her a sense of false security.

"Where is the True Master?" I asked.

I wondered if she was going to orgasm at his name, but she looked like she was suppressing the urge well. (I really wanted to escape this place now!)

"He is everywhere. He will come for you now. He will come for Lord Gillman. As a Master Gillman has to give him his pleasure now,"

The hairs on my neck started to stand up as I felt like something was starting to dawn on me but I couldn't say it. It was on the tip of my tongue what she was hinting at.

"Does Lord Gillman know this?"

"Course not, the True Master loves us all. He only picks one Master to give him pleasure at any one time. He is old-fashioned that way,"

Now it dawned on me.

"Will the True Master kidnap Gillman?" I asked.

The woman cocked her head. "It will not be kidnapping. We all love the True Master. We-"

I snapped her neck.

Running off.

I had to find Gillman.

I couldn't let the True Master take my only hope of learning about myself and saving the man I loved.

CHAPTER 10
44 Hours Until the Rebellion Falls

Coleman peeked around a corner of a little white house to look at the massive entrance to the main sewage tunnels that not only connected the impressive sewage system to the underground Temple, but provided a perfect entrance into the City for the enemy.

Coleman hated everything about the entrance with its large black manhole cover that was big enough to throw cattle down there without a problem.

But the smell of poo, raw sewage and rotten flesh was immense. The idea was ridiculous that the Overlord's soldiers would willingly travel into the underground Temple and into the sewage network. Yet the Overlord's soldiers were stupid, persistent and loyal to a fault (literally) to their Overlord Master.

Coleman focused on the massive amount of rubble, chunks of stone and corpses that littered the area around the entrance to the sewage tunnels. His beautiful sexy Assassin had done amazingly on their last mission when she burned down the Cathedral.

But now the little square (or what remained of it) looked sad, dystopian and horrific without a complete building. Yet that was the cost of war with the Overlord.

The sound of something tapping against metal and metal moving made Coleman stare at the manhole cover as it moved and it was lifted up.

Revealing an endless stream of foul armoured soldiers pouring into the City like they owned the place. Coleman might be able to understand them if they had tried to be sneaky or at least careful about their infiltration. But that was the last thing they were doing.

These soldiers looked so confident, so assured, so arrogant that no one was going to notice if they slipped and killed a bunch of people who only wanted freedom. And that really pissed Coleman off.

He took out his swords and looked at his ten Rebels (more had sadly died on the way here) and the five personal archers that Richard had lent him. They were all ready with their weapons to storm over and slaughter the enemy.

They all nodded to Coleman.

Coleman whipped out his sword and charged.

Feet pounding into the cobblestone.

The soldiers turned.

Their eyes widened.

They were too slow.

Coleman jumped into the air.

Twirling his sword

Slashing their throats.

They screamed.

The Rebels stormed over.

Swinging their swords.

Hacking into the enemy.

Blood flooded the ground.

The enemy died.

More soldiers kept coming out.

Coleman kept fighting.

The Archers fired. Again and again.

Arrows screamed through the air. Ripping into the soldier's flesh.

Someone whacked him in the head.

Throwing him to the ground.

They picked him up by the throat.

They started crushing him.

Coleman looked at the muscular woman. She was twice the size of him.

Her muscles bulged.

She was going to kill him.

Coleman struggled. It was useless. His vision blurred.

Arrows shot into the woman's brain. It didn't help.

Rebels slashed at the woman's head.

The Rebels stabbed her muscles.

Cutting them away.

She dropped Coleman.

Coleman gasped for air.

More enemies came out.

Coleman picked up his sword.

He flew at them.

Their blades slashed.

Sparks flying.

They were stronger.

They merciless swung at Coleman.

There were too many.

The City shook again. More flaming rocks slammed into the Wall. More of it collapsed.

The air whistled.

The air turned warm.

Coleman kicked a soldier.

He looked up.

A flaming rock was hurling toward them.

Coleman ran.

The rock smashed into the square.

Creating a shockwave.

Creating a dust cloud.

Throwing Coleman forward.

He smashed into a little white house.

As Coleman kept coughing more and more as the dust invaded his lungs, he shook his hands around to try and clear the dust away. He was horrified to see the massive flaming rock was burning uncontrollably in the square.

But Coleman had to smile as he saw the smouldering corpses of the enemy soldiers lying there, and when he closed his eyes and truly focused, he could barely hear the screams of agony of the soldiers underground as the flames caught them.

And one of the most scary things about sewages was how flammable they were, all that sewage, rot and poo created more than enough methane to ignite and Coleman had little doubt it had already gone off.

In that moment he was extremely grateful for the thick stone walls of the sewage network, at least the methane explosion was contained.

Coleman looked around but it dawned on him that so few of the Rebels and Archers were standing. There was a group of three Rebels standing next to some flaming corpses and the two Archers were kneeling on the ground in front of some more.

A wave of discomfort washed over Coleman as he realised he might have succeeded in fighting off the soldiers, but he had failed at protecting the brave men and women that looked to him.

The entire City shook again as more flaming rocks smashed into the Wall and a massive whoosh echoed around the City as an immense chunk of the Wall collapsed. Creating a thick choking dust cloud.

As Coleman focused on the Wall, he was glad that the chunk that had collapsed was still too high for the ten thousand enemy soldiers to jump, walk or climb over.

But that would happen in only a matter of time.

Coleman had to destroy the Catapults. He had to buy his beautiful Assassin more time. He had to risk his life to save the City.

And he wouldn't have it any other way.

"Want to destroy some Catapults?" Coleman asked.

All the remaining Archers and Rebels went over to Coleman and to his surprise they smiled.

"Let's burn them to the ground," Coleman said.

CHAPTER 11

42 Hours Until the Rebellion Falls

This was ridiculous!

How dare these stupid Masters allow themselves to give pleasure, servitude and lives to this so-called True Master. When I found him I was going to gut him from head to stomach and legs. I was not kidding around here.

No one even thinks about threatening my only hope and gets to live.

But as I went into his office with the massive golden bed in the corner and the small desk, I realised someone had gotten here before me. And I was livered.

The desk was knocked off and the bed was completely dirty and unmade. Completely outrageous and stupid because I now had to find the True Master, but of course I do not know what he looks like. I then need to save Lord Gillman and I need him to give me his private army.

I went to go over to the small desk when I felt something wet under my feet. It was blood. I loosened my long black cloak and hood as I knelt down to inspect it.

The blood was in a large pool in front of me, it was fresh. I tasted it. Definitely human, had plenty of iron it so clearly from a man and there was a hint of vitality in it. So I was looking at the blood of a young man.

Then as I knelt on the ground, I noticed that a good amount of blood was starting to drip down onto the ground from the bed. So I went to it and lifted up the sheets. Revealing a corpse.

The young man's corpse was still warm to the touch, the man himself was probably 25 years old and had massive scars all over his body. Probably from his Masters (I was more than glad I had killed them now). But the killing blows looked weird.

There were two large blows on the front and back of his body, and in my experience those blows looked like ones you get if you were trying to protect someone against a much larger, stronger and tougher opponent. (Believe me, I know my stuff about that!)

It made sense in a way. I know Lord Gillman was a friend of the slaves and he always tried to help them, so he probably went to collect me an army, came back here for some reason and on the way he picked up a slave or two.

Then I know (or like to think) he would have tried to help them. Maybe he healed them, gave some food or just showed them a piece of kindness that the other Masters would never have given them.

Of course solving that mystery hardly helped me find Lord Gillman.

I knelt on the ground again when I could have sworn I'd heard the sound of breathing coming close by.

The sound got louder and louder. It sounded like someone was breathing heavily out of fear, not physical excursion.

It was coming from under the bed so I tapped on the bed frame and a door popped open.

Someone screamed. They crawled out and started running.

I tackled them. Covering their mouth with my hand.

Knowing this place I probably didn't need to make someone quiet because these disgraceful people would probably think I was having fun with someone, but I didn't want this person to be scared.

They kept struggling.

"Relax, I'm not a Master. I'm not a person who would use you. I am here to help you,"

Now the person had stopped struggling a little, I managed to see that this was a strong young woman with golden eyes, long gold hair and she was wearing nothing more than cheap cloth.

"What's your name?" I asked.

"Number 329," she said.

Wow. Of course, this place doesn't value people

enough to give them a name, only a number.

"What's his name?" I asked, pointing to the top of the bed.

"He was ma boyfriend Number 490,"

I didn't know if it was touching or strange that these slaves actually had relationships.

"I am here to help you. Can I get off you without you running away?"

"Yes Master," she said.

I didn't have time to argue with her that I wasn't a Master. I hated the term. I hated everything about this place, but it was probably just automatic for her to say that.

I got off her and helped her up. She looked so terrified as I helped her. It was probably confused by the offer and act of help.

"I am looking for Lord Gillman. Where is he?"

The woman looked at her boyfriend. "The Creature took him,"

"The Creature? Does the Creature work for the True Master?"

The woman didn't answer.

"Where would the Creature take my friend?" I asked.

The woman looked so confused by that question.

"You really aren't from here, are you?"

I smiled and shook my head.

"The Creature took your friend to the Shrine Of Pleasure at the very base of the Spires,"

I hugged her. "Thank you!"

I was about to leave when she grabbed my arm.

"Master Gillman instructed me to gather up Rebel Slaves. Is that still my Orders, Master?"

I just went along with her. "Yes,"

"Okay Master,"

It was heart-breaking telling a young woman these things.

I looked at her arm that was still grabbing mine and I gestured her to remove it.

She did but slowly.

"Um Master, the Creature isn't working for the True Master. The True Master is the Creature,"

CHAPTER 12

40 Hours Until the Rebellion Falls

Coleman felt his stomach churn as he looked over the edge of a small sandstone hill that allowed him to stare at the massive Catapults slowly moving below him.

If going through the underground temple, fighting more soldiers and having to evade the enemy long enough to get into position hadn't been bad enough, Coleman was getting more and more irritated by the massive brutes guarding and pushing the Catapults.

Unlike normal guards these Brutes wore bright red armour with budging muscles almost popping out of their armour, their arms, legs and chests were muscle factories, and their entire purpose seemed simple enough to Coleman. These brutes were born, bred and created for the sole purpose of killing and pushing Catapults around. It was hard from a perfect life, but Coleman had little doubt these people weren't intelligent enough to know what a good life was.

Especially as the only sound that came from these brutes were groans. Coleman doubted these people could just speak, bless them.

But just because they couldn't speak didn't mean they wouldn't kill Coleman, the two Archers and three Rebels that were left. Coleman had to be smart here or risk everything and the fate of the Kingdom.

Whooshing, cheering and shouting filled the air as the catapults fired again and Coleman forced down a hiss of pain as he saw the flaming rocks smash into more of the wall.

Considering he had been gone for hours trying to get here, Coleman was impressed that Richard had managed to ensure the Wall held together as even from this distance Coleman could see the Wall was failing. Especially with five catapults attacking it every few minutes.

Taking out his sword, Coleman was about to think of a plan, then the five remaining troops he had knelt down next to him.

"We can't fight 'em," someone said.

Coleman really wished Abbic was here. He needed someone he could trust by his side and Abbic was an amazing fighter so if things went south then at least there was a tiny chance they would make it back to the City.

"Bombo, got any knives on ya?" one of the Archers said to the other.

"Aye," Bombo said.

Coleman's eyes narrowed on the tall skinny man called Bombo with a massive ginger beard, grey hair and shaky hands. He was a bit surprised the Archer would fire straight.

"Coleman," Bombo said, passing him the knives.

Coleman's eyes widened as he realised what the Archers were hinting at. They clearly wanted him to throw the knives at the ropes that supported the Catapults. And the best thing was (at least to Coleman, not the enemy) that he didn't need to cut them completely, all he needed to do was damage the ropes enough so the strain of firing the next rock would destroy the ropes.

It was risky. Coleman hadn't practised throwing knives for years, decades even.

He held out the knives for someone else, but everyone smiled and shook their heads. Typical!

Coleman saw massive groups of brutes down below start to load up the catapults.

"Now or never," Coleman muttered to himself.

Coleman checked to see how many knives he had. He only had five shots to do as much damage as he could.

He raised the first knife. Aiming it at the catapult directly below him. Its main rope that attached the throwing arm to the frame was exposed enough.

Coleman threw it.

The knife chomped into the rope. Slicing it.

Coleman closed his eyes and listened for the

characteristic squeaking of the rope against the pressure of the throwing arm.

It was there.

Coleman took out the second knife. He aimed for another catapult a bit further out. The needed rope was a bit harder to see.

Coleman threw it.

The knife ripped into the rope. Slicing it cleanly. Then the knife dropped. Landing on a brute's head.

Coleman and the others ducked. But the brutes dismissed it.

Bombo came up to Coleman's ear to whisper.

"Coleman, aim for the catapult at the back. If you bring it down the others will be trapped,"

Coleman nodded. He focused on the back catapult but he could barely see the rope he needed to cut.

Coleman threw it.

The knife missed. Slamming into the throwing arm.

The brutes groaned.

Coleman threw again.

The fourth knife missed completely. It flew towards a brute. It slammed into a brute's eye.

The Brutes were alerted.

They pointed to Coleman.

Coleman threw the final knife.

It sliced through the rope.

The Catapults fired.

The rope screamed.

The wood screamed.

They smashed to the ground.

Creating a cloud of dust.

Coleman jumped up.

Everyone else did.

They ran back away.

Coleman wasn't going to fight thousands of men to destroy two catapults.

Cannons exploded.

People screamed inside the City.

Coleman kept running.

He knew the attack from the sea had begun.

Time was seriously running out now.

And Coleman didn't know what to do.

CHAPTER 13

40 Hours Until the Rebellion Falls

Damn it!

I am really, really starting to hate this True Master. Because of him I missed my deadline with the Hunters so no doubt I'm going to have to fight, struggle and hopefully survive an attack from them. I don't even know if that's possible.

I took out my swords and pulled my long black cloak and hood over me as I entered the so-called Shrine of Pleasure. Considering it had taken me hours to climb down here through the Spires, I was at least expecting something a bit grander.

The massive dirty stone arches lined an even larger (and horrible) circular chamber that I entered. The marble floor was covered in some strange symbols and the smell of blood, semen and sweat assaulted my senses.

I might not have been able to see the True Master or Lord Gillman but this was definitely the place where the True Master pleasured his victims.

The sound of strange groaning, moaning and hissing made me look up to see something that utterly horrified me. On the ceiling of the Shrine was a strange beastial looking creature with a long worm-like hairy body and eight limbs.

But these limbs weren't like arms, legs or claws. They were more akin to strange sex objects with the very tip of the limbs leaking something. This was beyond strange and I just wanted to leave.

No, actually I tell a lie. I wanted, needed to grab a flaming torch, throw it at the Creature and watch its corpse burn to ash. Then it would feel a lot safer. But what really disturbed me (out of the millions of things that this situation that did) was I couldn't see a head or a worm or insect equivalent.

A massive groan came from the Creature and I watched its limb move around and in the very centre of this monstrous sight was Lord Gillman. At least it looked like him. His entire body looked to be covered in a strange type of white silk that covered him completely.

Through the white silk I could just about see his face and it was a horrific mix of pure, utter pleasure and sheer terror. I wasn't sure if he wanted this or not. But judging by the hissing and moaning that I now understood was coming from him, I think it's fair to say he didn't want this.

Then the white silk started to turn red. Blood dripped onto the ground. The Creature was killing him.

I couldn't let Gillman die. I needed him.

"Stop!" I shouted.

I threw my swords at the Creature.

They sliced into its flesh.

Thick white blood poured out.

My swords fell. I rushed over. Picking them up.

The Creature shrieked.

Dropping Gillman's body.

I dashed. I was too late. His body slammed into the ground.

The Creature hissed.

It flew at me. It was quick. Dangerously quick.

It wrapped around Gillman's body.

One of its limbs whacked me.

Knocking me away.

I stood firm. Whipping out my swords. I charged.

I flew at the Creature.

Four limbs swung at me.

I jumped into the air.

Swirling and whirling.

I sliced through the limbs.

I ducked. Slicing through more.

The Creature hissed. It screamed. It moaned.

It thrusted a limb into Gillman. I could hear him screaming. Part in pleasure. Part in agony.

I charged over.

The Creature unleashed a supersonic shriek.

I collapsed to the ground. Covering my ears. My

vision blurred.

Gillman screamed.

Something whacked me across the Shrine.

Slamming me into a wall.

My vision cleared.

As my eyes fully adjusted to the Shrine once more, rage filled me as I stared at the bloodied dying body of Gillman. The Creature was gone, a small trail of white blood led away from the Shrine. But I didn't care at that moment.

I went over to the dying bloodied body of Gillman and just held him in my arms. He looked at me. As the life slowly drained from him, he had the decency to place his hands over his manhood where I knew there was a massive hole from the Creature's limbs.

Gillman didn't stare at me like I had failed him. Like I had failed to protect him, his people and my Rebellion. He looked at me as if he was the failure. I couldn't have him dying feeling like that.

"You did your best. You gave me hope. The first person in a long time," I said.

He smiled at that and as bright pink blood floated out of his mouth he tried to force out something. I couldn't understand it in the slightest, but there were three words that I did understand enough.

Smash my desk.

Of course I didn't know what that meant, why I needed to but considering I was now out of leads, my mission was as good as dead and my beautiful Coleman could be killed for my failure. I had to try.

Gillman grabbed me.

His eyes were glassy. His skin cold. Pink blood leaked from his eyes.

He smiled at me. It was a smile of a predator.

He pulled me closer.

His mouth opened. A massive worm-like limb poured out. Leaking something.

I shot back.

Whipping out my swords.

Ramming them in his throat.

As Gillman's body turned to ash I knew something was extremely wrong now. That Creature or True Master wasn't having sex for pleasure, it was reproducing, creating those monsters or slaves or whatever it called them.

I ran out of the Shrine knowing I had to save the City of Pleasure not only from the Overlord's control but something far, far darker.

CHAPTER 14
36 Hours Until the Rebellion Falls

Coleman whipped out his sword as he, the two Archers and three Rebels returned to the City of Martyrs to see it in utter chaos. Most of the little white houses were a raging inferno. The yellow cobblestone roads ran with blood.

Coleman led everyone through the City towards the main port where presumably the ships with cannons were attacking. Everyone kept their swords and bows aimed at corners of the streets, the doorways and roofs of the little white houses.

No one wanted to be caught off guard here.

Coleman couldn't believe this was happening. He had tried to plan for everything but two days was not going to be enough to plan for a sea invasion.

He had ordered countless ships to be wrecked to stop Overlord Battleships from entering the port but apparently that had been repeatedly vetoed by Richard's posh friends.

The idiots!

Now Coleman was really starting to understand why the Assassin hated politics, politicians and everything to do with them. They hardly ever did the right thing and at the end of the day, it was always down to people of action and more practical people to save the day.

Coleman had no idea where these posh friends were right now, but he knew they weren't fighting for their lives.

Two enemy soldiers ran at Coleman.

The Archers fired.

As Coleman nodded his thanks but the enemy was everywhere and the more Coleman focused on the corpses of the soldiers, the more he felt like something terrible was happening.

The soldier's uniforms weren't black like the Overlord's other soldiers, their uniform was dark, dark blue and Coleman felt as if he had seen these types of soldiers before. He had. Coleman didn't remember all the details but he remembered something about Naval elites.

Coleman sat at the corpses as he now had a very dangerous question to answer. In the rare case that the battleships weren't in the port, how did these enemy elites get into the City?

A cannon fired.

Little white houses shattered.,

Coleman jumped to one side.

A cannon flew past him.

He looked at the others. They nodded. Everyone ran towards the port.

The heat of the fires licked their flesh. The sounds of crackling fires were everywhere. The smell of black smoke infected every breath.

Coleman kept moving.

He had to get to the port.

When he reached the top of the hill, he stopped immediately. The long yellow cobblestone path down to the port wasn't yellow anyone. It was pure red as corpses of Rebels and soldiers like littered the path.

The smell of black toxic smoke was overwhelming but at the very bottom of the path at the port where a legion of tiny wooden boats docking, shouting and unloading hundreds of elites.

When each person got off their boat, they didn't wait to form a formation with their brothers and sisters in arms. They whipped out their swords and charged into the City.

Enemies were charging towards Coleman, the Archers and Rebels.

There were no reinforcements nearby. Coleman was alone.

He saw well over ten flashes as cannon balls were fired. All heading in his direction.

Coleman was ready to make a final stand.

351

CHAPTER 15

38 Hours Until the Rebellion Falls

Something was definitely happening outside on the streets of the City as I stormed into Gillman's office. All I could hear outside was people screaming in utter terror as something was shrieking.

It had to have something to do with the Creature and his reproducing. I wanted to go and check but something inside me was shouting at me to smash up Gillman's desk. If there was any hope for the City of Pleasure I was hoping, praying, demanding that there would be something inside the desk to help me.

I completely ignored the bloody corpse on the large golden bed and I went straight over to the small desk. I didn't look special or important but maybe that was what Gilman wanted. In my experience there's no better hiding spot for anything than in plain sight.

I opened the draws in the desk and hissed as my long black cloak got caught on a corner. The desk were filled with sexual objects, erotic drawings and packs of food. All great for him and the slaves but useless to me.

Taking out my swords I struck the desk repeatedly. Beating it into a wreckage of its former self.

When only large chunks of wood were left of the desk, I huffed as this was really started to annoy me now. So I kicked through the chunks of the wood and I sound something. It sounded like something metal hitting wood.

I knelt down on the ground and searched through the chunks and found something. It looked to be a small metal box. It was hardly that big, it was a lot smaller than a cash box but slightly bigger than the sort of box you get when you gift something expensive jewellery.

I grabbed a sword and popped it open.

There was nothing of great interest in the box, there was only a journal inside. I flipped through the journal and coughed as the sound of musty old paper filled my nose.

But when I actually started to read it, it was filled with journal entrances about the slaves, the ones they sent to the capital and something about baby Jasper.

A lump formed in my throat as I realised I was the baby Jasper. There were a few details I knew in the journal, including a rather passionate and rageful entry about hearing the Overlord throwing me and my brother in the river.

I tucked the journal safely away from in my long black cloak and prayed to the Gods and Goddesses that I got to read it all at some point. I had to have my answers.

I got up to leave when I noticed something off about the metal box itself. It seemed bigger on the outside than the inside. I mean the inside of the box should have been deeper than it actually was, not by much, maybe a few centimetres.

So I grabbed my swords and pounded the box until it cracked. Revealing two things, a long ivory dagger that was covered with white blood at the tip and a simple note.

I put the ivory dagger in my pocket along with the white shard I had from the mask of the Maiden of Light to use against the Hunters that I got a while ago.

When I read it, it couldn't really understand it at first but by the time I finished it, it was clearly about the Creature and what it was doing. It seemed there had only ever been one survivor (my mother) and she had described the experience, the powers and the wants of the Creature.

But it was the last part that really interested it.

The Day of Enlightenment shall come sooner than anyone ever thought. The City will embrace Master's pleasure and be longing for it. For He is divine and the pleasure is amazing, the only hope is the Ivory dagger to be forced through his mouth, just as I did.

Wow! I didn't know much about my mother but

she sounded like a bad-ass. But this was all too much, I didn't know how to handle all this information. Ten minutes ago, I had known nothing about her to almost knowing everything.

It was too much.

A deafening scream came from behind me.

I jumped up. Spun around. Throwing my sword at one of the Creature's Monsters.

"Thank you," someone said. And I hadn't noticed that the young strong woman from earlier with her long golden hair and golden eyes was there before now.

"You're welcome," I said simply enough. But there was something off about all this, why was the Creature attacking now?

"Master Gillman would have wanted you to have that?" she said.

"Do you have my army?" I asked, probably colder than I wanted.

"Yes Master, the slaves are coming here. But…"

I stepped forward. "What?"

"Master, the slaves are being swarmed, infected, turned,"

I held both my swords in my hands and sighed. "Come on, take me to them. We're going to save them, kill the Creature and then you will help me,"

"Yes Master. Anything Master," she said.

As we left the office, I subtly padded the journal and the ivory dagger in my pockets. I had no idea what I was walking into but I had to be ready. And I had to try to protect these slaves. I needed them to save my beautiful Coleman.

But this Creature would infect and turn people into mindless Monsters.

And that terrified me.

CHAPTER 16

35 Hours Until the Rebellion Falls

Coleman was going to gut each and every one of these foul elites that tried to attack his City, kill his people and threaten their freedom. It was bad enough they had been stupid enough to attack in the first place, but now they were swarming Coleman and his friends. He had had enough.

He was going to stop them no matter what!

The blood-red cobblestone path down to the port was a graveyard. Bodies covered every inch of the path. More and more cannons fired.

More little white houses shattered.

Fatigue flooded Coleman's body as he slashed the throat of another elite. They had all been fighting for an hour now. No help was coming.

Coleman had sent two of the Rebels away to get help. They hadn't returned. They were probably dead.

The dark blue armoured elites kept running up the path towards them.

The Archers fired.

Coleman slashed his sword.

Slicing into the enemy's throats.

More blood splashed onto the path.

Coleman kept cutting them down.

More cannons fired.

Coleman saw the cannon balls.

He jumped out the way.

The balls smashed into the cobblestone.

Shattering it.

Deadly shards flew at them.

Coleman heard a Rebel scream.

She bled out in seconds.

A shard sliced Coleman's forehead.

Coleman hissed.

Blood dripped down his face. Into his eyes.

Two enemies grabbed Coleman. Forcing him to the ground. They smashed their fists into him.

Coleman's vision blurred. His teeth chipped. His mouth bloody.

Explosions echoed throughout the City.

It wasn't cannon fire. It was the exploding of wood. The two elites let go of Coleman.

Coleman jumped up.

Smashing their heads together.

The elites fell.

Coleman stomped on their heads.

With no enemies nearby Coleman took long deep breathes of the smoke filled air and watched as one by one the massive wooden warships of the Overlord exploded, water flooded each ship and they all sunk rapidly.

The air moved behind Coleman.

He ducked.

A sword rushed past.

Coleman spun on the ground. Kicking the enemy. Knocking their legs out from under them.

Coleman leapt on top of them. Grabbing their head. Smashing it into the cobblestones.

Shouting filled the path.

Coleman looked down at the port.

More enemies were charging up to him.

Coleman whipped out his sword.

A crossbow bolt shot at his sword.

Causing it to fly out of Coleman's hands.

Coleman was unarmed.

The enemy jumped.

They were about to tackle Coleman.

Glass bottles flew through the air.

Smashing into the enemy.

The enemy exploded.

Coleman jumped back. Shielding his eyes.

Bright blue fire engulfed the enemy. Turning them into liquid.

As more and more glass bottles smashed into the enemy, Coleman picked up his sword and was surprised to see enemies running away from the City as quickly as they could.

Most of the so-called elites were even pushing their wooden boats back out. Coleman had no idea where they would go now their ships were sunk, but Coleman was never going to underestimate these foul soldiers again. Once this was over, Coleman would definitely send out people to hunt these elites down and kill them all.

But now Coleman had much larger problems to deal with.

"That okay for ya Bossie," a very familiar voice said.

Coleman felt his body fill with excitement and his stomach flipped with happiness at the sound of Abbic's common voice. Her voice might have been rough but he was so glad to see her.

He ran over to her and hugged her. Then he realised she was carrying plenty of glass bottles filled with toxic, deadly and just plain old explosive chemicals. So he made sure not to hug her too much.

But it was great to see her in her bright shiny armour again. She wasn't here to deliver her chemical concoctions to him, she was here to fight and that delighted Coleman.

Panic screams filled the air as Coleman and Abbic spun around to the Wall.

Everyone was running as quickly as they could away from it.

Coleman wanted to run over. He didn't.

A deafening boom echoed for miles around as the Wall shattered. Creating a thick deadly cloud of dust, ash and powdered sandstone.

Coleman felt cold sweat drip down his face as

now the ten thousand enemy soldiers outside the Wall could happily storm the City.

And kill every single person.

CHAPTER 17

34 Hours Until the Rebellion Falls

This was worse than anything I ever could have imagined.

After hours fighting through these horrible narrow streets and watching the Creature's monsters hack away at the little wooden slave houses and infecting everyone they could. I stood at the very edge of the City of Pleasure on the massive stone wall that circled the entire City.

My swords were drawn and all around me stood hundreds of brave men and women armed with whatever they could find (which wasn't more than kitchen knives and pots and pans) as we all watched the foul horde of thousands of infected Slaves march towards us.

I hated the sounds of their groaning, moaning and hissing but I had to defeat them, protect these brave men and women and hopefully gather some forces to save the man I loved.

I raised my swords and jumped off the wall.

I landed hard.

I swung my swords.

Slicing into enemy flesh.

White blood poured out. Splashing everywhere.

I didn't stop.

My swords swirled in the air. Slashing enemies.

Slicing their flesh. Slicing their throats. Slicing their heads off.

Their groans got louder. They attacked harder.

I kept swinging my swords.

Hacking off their hands.

Chopping off their arms.

Shattering their heads.

They still came.

The brave men and women fought too. They threw stones at the enemy.

The stones smashed into the enemy. Shattering bone. Splitting open heads.

I jumped into the air. Spinning around. Becoming a hurricane of death.

My swords chomping on all they touched.

The enemy hissed.

I kicked them. Breaking bones.

They were moving faster now. They kept coming. They focused on me.

I was being overwhelmed.

Screams came from above me.

I swung my sword in a bloody arc. I looked up.

The brave men and women were being attacked.

They were being infected.

I had to save them.

I kept swirling. I kept hacking the enemy apart. I had to get to them.

Hands grabbed me.

Pulling me to the ground.

I fell.

Warm liquid covered me.

I stared at the enemy. I struggled.

The enemy grabbed my arms. I couldn't swing my swords.

Their mouths opened. Something grew out of their throats.

They were coming towards me. Leaking something.

I screamed.

Something burnt in my pocket. White light shone out.

The enemy released me. Moving back. I whipped out the ivory dagger.

They hissed louder and louder.

I charged at them.

Slashing them with the dagger.

They turned to ash.

They screamed as loud as they could. They were calling something.

I had to silence them.

Something screamed back. They flew at me.

I swung the dagger wildly. Turning the infected to ash.

There were so many.

They whacked me against the outer wall.

I dropped the dagger.

They laughed.

They came to me.

Their mouths opened.

Then everyone stopped as we heard something stomp towards us. The silly infected people stepped to one side to create a path. My mouth dropped as I watched the massive Creature move towards me.

I didn't know how it was moving but as the sounds of cracking wood, falling buildings and screams filled my senses, I knew it was moving through the City and crushing whatever it wanted. I could see the hairy worm-like body of it and my stomach churned.

I didn't want to fight it. I didn't want to die.

I rushed over and grabbed the ivory dagger. The Infected slaves didn't seem to bat an eyelid. They truly didn't believe I could kill the Creature.

Three whooshes filled my senses.

The Hunters appeared in front of me.

They whipped out their swords.

I pointed behind them.

They hissed.

They ignored me. Their shadowy swords pointed at the Creature.

The Creature roared.

Charging towards us.

CHAPTER 18
34 Hours Until the Rebellion Falls

Coleman felt horrible sand, dust and ash coat his skin and throat as he marched up to the shattered Wall where ten thousand Overlord Soldiers were pouring into the City like an unstoppable tidal wave.

He grabbed a bow and arrows from a corpse.

Coleman aimed.

He fired.

An arrow flew through the air. Ramming itself in an enemy's brain.

More flew at him.

Coleman fired again.

And again.

Two more corpses dropped.

The enemy were getting too close.

Abbic ran over. Throwing her glass bottles.

Soldiers screamed as they melt. Their liquified flesh covered the cobblestones.

Coleman whipped out his sword. He had to find

Richard. He had to find survivors.

Coleman dived into the battle.

He swung his sword rapidly.

Chopping down the enemy.

Abbic covered him. She threw bottles.

More enemies burnt alive.

Coleman hacked through the soldiers.

Swords flashed past him.

Coleman ducked.

Abbic hissed.

Coleman heard shattering glass.

Abbic screamed.

Coleman slashed the soldier.

He spun around. Abbic was burning.

He grabbed her. Ripping off her armour.

Coleman threw the burning armour into the soldiers.

They screamed. They burnt. They died.

Coleman threw Abbic to the ground. She rolled around until the fire was out.

Someone whacked Coleman round the face.

They picked him up. Throwing him into the soldiers.

Swords sliced at him.

Coleman tried to jump up.

Soldiers stomped on him.

Coleman wrapped his arms around his head.

Magical energy crackled around him.

Lightning shot through the enemy.

Someone grabbed Coleman. Coleman jumped

up. Abbic pulled him away.

Richard stormed towards the soldiers. Magical energy scouring them.

Coleman raised his sword to join him. He went to charge over. Abbic grabbed him.

Whooshing filled the City. Tens of arrows screamed through the air.

Slamming into Richard. He dropped to the ground.

Coleman looked at Abbic. He had to save his friend. Abbic nodded.

Coleman ran towards Richard.

Abbic followed him. Throwing her bottles. The enemy slowed.

Coleman grabbed Richard. Pulling him away.

Richard tried to stand. He couldn't. Coleman kept pulling him.

Abbic stopped throwing bottles. She was out of them.

She grabbed Richard. Helping Coleman. This wasn't what Coleman needed.

Posh snobs ran past Coleman. He wanted to stop them.

The enemy open fired. Slaughtering the rich and powerful snobs.

Coleman kept pulling.

The rich snobs were buying him time.

And now Coleman knew that his entire fate rested in the hands of the Assassin.

She had to get here soon.

CHAPTER 19

34 Hours Until the Rebellion Falls

I flat out hated the Creature.

It charged at me and the Hunters. The Hunters disappeared. I dived out the way.

The Creature swung its limbs at me.

I jumped up.

Swinging my swords.

My swords sliced the limbs. No blood came out.

The Creature screamed.

They infected slaves charged.

The Hunters appeared.

Each one in front of a third of the infected.

Their shadowy swords sliced them.

Cutting them to pieces. They were stopping the infected from hurting me.

I flew at the Creature.

My swords swinging wildly.

The Creature's limbs met my swords.

The force making my hands ache.

Pain shot into my arms.

The Creature surged forward.

Knocking me back.

The Creature dived for me.

I threw a sword.

My sword slammed into its stomach.

It screamed.

I rolled. Jumping up. Whipping out the ivory dagger.

The Creature shrieked at the sight.

I ran at it.

Jumping into the air.

The Creature's limbs flew at me.

Wrapping around my waist.

Wrapping my head.

Wrapping around my wrists.

They squeezed.

I dropped the ivory dagger. The limb around my head stopped. It grabbed the ivory dagger.

Crushing it. The dagger shattered. My heart dropped.

Rage filled me.

I swung my sword. It sliced the Creature.

The limbs released me. I fell to the ground. I landed hard. My knees ached.

The Creature whacked me against the wall.

The back of my head cracked against the wall. My sight went black.

I couched at the ground with my world completely black except for the odd slivers of light at the very corners of my vision.

I was expecting the Creature to just finish me off but I heard it turn and started attacking. He was presumably attacking the Hunters.

The Hunters deserved to die for what they tried to do to me. But they were innocent. They were trapped by a magic bond of some sort. I had to save them.

Something wet slammed me against the outer wall. I felt something growing over my skin. It felt great. Wonderful. It felt pleasurable.

No!

I wasn't letting the Creature do something to me. A wave of strange energy dripped into my blood as more and more of my skin started to tinkle.

This had to be the Creature pouring his corruption into me but the energy felt as if it was coming from my cells and within me. It wasn't coming from the stuff on my skin.

Then it twigged. My mother was the only survivor of the Creature. She apparently had strange magical powers. Maybe I inherited them!

More and more energy filled me and my sight started to return. I was covered in fine white silk and I felt myself smiling.

I stopped that. I was not smiling. I was not happy. I was fuming!

Magical energy surged inside me.

I thrusted out my hands. Shattering the white silk and limb like it was nothing.

It was nothing. I hated this Creature.

The Creature shot back at the sight of me.

Even the Hunters disappeared.

White magical energy shone out of me.

The Creature froze. I didn't.

I charged forward.

My swords flew over to me.

I raised them.

Jumping into the air.

The Creature swung its limbs at me.

I sliced them.

The limbs turned to crystal.

They shattered.

The Creature tried to run.

It couldn't move.

I bought down my swords.

Magic energy shot out of them.

Turning the Creature to crystal.

I punched it and the entire Creature shattered. Turning to dust.

I blinked a couple of times as I felt the strange magical energy absorb back into my cells and I had no idea what had just happened. All I knew was that it had something to do with my mother.

People muttered to themselves and I realised that everyone who was still alive was no longer infected and they all stared at me with that annoying as hell human curiosity.

Someone clicked their fingers at me (the nerve!) and I looked up at the outer wall to see the strong young woman with her golden hair and eyes stared at me.

Then she bowed.

Everyone bowed at me. I didn't want their praise. I wanted them to help me, help free my people, help me save the man I loved.

But as I looked around at their City, I realised it was all destroyed. These people had nothing left, not that they had a lot in the beginning. They were sex slaves.

Well, they *were* sex slaves. They were people now. People free to do as they pleased.

"Rise," I said.

Everyone looked at each other and then they rose with massive smiles on their faces. But all the previously infected people started coughing out of ash as presumably the thing inside their throats was now dead.

As dead as beautiful Coleman if I didn't hurry.

So I did something that I swore never to do. I knelt on the ground like all these people were superior to me. Because in that moment they were.

"You're welcome to your freedom. But I beg you, I truly beg you to help me. Come with me to the City of Martyrs and please, please help me save my friends,"

"Assassin!" the young strong woman shouted gesturing me to look at something.

I climbed up to the outer wall and looked over the area and my mouth dropped as maybe tens of thousands of different people from all different Cities, regions and every single part of the Kingdom rode past the City as fast as they could.

Coleman's message had inspired people to risk their lives.

"We Stand With the Rebellion," the young strong woman said.

I smiled. Maybe I could save the man I loved after all.

CHAPTER 20
0 Hours Until The Rebellion Falls

Coleman hated his idea of the Rebellion having over 30 hours to live. That was never going to happen. The Rebellion's time had ran out and he hated himself for it. How could he have been so arrogant to think they could have defended themselves. The Overlord was always going to win. That was the simple truth.

A massive thud echoed around the little house Coleman, Abbic and Richard were hiding in. The room was disgusting with its tiny size, layers of mould and pathetic door.

But it was all Coleman had time to find. Him and Abbic had tried to board up and reinforce the door as best they could and finally their building skills could be tested.

Another thud cracked the door and Coleman could see the soldiers outside with their battering ram.

Coleman looked at Abbic who was staring at the

door and like Coleman, she had cold fearful sweat dripping down her forehead. Coleman hated all of this, he wanted to do something.

He didn't know how many of his friends lived, how many of them were fighting or even how many of them hadn't been captured. Coleman just wanted to know they were okay.

He would happily give up his life for theirs. His friends never deserved to die.

Richard groaned a little as magic energy crackled around his wounds as he presumably tried to heal himself. Coleman wished he could help but medicine was never his specialist subject.

A final thud shattered the door.

Wooden shards flew towards them.

Coleman dived over Abbic and Richard.

Shards rammed themselves in his back.

Coleman hissed.

The soldiers poured out.

Ripping him away from Abbic and Coleman.

Another soldier kicked Richard in-between the legs.

Coleman felt a cold blade touch his throat.

Two other soldiers grabbed Richard and Abbic.

"See Commander Coleman. Watch your friends die," a man said.

The other soldiers with Abbic and Richard whipped out knives and raised them.

Coleman had to do something. He wouldn't let them die. His Assassin might have failed him. She wasn't coming. Coleman couldn't fail these two.

"Stop! I know something," Coleman shouted.

"I don't believe you. Kill them," the man said.

"If you kill them I will never tell you the secret,"

The man laughed. "Just do it,"

The two soldiers pressed the knives against Abbic's and Richard's throats. Coleman couldn't bear it. Blood dripped down their bodies.

Richard blinked at Coleman in a beat. He didn't know what it meant.

Coleman needed to half-act. "No. Please don't! Take me. Kill me please! Let them go!"

The man laughed again right in Coleman's ear as he gestured the soldiers to slowly kill them.

Richard smiled. He shot out his hands. Magical lightning shot out. Killing the soldiers.

Coleman grabbed the man's sword.

More soldiers poured in.

Coleman slashed their chests.

Abbic grabbed two more swords. She attacked. Hacking the enemy to pieces.

A deafening sound echoed throughout the City. Coleman didn't know what it was but it made all the soldiers run away from them and towards the Wall.

Coleman went out of the little white house they were in and looked at what the soldiers were so scared. And utter delight filled him as he saw in far, far distance tens of thousands (probably hundreds of thousands in reality) of people were riding towards them.

And there was a little black dot at the very front of the mass of people. A little black dot with a long black cloak and hood flapping in the wind.

Coleman's stunning sexy Assassin had come for him at last.

CHAPTER 21

0 Hours Until Rebellion Falls

I was finally going to save the man I loved. The man I needed to protect, treasure and made sure he survived. Not only for me but to ensure the freedom of the entire Kingdom, and that was why tens of thousands of amazing people rode behind me.

I kicked my horse to ride faster.

My horse went faster and faster and faster. We had to reach the City of Martyrs. I could see the thousands of foul enemies in the City. They weren't claiming my beautiful Coleman today, or any other day for that matter.

I was leading the mass of riders towards the City. I just wished they would hurry up and help me storm the City but the wind was awful so I couldn't blame them too much. My long black cloak and hood was flapping about wildly.

The Hunters appeared in front of me. They flicked out their hands.

Throwing me off my horse. My horse kept riding.

I jumped up. Staring at the Hunter's black cloaks and shadowy faces. They whipped out their shadowy swords.

I whipped out my swords. The Shadows flew at me.

Our swords clashed.

Magical energy crackled around us.

I jumped into the air. Swirling around. My blade whirling.

The Hunters' swung. Knocking me to the ground.

My back pounded the ground.

The Hunters grabbed me. I screamed. Their icy touch burning me.

I struggled. I kicked. I punched.

More icy pain flooded my senses.

In the back of my mind I heard Coleman's voice. He needed me. I had to protect them.

I screamed through the pain. I leapt up. Swinging my swords in a bloody arc.

The Hunters shot back.

Raising their hands.

Black energy shot out.

It slammed into me. Burning my cloak.

I sank to my knees in agony.

I heard horses thunder towards us. Tens of thousands of people were close. I felt the hooves pound behind me.

The pain lessened. Hunters were distracted.

I dived forward.

Whipping out the white shard. The Hunters screamed at the sight. The shard shone bright light.

A ghostly form of the Maiden of Light appeared.

The Hunters screamed in terror.

I jumped forward.

Slicing a Hunter with the shard.

It shrieked.

They all disappeared.

But when I looked back at the white shard from the mask of the Maiden of Light (the woman who birthed them), all I saw was ash in my hands. I might have saved myself this time but now I didn't have a weapon to use against them.

My only hope now was to find that oath rode if such a thing even existed, and then I just had to hope beyond hope that the Hunters wouldn't kill me after I freed them.

With the sound of tens of thousands of amazing men and women thundering behind me, I whistled for my horse and hopped on.

Riding towards the City of Martyrs to save, protect and treasure the man I loved.

I just hoped he was still alive.

CHAPTER 22

1 Hour After Rebellion Was Saved

Commander Coleman felt immense waves of happiness, delight and affection wash over him as he stared at all the wonderful people around him.

In amongst the wreckage, the burning little white houses and corpses stood tens of thousands of people that had dared to do the unthinkable. They had all left their comfortable homes and Cities and rode for Gods know how long all to come to his aid.

A man denounced by the Overlord as a crazy, traitor that wanted everyone in the Kingdom to die. But all these people had come.

Coleman had never seen so many people from so many different classes, regions and Cities. He didn't recognise half the accents, the dialects and even some of the food these people had bought for him and his friends.

He might have not have known these people, leaders or their interest in the Rebellion, but as

Coleman breathed in the wonderful sweet fruit smells of the mini-desserts of these people. It was clear these people wanted him to do well.

Later he would have to talk seriously to each of the leaders so he could understand what was happening better, but for now, he just wanted a little moment of peace. After all him, Abbic and all the other survivors had just survived a massacre.

All because of his girlfriend the Assassin with her stunning dark eyes, long black cloak and hood and her wonderful smile that would always melt his heart.

When this mass of people stormed the City and immediately started killing the Overlord's soldiers, Coleman had tried to look for the Assassin but he couldn't find her. He knew she was alive, he would have liked to think if anything had happened to her he would feel it in his bones.

People cheered, shouted and laughed as they picked through the wreckage, and there was something so warming about it.

After days of fighting, bloodshed and sadness, it was amazing (to Coleman at least) to see people who had never met before laughing and bonding over mocking the Overlord. A few metres from Coleman was a man with dark skin laughing with another man as he gave him some of the corpse's armour.

Coleman didn't know what they were laughing about, but they weren't the only ones. Even in this strange time after a massive loss and a victory, everyone was finding the joy in it.

Maybe they were happy that the Overlord could be defeated.

And that reminded Coleman of one of his worse fears that was thankfully proved wrong. At the start of the slaughter, Coleman had been terrified that if he lost it would send a message throughout the Kingdom telling everyone how the Overlord could never ever be defeated.

As Coleman looked around with a massive smile on his face, he knew the Overlord had been proved very wrong. He was even more impressed when Lord Castellan Richard had sent out ten messengers sending in every direction in the Kingdom to tell others about the Overlord's defeat.

That was bold.

Yet it was needed. The people of the Kingdom needed to know the power of the people and the Rebellion when they helped each other anything was possible.

Coleman might not have known what the future held but he was looking forward to it. He looked forward to storming the capital, killing the Overlord and freeing the people of the Kingdom.

As he walked off into the crowd, he realised the storming of the capital was definitely something for thinking about tomorrow, today he wanted to talk to the other leaders then see the most important person in the entire City.

Coleman was going to have a long overdue catch-up (and hopefully more) with his beautiful

Assassin.

Finally.

CHAPTER 23

Two Hours After Rebellion Was Saved

After a couple of good hours, I had finally found a person who was willing to make me a good cup of coffee without any of that horrible almond syrup. That was probably the highlight of my day!

With most of the City burning, destroyed or just no longer standing, I sat on one of the few remaining granite towers of the Wall with my legs dangling over the edge with a wonderful view of the City below me.

Of course the idea of sitting on the edge of a building that could collapse was scary to most people, but after the past few days I just wanted a quiet place to sit and get a precious few moments of silence before something else happened.

I loved the amazing warm feeling of the mug of coffee in my hands and I loved the bitter smell of the coffee even more. It was a great contrast to the foul smells of the past few days.

But I will mention one thing I am surprised about. Normally when Coleman sends out a note, a message or anything, no one cares. No one cares about the Rebellion, no one wants to help them out because of fear of the Overlord burning their family to ash. And yet this time they came.

When I was riding here with the City of Pleasure and the other tens of thousands of people, I actually asked them why did they come. Their answer surprised me. It was all because of me.

Apparently news of my skills, hatred for the Overlord and actions had reached every corner of the Kingdom and it inspired people. Then apparently because I believed in Coleman, people trusted my judgement so they followed him.

I'm not really sure how to take that really. I have never seen myself as a great warrior, an inspirational person or even that good at all that moral character stuff. I'm just an assassin who got caught up in the Rebellion's great cause.

Damn them!

The laughter, talking and shouting of tens of thousands below me was such a strange sound after everything. People were happy here and in all honesty I could understand it. I really could. For them there was a chance of happiness and freedom, a real chance for the first time in fifty years.

Forgetting about the battle and fighting for each City for a moment, I picked the journal and opened it on the very last page. It turned out Lord Gillman didn't fail me or himself anything.

There was a map on the very last page but I couldn't understand it. It was made up of so many crazy lines and symbols and words in another language. I would have to scout out the City of Martyrs tomorrow to find someone who could understand all this.

But the journal. It made for interesting reading and now I sort of felt like I didn't know myself anymore. Turned out my mother was a simple farm girl who was captured, shipped and trained in the City of Pleasure decades ago. She rose through their ranks and became the most popular slave in the entire City.

The Masters treated her well and the other slaves were so jealous they tried to kill her on at least ten occasions over the decades. Then the True Master selected her for a pleasure session and that's when everything changed apparently.

Whilst Lord Gillman might have been her only true friend in the City, he didn't have a gift for describing what had happened next. All I could gather from his writings were my mother fought back using the ivory dagger, resisted its corrupting influence and become changed somewhat.

Now I don't know what my mother was truly like but Gillman made it sound like she become a sort of Seer. Able to see the future, perform most types of limited magic and something about her being a holy figure except when she was with him.

I have no idea how I feel about that personally, it seems so strange and made-up but I don't know how to explain my own magic during that battle. It had to come from my mother.

I really don't know what to think about at this time.

Then the Overlord came, collected her and that was the end of the writings really. After that it was simply Gillman journaling and channelling his rage at what the Overlord had done to my mother, me and my brother.

My beautiful precious brother, the Overlord will pay for killing him.

I felt someone wrap their strong amazing arms around me and I was pulled towards someone. Coleman kissed me on the head and I stared into those wonderful dark emerald eyes.

Then I realised none of this stuff about my mother, the Overlord or the Rebellion mattered, at least not for a few hours.

I rolled over, pushed Coleman on the ground and I smiled.

With everything right with the world and everyone safe once again, I wasn't going to be an Assassin for a few hours. I was just going to be a woman with her boyfriend and I was going to enjoy it. A lot.

And that was fine by me.

After saving the Rebellion, the City of Pleasure and the Kingdom, I think I deserved a bit of pleasure myself.

And I was going to savour it.

AUTHOR'S NOTE

Thank you for reading, I really hope you enjoyed it.

In the Author's Note, I always like to mention quickly what inspired the book, and the main inspiration for this book was a very strange picture I saw once.

I think I must have been watching a history programme and they were talking about Pleasure Gardens in England during the 18th Century, so I was interested in that because I had never heard of Pleasure Gardens before.

Therefore, I started watching it and it turned out that one of the functions of Pleasure Gardens were brothels and as I was starting to write the City of Assassins short stories that got me thinking.

Then the programme showed an image of the Pleasure Gardens with tons of young women dressed in scandalously short stuff with their arms and ankles showing skin, (at least back then it was scandal) and they were all cramped together.

As well as you also have the fact that Coleman mentioned that he came from the City of Pleasure so it was worth exploring for that alone. Then the idea of the Masters, True Masters and monsters came from different places of course.

But in the first and last chapters, I mentioned the Assassin didn't like almond syrup in her coffee. Now I did this because at the time of writing, I got a range of flavoured coffee syrups for Christmas and there was a syrup I really didn't like.

It turns out it was actually an apricot syrup but I thought it was an almond so hence the dislike from the Assassin.

Overall, I really hope you enjoyed the book and see check out the rest of the series in electronic and print format at your favourite bookstore.

I hope to see you in another book soon.

Have a great day!

CITY OF
POWER

CONNOR WHITLEY

cccxcvii

CHAPTER 1

Whenever I normally go to see a contact, asset or spy, I always make sure we meet in a public space with multiple escape routes and with minimal guards. That was in normal times.

These were far from normal times.

As I pulled my long black cloak and hood over my body to cover me, I made sure my swords were easy to get to and my movements were unrestricted. Because I was going to need to be free in this place, that was a certainty.

I leant against the cold wooden walls of a local pub in a large market square lined with every single shop, stall or table you could imagine. There were blacksmiths, bakers, toy makers and more all in this single little square where rows upon rows of them were.

The amazing smell of freshly baked bread mixed in with the hints of smoke that I tasted in the air, it all smelt incredible. But I wasn't here for any of those things. I was here for a simple purpose, I needed to meet someone.

People strolled around the market talking, muttering and barring at everyone else as they went around their daily business and considering how cramped the square was, I was surprised how calm everyone was.

And that concerned me. This wasn't ideal for escaping, fighting or killing in. The risk of me hurting innocent people was too high and black armoured guards were everywhere. I could see at least twenty from where I was standing.

There was the real problem. I will never deny being a female assassin is wonderful, I get to kill whoever I want for money, I get to help me and most importantly I get to be my own boss. But ever since that damn Rebellion, who wanted to kill the tyrannic Overlord, seduced me with their amazing cause wanting to free everyone, I only get to kill for them.

But their leader, Commander Coleman, is pretty sexy, hot and adorable with his amazing body and deep emerald eyes. He is a pretty boyfriend too.

A bell ringing in the middle of the square reminded me it was getting close to midday and I needed to get a move on before the typical lunch crowd came out and swarmed the market. Then escaping would be next to impossible if something went wrong.

So I made sure my long black cloak and hood were covering me and I made my way through the crowd and deep into the market.

Now by this point most people would call me paranoid, crazy or just overly cautious, well, for starters being like that keeps you alive as an assassin. And when the Overlord is your father and he's hunting you down, you tend to get very wary of spending too long in a place he controls.

Believe me, if I didn't have to be here right now, I wouldn't. I would be with the man I love but because some supernatural Hunters are, well, hunting me down and want me dead, and I found some map that I can't read. I needed to find someone who could read my map and luckily there was apparently someone here who could help me.

As I continued through the crowd, all that wonderful fresh bread and smoke smell was gone and replaced with the horrible smell of sweaty people. I really hoped this mission wasn't going to take that long.

After a few more minutes of pulling, gliding and forcing my way through the crowd, I saw a long wooden table covered in maps (that were far from accurate) and a tall woman stood there talking to a man. I didn't like her dirty black clothes that were falling apart, but I suppose I couldn't judge too much. This long black cloak was about two decades old.

I went over to the woman and watched her deal with the people in front of me.

"And that will be twenty-five coins for the Black Valley Map," she said.

The man smiled. "Oh thank you, that is just brilli! Thank you!" He gave her the money, took the map and rushed off smiling.

I went up to her. "Ever been to the Black Valley?"

The woman smiled. "Of course not Assassin, and of course the map's wrong, these people don't know any different,"

For some reason I was both impressed and extremely concerned that she knew who I was.

"Coleman tells me you're the best scholar on ancient languages outside the Capital. But judging by your maps I doubt that highly," I said coldly.

The woman laughed. "Oh Assassin, before the Overlord came to power and he killed my parents. My mother was Lady Jones Of Green Valley,"

She paused as if that was meant to mean something to me. It really didn't. I think there was a Green Valley in the far, far south of the Kingdom. Besides from that I was happily clueless about that lawless part of the Kingdom.

"The famous explorer," she said.

I just nodded.

"Assassin, I am Margret Green-Valley. Exploring, history and languages are in my blood literally. I know all of the Kingdom's history, languages and everything else. I… I just can't draw them," she said gesturing to the maps.

She wasn't lying about her inability to draw. Even I could have done a better job at this than her and

401

according to my teachers at the Assassin Temple as a child, my drawings of men look like donkeys, and my women look like horses.

I took the journal that contained the map and opened it to the very last page to show it to her. I hated the craziness of the strange lines, ancient symbols and words that meant nothing to me. But as she looked at the map, her eyes lit up and her eyes were moving. She was reading this!

I have no idea how but she was glued to the map like it was the most fascinating thing ever.

People moaned, shouted and argued as black armoured guards pushed through the crowd. Damn it. They were on to me I needed answers now!

Margret saw the guards. "Arg! Those guards have to go. Don't have much time. The map speaks about something. A dragon's resting place. A Capital of all power. A Rod of Ultimate Sacrifice,"

I rolled my eyes. The guards were getting closer.

"Come with me," I said.

Margret stood away from her table and pulled up some of her clothes. Her legs weren't there, she was only able to walk because of two wooden sticks that had been forced in.

"A present from the Overlord," she said. "Kill him for me,"

I nodded.

"Stop!" a guard shouted.

I whipped out my swords.

Guards stormed over.

Thrusting their swords into Margret.

The guards flew at me.

I slashed my swords.

Our swords met.

I jumped into the air.

Kicking them in the heads.

People screamed in terror.

They ran out of the market.

I slashed the throat of a guard.

I ran.

Guards were too slow.

I kept running.

I dived into the chaotic crowd.

Making sure they couldn't find me.

CHAPTER 2

Commander Coleman sat on the freezing cold wood of his favourite chair inside one of his least favourite rooms in the City. It wasn't that he hated the room's so-called fine art, long oak table and chairs. It was more of what this room had come to represent in the City of Martyrs.

Even since the Rebellion had claimed, freed and defended the City Of Martyrs, so many vital decisions had been made in this room by posh snobby people who ultimately didn't know what they were talking about, so the decisions were bad and far too many lives were lost.

Coleman really wanted to never make those same mistakes as those people but as they were all dead now and the ruler of the City, Lord Castellan Richard, had named Coleman as his second-in-command, Coleman didn't have much of a choice in the matter.

Sweet oranges that tasted like the amazing bitter orange tarts he had as a child made Coleman wonder about when all this chaos would be over. He had been leading the Rebellion for a good few decades now and he just wanted it all to be over. He wanted everyone to be free, peaceful and able to enjoy life.

Coleman listened to the sounds of people being happy, laughing and cheering outside as he assumed his beautiful Assassin had returned and his people were happy to see her. He could imagine her outrage and horror at receiving the welcome now, she would hate it but she deserved it.

Coleman wasn't sure what the Assassin had wanted the map to be but for his sake and the sake of the Rebellion and Kingdom, he hoped she was in a good mood. He might not have been her boyfriend for too long but he had been it long enough to know how angry she could get!

"You okay Bossie?"

Coleman smiled as he looked at a short beautiful woman to his left with her long perfectly straight hair and leather armour. She was called Abbic and Coleman loved her as a father in a strange way, she had saved him more times than he wanted to admit and she was as strong (probably stronger) than any man he had ever met.

"Ya boss, what up?"

Coleman rolled his eyes as now he had both of his closest friends worried about him. The man to his right was Dragnist, a wonderful man, a clever man with his long beard and dirty armour.

"Relax I'm just thinking," Coleman said. Not

sure what to tell him. He just wanted his beautiful Assassin's mission to go well and hopefully she would have an answer to their Hunter problem.

Coleman had only met the Hunters once when the Assassin saved the Rebellion from extinction but they were supernatural, made from shadow and just deadly. The Assassin had fought them many more times since and just the idea of the woman he loved being killed by them was too much.

The Hunters needed to go but Coleman hated how the Overlord had trapped them and bound them to his Will using a so-called Oath Rod.

Coleman had always believed them to be myths, the stuff of legends but they were real. He wasn't sure how the magic inside the Rod made the oath between the parties unbreakable, but he never ever wanted to find out.

It still didn't make the mission any less real. The theory (which Coleman wasn't completely sure on) was to find the Oath Rod, break it and hopefully the newly freed Hunters would return to their supernatural place and leave the Kingdom alone.

Coleman wished that thinking was right but he really wasn't sure.

"Bossie?" Abbic asked.

Coleman placed a gentle hand on hers and rubbed it. "I'm okay really. I just want my Assassin back,"

Coleman felt a hard hand grab his shoulder and run down his back as someone kissed him. He raised his head, saw it was his lover and kissed the Assassin on her soft beautiful lips.

Coleman gestured her to take a seat but she shook her head. He wished she would let him hold her hand or do something more intimate than just standing next to him but he knew she would never allow that. Sadly.

"Ya mission good?" Abbic asked.

The Assassin knelt on the ground so she was in line with the table.

"What do you guys know about A Dragon's Resting Place?" she asked.

Coleman had no idea why she would be asking about a dragon. They were made up creatures, they weren't real. Coleman remembered the Assassin mentioned them a few times but he never believed they were real.

Dragnist pointed at the Assassin. "Know there were stories. Massive Stories. Dragons in Central regions,"

"What stories?" Coleman said.

"Know kiddy ones. Dragon in dead centre of Kingdom," Dragnist said to the Assassin.

Coleman looked at Abbic. She was nodding.

"Seriously Abbic? You heard the same stories?" Coleman asked.

"Yea Bossie, me heard lots of stories about Dragons. Dragons big, tasty and cuddly. One lays in the dead centre of the Kingdom. Where Capital is. I saw it,"

Coleman and the Assassin just looked at each other. "Go on,"

Abbic leant forward. "Yea Bossie and Assassin, I went there with traitorous Sis once on a mission. We went down into the sewers. Lost for hours. Found a massive chamber. Size of the City,"

Coleman really hoped his face wasn't as puzzled and doubtful as he felt.

"Then it was there. Massive skeleton of dragon, even have a dragon tooth on me," Abbic said, standing up and getting something out of her pocket.

Coleman and the Assassin looked wide-eyed at each other as Abbic threw something on the table. It was a wonderfully long tooth, easily the length of a dagger.

Dragnist picked it up. He dropped it. Licking his finger.

"What's wrong?" Coleman asked.

"Bloody thing sharp," Dragnist said.

The Assassin used a bit of her sleeve to pick it. She hissed as she put it back down. Coleman could see a part of her sleeve was sliced wide open. That tooth was sharp alright.

"How do you know this is a dragon's tooth?" Coleman asked.

The Assassin placed a hand on his shoulder. "It matches all the records and when I met the Dragons their teeth were this good. So we need to head to the capital,"

Everyone went silent.

"The map contact I met with told me three things about the map before she was killed. Something about the resting place of a dragon. A Capital of Power. A Rod of Sacrifice,"

As right as she might be, Coleman felt his stomach churn at the idea of attacking or even going anywhere near the Capital. That place would be crawling with the Overlord's guards and everything.

Coleman cocked his head when he realised it actually wouldn't be as difficult as that. When the City of Martyrs was facing annihilation and Coleman sent his message for aid out to the entire Kingdom, tens of thousands of people came to his help.

Hundreds of thousands (if not millions) had turned up since. They had the numbers to storm the capital and everyone had received basic combat training. They had an army.

A peasant army, but an army nonetheless.

Coleman stood up. "The Dragon's Resting Place, a location for the Oath Rod?"

"Yes, the Rod of Sacrifice must refer to the sacrifice the Hunters made to give up their freedom," the Assassin said.

"Bossie, we attacking Capital?"

Coleman looked at the Assassin. If she wanted to storm the Capital, kill her father and free the Kingdom he would support her, he just hoped she would love him after the battle, if he was still alive.

"Attacking Capital would be best," the Assassin said.

Coleman nodded and looked at Abbic and Dragnist. "We need a plan. But only if you two want to. I don't attack if you think it's a bad idea,"

He could feel the Assassin smile and agree with him from behind.

Abbic and Dragnist exchanged glances and started laughing. "Of course we wanna attack Bossie. We gonna kill the Overlord and free us,"

Coleman hugged the Assassin. She hugged back. Hard.

The Assassin whispered in his ear. "So we go to war my love,"

"And so the final battle begins here," Coleman said.

CHAPTER 3

Whenever I come to these meetings, I only know one thing for certain. I'll get to see the most beautiful man in the world, my stunning Coleman. The rest of the meeting tends to goes towards the slow and uninteresting end of the excitement spectrum, which is why I avoid them like the plague and I tend to go on killing missions. You know, to liven things up for myself.

Or I tend to make sure my long black cloak and hood are extra tight so I look terrifying. You wouldn't believe some of the screams I've got from scaring people like that. Good times!

But as I stood there in this rather tasteless room with its awful art and even worse oak table and chairs, I never would have expected to end up planning to invade the Capital, also known as the City of Power in the ancient language.

In all honesty I had absolutely no idea how I felt. Sure, I've wanted this from the day my bastard father threw me and my brother in the river, trying (and failing) to kill us. For as long as I could remember I've wanted to slash my swords across my father's throat, but now it was actually happening, I didn't know how I felt.

A part of me was happy, another part of me was excited and the last part was numb. I was like I didn't want this time with Coleman to end because I didn't know what he or I would do after this was all over.

My face must have spoken a thousand words as Coleman gently rubbed and kissed my hand and I looked at him and smiled.

I was about to say something when the temperature dropped. The air turned icy cold.

The Hunters appeared.

Their shadowy swords swung.

Everyone jumped to one side.

I whipped out my swords.

Charging forward.

They met my swords.

One thrusted out their hand.

Flying me across the room.

I shrieked. Whacking my head at the wall.

Coleman and the others whipped out their weapons.

They fought.

I flew over.

Jumping into the air.

Twirling my swords. Becoming a hurricane of death.

The Hunters flicked their hands. Throwing everyone else across the room.

I slashed my swords. The Hunters disappeared.

They rammed their swords into me.

I screamed in agony.

Coleman rushed over. I heard the swords. He screamed.

Warm blood splashed up my back.

Magical energy hummed.

Lightning shot across the room.

As I fell to the ground and forced myself to turn over, I stared at my beautiful Coleman who had his hands so tightly around his throat his knuckles were white. It still didn't matter too much, I could still see the blood gushing out of his wound.

I couldn't let him die. I fell forward and forced my bleeding body to crawl over to him.

White magical light in long strings wrapped around me and stopped me from moving. I couldn't allow this, I couldn't let my Coleman die alone! I wasn't going to let him die!

Then I felt the magical strings of light wrap around me and forced themselves into my back wounds. I saw Lord Castellan Richard storm into the room and my stomach churned in agony as I didn't know what was going on.

I kept wanting to fight against the strings, they might have been healing me but I had to get to Coleman. I had to be with him. I watched Richard knelt next to Coleman and Dragnist and Abbic were standing next to him blocking my view.

If I wasn't as stable as I was, I would have grabbed my swords and swung it at them only to get them away from Coleman. I had to see him. I had to see if he was okay.

Each of them exchanged concerned looks and I knew I had to do something but these damn strings kept healing me. All I could feel was a strange icy coldness cover my back.

"Strange. I was sure they would kill you," the Overlord's seductive voice said in my mind.

I rolled my eyes.

"See beautiful Daughter. We are connected now. Don't worry I cannot read your thoughts so to speak, I can only talk to you whenever I want,"

"Go away," I muttered.

"The Hunters failed me this time. They promised to kill you after their mysterious six hour disappearance in the City of Pleasure,"

I smiled at that memory. When I was freeing the City of Pleasure I was surprised that the Hunters agreed to give me six hours of freedom to try and find the object that would give them their freedom.

I know they're evil, supernatural killers but I actually felt sorry for them.

"What will you do to them?" I asked.

I heard my father laugh in my head. "Daughter, just like your mother, always a failure, a abnormal bitch of a woman, and a person who I'll enjoy killing,"

A small headache pulsed through my head as I presume the Overlord cut this strange mental connection, but another strange feeling was taking over my body. It felt familiar almost as if some strange energy was coming out of my cells.

My eyes widened as I realised this was the same sort of feeling I had in the City of Pleasure where I learnt I might share some of the same powers my mother did.

I focused back on Richard, Abbic and Dragnist as they knelt around Coleman and their faces grew paler and paler and sadder and sadder. I knew Richard with all his magical power couldn't heal Coleman, but maybe I could.

Maybe my mother gave me some kind of healing power or something. I don't know. I had to try, I wasn't going to let the man I love die without a fight.

I crawled forward and I felt the magical strings of light finish their healing work as I moved and I slapped Richard on the back.

He moved, which was good for him as I would have happily hurt him to clear the way to the man I loved. I kept crawling over to Coleman who was nothing more than a pale man covered in deep red blood and barely clinging to life.

I grabbed his leg and closed my eyes. I had no idea how this magic thing worked but back in the City of Pleasure it felt as if it came from a need, like I needed the Hunters gone and my magic allowed that to happen.

Now I needed to save my beautiful Coleman.

Slowly I felt my strange magical energy ooze into his leg and travel up into his body. It felt strange as if I was actually inside his body, feeling his wants, desires and his heart barely beating.

After a few seconds I could see out of his wound and could even see myself laying on the ground with my eyes closed. So I focused on absorbing his blood once more and closing the wound.

I opened my eyes and to my amazement, Richard, Abbic and Dragnist were staring at me like I was a crazy person. But I didn't care about them at this moment, I forced myself to my knees and grabbed Coleman's cold hands.

As I gently rubbed them I wasn't sure if he was alive or dead, he couldn't die. The Rebellion, Kingdom and most of all I needed him to lead, love and free us all. Then his eyes flickered opened and he weakly smiled.

I hugged and kissed him.

"Good job. One more person for me to kill," the Overlord echoed into my mind before leaving.

As I kissed Coleman, I knew there was only one way for me to protect my love forever. I had to kill the Overlord and I had to kill him quickly.

I was really looking forward to that!

CHAPTER 4

Commander Coleman couldn't believe what had just happened, this was all impossible. He was just on the edge of life and death, then he wasn't. It was so strange, so unnatural, so unnerving.

He had felt his beautiful, sexy Assassin inside him. He felt her moving through his body and that was just wrong, it didn't feel right in the slightest.

But at least she had saved him and Coleman was more than grateful for that, yet it was impossible that Richard who was a Lord Castellan, a god amongst men in his own right, couldn't heal him but the Assassin had.

How?

When his beautiful Assassin helped him to his feet, all Coleman wanted to do was stare into her amazing dark eyes and admire her long black cloak and hood. But he could feel Richard, Abbic and Dragnist staring at him wide eyed.

"Thank you," he said to the Assassin.

She smiled at him. "Your welcome but... but we have a problem,"

"What?" Richard asked.

The Assassin turned to face everyone. "My father can... mind talk to me now,"

Coleman and Richard started nodding.

"What Bossie? What do ya know?"

"You know the Assassin has tons of half-brother and sisters, right?" Richard asked.

Coleman held the Assassin's hands tight as he could see how uncomfortable she was becoming.

"Ya," Abbic said.

"Assassin, I hope you don't mind but I've been hunting them for years. Even before you Rebels came to the City of Martyrs whenever one came here I killed them,"

"Believe me Richard that isn't a problem," the Assassin said firmly.

Coleman couldn't believe how relieved Richard looked.

"But whenever I killed one it was like... like an echo in my mind was left of the Overlord's voice. It only lasted for a second but it was like they were talking to him seconds before they died,"

The Assassin nodded. "So... this power's from him?"

"We don't know that-" Coleman said.

"If both your mother and father had magic then it makes sense you get powers from both of them," Richard said.

Coleman just looked at Abbic and Dragnist were looked like they were watching a gripping play.

"Is it dangerous!" the Assassin shouted.

Everyone took a step back, even Coleman.

"I'm sorry," the Assassin said.

Coleman hugged her.

"No. It shouldn't be dangerous but the Hunters can come here now. This is no longer a safe place from them. I heard you found something about getting rid of them?" Richard said to the Assassin.

Coleman stood up straight. "Richard, Abbic, Dragnist, I need a full military plan for the Capital in three hours. Tell everyone to take up arms. We leave in twelve hours at first light,"

Coleman felt great. It was amazing to take charge again.

The three of them smiled and left. Coleman wasn't sure what he had just done. He wanted to invade, storm and free the Capital, but something felt wrong. It wasn't that this attack felt rushed, they had millions of potential soldiers that had all gone through basic combat training.

But this was the point his entire life had been working towards. He hoped his dad would be proud.

"And what do you want me to do?" the Assassin asked, pushing her head into his neck.

Coleman had never heard the Assassin this vulnerable, fearful or dare he say it scared. "I want you to… I want you to be safe,"

She laughed at that.

"I'm serious. The Hunters almost killed you today. I never want to lose you," Coleman said.

"I never want to lose you too, Coleman,"

"All know in all the history scriptures, the man and woman have passionate *exercise* tonight and swear their love for each other in case something bad happens,"

The Assassin playfully hit Coleman. "I don't believe in the Gods and Goddesses so I don't believe in marriage, but I would marry you Commander Coleman. And I love you from the bottom of my heart,"

Coleman felt his stomach do happy backflips at the sound of that. This cold, brutal assassin had just confessed her love for him. That was amazing, that was shocking, that was what he had always wanted.

"Whatever happens in the next few days, I will find you. In this life or the next," Coleman said.

The Assassin broke away from Coleman and closed the doors and windows to presumably make sure no one could see them.

"I don't plan on seeing you dead in the next few days," the Assassin said, loosening her long black cloak and hood. "But in case something happens to me, let's make the most of the next three hours,"

As blood rushed to wayward parts, Coleman wished these hours would never end, but he knew once they did. He would only be seeing blood, rage and death for the next few days.

And that was if he survived.

CHAPTER 5

I never wanted to leave Coleman and the rest of the Rebellion behind, but fighting on the front line was never going to be my style, my way or my purpose in finishing off the Overlord. As an assassin, I have and always will work behind enemy lines, killing a critical person here, there and everywhere.

Yet as much as I wanted to say I was simply being an assassin when I said I was leaving the Rebellion before they left, I was actually going to hunt down the dragon's resting place and try to find that Oath Rod. After almost losing the man I love, I had, I absolutely had to get rid of these Hunters.

My large black horse rode softly along the soft sand road onto the Capital as me and Abbic went, with a horrible wind making my long black cloak and hood flap in the wind. The desert that led up to the Capital was as bare as anything and a hellhole in its own right, but in the far, far distance I heard the whirling river.

I hate that river more than anything else, that damn river that almost claimed me and my brother when we were just children. I was so confused back then, I didn't know why my father had just killed my mother and was dragging us over to the river.

Yet as I felt the water drag me under, it didn't matter that I didn't understand, my survival was the only thing that mattered.

Like it does now.

As I listened to Abbic riding next to me, singing a merry little tune to herself, I was starting to really wonder why I had bought her. It was, of course, because she could lead me to the dragon's resting place, but me and her were so different.

Sure, she was a great fighter, "friend" and person, but I almost didn't want to be escorted around the Capital. For the simple reason that if my father was there, no matter how risky the shot, I was going to kill him.

A gust of hot desert breeze made me shiver for some reason and I saw that Abbic was staring at me like she had a question on her mind.

"What?" I asked.

Abbic smiled at me. "What ya gonna do when Coleman's King?"

I... I actually didn't know how to answer that. From all the conversations Coleman had had with both me and his Rebels, I had always been given the impression he was going to do a thing called democracy. I had no idea how it worked, but apparently a few decades before the Overlord came to power, that was how the Kings and rulers of the Cities were decided.

It sounded strange, problematic and just crazy to me, but I suppose after the Overlord, he needed something to happen. So why not let the people decide who they want. If they abuse their position, I'll just kill them anyway.

But given Abbic's question, she must know that and I don't know, she must be thinking that Coleman would be elected. I couldn't blame the people for wanting him as the Supreme Ruler of the Kingdom.

"I don't know. I'll be around. I'll still love him," I said coldly.

"I wanna be tha Security Chief!"

I snorted. "Ha!"

Abbic smiled too. "Just kidding, I wanna be something important,"

In the distance, I could see the very top of the massive spires of the City of Power and I felt my stomach turn, churn and flip as it finally sunk in what we were doing.

"Coleman likes you Abbic. You'll be fine, I'll make sure he gives you a good job,"

"Ta!" Abbic said with a massive smile.

As I kicked my horse a bit more, we both started to travel faster and I started to see more and more of the City of Power. The massive crystal spires that rose high into the sky and the rest of the bejewelled City shone in the desert sunlight. This wasn't going to end well, I just hoped Coleman would be okay.

"Where we heading?" Abbic asked.

I made my horse start to ride off the soft sandy road. "We need to go to one of the outer sewage drains. There's one about a mile outside the City,"

"Got ya," Abbic said.

As we both rode off deeper into the desert, the hot sun pounding on us and the sweat starting to pour down our backs. I had a terrible feeling that my father already knew what I wanted to achieve and had planned for everything.

But that didn't scare me.

It terrified me.

CHAPTER 6

Commander Coleman forced himself not to think about his beautiful Assassin, those three amazing hours were... amazing and the best three hours of his life. But Coleman was a leader, a fighter and a beacon of hope now so he had to remain focused.

As he walked along the yellow cobblestone streets of the City of Martyrs, he loved listening to the hopeful mutterings, laughter and general talking of everyone. He was a bit surprised that everyone was excited and looking forward to the attack, but he could understand.

Yet it was more than strange that when he spun round to look at the long lines of people behind him, he looked at where the old protective Wall used to be with its strong granite towers still standing, and he could have sworn one was missing. It was strange but Coleman was tired so he dismissed it and focused back on the amazing people around him.

Whilst Coleman knew the Assassin could never truly understand it, he did. Everyone in the entire Kingdom that wasn't a rich powerful person had lived for the past fifty years under a tyrant and as a slave. Coleman hated the City of Pleasure, he hated the constant fear of reaching age where the Masters or guests could grab him and use him for their entertainment. Or even worse, Coleman hated the odd Master that liked slaves a little on the young side that would grab him.

But this was everyone's chance to either free themselves and their unborn children of the tyranny, or die trying. And amazingly enough, Coleman actually didn't mind that, sure, he wanted to live, enjoy his freedom and be with the Assassin for decades to come.

Yet if he did die on the battlefield, as long as he died fighting for the freedom of his people, then he honestly didn't care.

Hints of sweat, metal and rust filled Coleman's senses as he went past a long line of blacksmiths that were producing swords, arrows and armour like there was no tomorrow. Then the scary idea of there actually being no tomorrow hit him, Coleman might have already said his goodbyes to his beautiful Assassin and wonderful Abbic, it still didn't make him feel any better.

"Commander," Richard and Dragnist said behind him.

Coleman turned around and nodded at them

both.

"We have the plans," Richard said, looking around.

Coleman gestured them to walk to him closely and in quiet voices. "What is the master plan then?"

"We storm it," Dragnist said.

Coleman had always admired Dragnist with his long beard, scar across his face and armour for his short conversations and honest opinions, on this occasion though he needed a little more.

Richard came close to Coleman's ear. "We have three million people here at last count. That's nothing to march up to the City of Power's Gate and blow it,"

Coleman cocked his head. "I remember that gate well from my dad's stories. It's two metres thick, twenty metres high at least. We don't have the explosives for it,"

"We have enough then magic can do the rest," Richard said.

That was risky. Coleman didn't know how magic worked, he didn't have magic, he didn't even know how well it could be trusted. Could he really rely on magic to save him, his Rebels and the Kingdom?

He wasn't sure and he didn't really want to find out.

"Coleman, I'm powerful enough. I can do it. I ran some tests earlier,"

Coleman's eyes widened as it dawned on him what happened to one of the granite towers that used to belong to the protective Wall around the City of

Martyrs, and what disturbed Coleman more was he realised he actually heard the collapse of the tower, but he thought him and the Assassin had broken the bed.

He was wrong!

"I see," Coleman said, still not sure.

"Don't have another option Boss," Dragnist said.

"Fine. Get a group of blacksmiths and get them to make us some shields. We'll need them the closer we get to the wall. The cart or carriage with the explosives must get to the gate," Coleman said.

As Dragnist bowed and went off to complete his orders, Coleman felt his stomach tighten as he felt as if the entire operation to free themselves of the Overlord's evil rested on one part of the plan going exactly right.

Normally Coleman liked plans to have at least some wiggle room as things always went wrong, but if those explosives weren't there or if Richard wasn't powerful enough. Then the entire mission would fail before it had even begun.

Then Coleman, Richard and three million Rebels could be sitting ducks for the Overlord to massacre.

CHAPTER 7

I slid off my large black horse and landed on the wonderfully soft sand of the desert as me and Abbic approached our destination. Ahead of us was nothing more than a little wooden shack that served as the entrance to the sewage system.

Theoretically my amazing plan is simple. Me and Abbic go into the shack, open the entrance to the sewers and go for a little walk (or swim sadly) into the City of Power. It sounded simple but considering how boiling hot it was out here, I was really hoping the sewers would be cool.

And that's how you know when an assassin finds it hot, because they actually want to go in smelly sewers! I suppose I could easily take off my long black cloak and hood but that isn't my style.

Abbic crawled up next to me and her eyes widened as the smell of sick, dust and sand attacked my senses, so I focused back on the shack and to my annoying horror, I saw five black armoured guards

430

walking out of the shack.

Then another. Then another.

Damn it! I knew I was right about my father seeing this move, I hated it when I was predictable, I didn't want to have to fight, kill and slaughter these people so early.

But it was strange to see only seven guards, especially in black armour, so I suppose I had two choices. One, I could just wait for their black armour to heat up and they'll be forced to retreat. Or-

Abbic charged out. Roaring.

I rolled my eyes. I whipped out my swords.

I flew at the guards.

The guards were prepared.

They whipped out crossbows.

They fired.

I tackled Abbic.

We rolled into the sand.

I jumped up. Throwing my swords.

They ripped into two guards.

I charged.

Dodging the arrows.

I ripped my swords out of the corpses.

Abbic charged. She jumped on a guard. Hacking him to pieces.

I rushed over to the others.

Swinging my swords.

Slashing throats.

Shattering bones.

Blood splashed everywhere.

Within moments there were scattered pieces of seven corpses, I spat at each of them. It was ridiculous how my father had sent these people to hurt me. It was never going to work, it was cowardice that he hadn't even come, but it scared me that he would be waiting for me somewhere.

A ticking filled the air.

Abbic was about to open the shack.

I ran at her.

Tackling to the ground.

The shack exploded.

Sending deadly shards of wood everywhere.

I stood up and shook my head as I looked at each and every part of the flaming wreckage of the shack. Now that was silly, futile and pathetic, explosions weren't honourable and they were damn well cowardice.

It meant my father, the so-called grand Overlord was scared, so scared that his weak silly little daughter was coming for him. I was most certainly coming for him now and I was going to kill him.

"You alive little girl?" I heard my father asked into my mind. But the question was an honest one, he actually didn't know if I was alive or not.

I stayed silent. If I could gain an advantage over him then I was going to take it.

The Hunters appeared.

I raised my swords.

The Hunters dipped their heads and disappeared.

"Shame. It would have been nice for you to die. I

have more surprises coming my beautiful daughter, you will not reach the Dragon's resting place alive,"

I hissed as I felt him cut the mental link and I saw Abbic stare at me.

"Did he talk to ya?"

I nodded. "We have to keep moving and be careful. I don't want you to die Abbic," That sort of just came out of nowhere.

"Ah, me too Assassin. I wanna stay alive too. Be careful ya-self," Abbic said, walking off into the shack's wreckage.

I rushed over to her when she was about to pick up the sheet of metal that was covering the sewers' entrance. I took a step back and wedged one of my swords under it, using the sword as a lever in case the metal was booby trapped.

When the entrance was open, me and Abbic frowned when we saw the explosion had destroyed the ladder, there were no guards in the tunnel but the explosion had destroyed the small pathway too.

Meaning we had to go for a swim.

"Ya first,"

I rolled my eyes as I focused on the fast-flowing sewage. There were no lumps of solid debris but it was the worse colour and smell imaginable.

I took a deep foul breath.

And jumped.

CHAPTER 8

Commander Coleman rode his horse through the massive desert that led to the City of Power with one million Rebels behind him. To any other person one million might sound like overkill and a rolling death ball that was sure to kill the Overlord and defeat the City of Power.

But as much as Coleman wanted to believe that, he was hardly impressed that two million Rebels had decided to stay back at their base and Coleman hated how large the City of Power was. The Overlord easily had a million or more people behind those walls.

This was going to be far from easy but that excited Coleman a little. He wanted to get into the fight and killing the enemy.

Coleman listened to all the muttering, talking and worry behind him and he understood it all. Everyone was at least a bit concerned because no one really knew the layout or the capabilities of the Capital. Over the decades, there had been tons of rumours about horrific weapons that were capable of annihilating dragons from the stories, erasing entire armies and even turning the strongest men to ash within seconds.

Coleman didn't like any of those options but he hoped by the time the attack began, the beautiful Assassin would have finished her mission and might be able to help him, his Rebels and their master plan.

As the million people behind him went deadly silent, Coleman's mouth dropped as he started to see the tops of the massive crystal spires that the City of Power was famous for.

This was actually happening.

Worried voices and concerns started to spread throughout the Rebels behind him and Coleman just stopped. He wasn't having this, he was a leader and his leadership was needed more today than any other day in his life.

"We are here. They have probably seen us. They are probably preparing themselves to kill us!" Coleman shouted.

Everyone frowned.

"But we will fight. Because we are not fighting just for ourselves. I want to live in freedom, liberality and I want to live the life I want,"

Everyone nodded at that.

"Yet this Rebellion, this attack, everything about this is not for only us. What will do today will echo throughout history. We will be the fools that died like cowards,"

A wave of grumbling washed over the Rebels.

"Or history will remember us as heroes. Each of

us will be the brave men and women that dared to take on the Overlord. We will be remembered for millenniums to come. We will be the Saints and Demi-Gods that freed the Kingdom,"

Smiles lit up the faces of every single Rebel in front of him, and Coleman loved that.

"So my question is simple. How do you want history to remember you!"

"Victors!" everyone shouted from the top of their voice.

Coleman spun around. "Then we ride. Ride for Death. Ride for Victory. Ride For Freedom!"

Coleman kicked his horse. He charged off towards the City.

A million Rebels followed him.

The sound of two million hooves was deafening.

And that excited Coleman.

Coleman and the Overlord were going to clash and the result would determine the fate of history.

CHAPTER 9

I hate sewers!

They're disgusting, dirty and just utterly horrible. Even now as I climbed up a rusty metal ladder onto a little concrete pathway that ran along the sewers, I could still feel some disgusting mixture slipping down my leather-covered legs. I hated it!

And as for my poor long black cloak and hood, it was covered in dirt, smelly stuff so I quickly took it off and shook as much as the stuff off as I could.

But the smell was just awful and it was the worse thing I could even imagine, it was even worse than when I had hidden in a toilet to kill a target. I was more than glad after this mission, I would never have to deal with the Overlord again.

Abbic walked past me and I couldn't believe how happy she looked. She was covered in head to toe in some poo covered mixture, but she didn't even bat an eyelid (partly because she was still wiping her eyes clean). Abbic might have been an amazing person, but she was weird, but a strange loveable type of weird. (maybe I am going too soft on people now)

Both me and Abbic started walking along the small pathway and I was hoping there would be dents in the wall, loose hanging metal piping or something to grab on to, but there wasn't. I was so much concerned about falling because of a misstep, but more because this concrete hardly looked secure.

All along the path there were massive holes, cracks or chips where the concrete had fallen away. I didn't want to die before I had even reached the dragon's resting place.

"Not much further now!" Abbic shouted.

I still didn't understand why she was so happy, I was ready to kill someone, even more than usual. I had just spent hours floating, swimming and pulling myself through a range of sewer tunnels. I meant those things can bend around, separate and go into crazy patterns at a moment's notice. Believe me when I say I was happy to have Abbic with me.

But even worse! I had even been pulled under the sewage at one point!

"How much further?" I asked, trying to ignore the funny taste in my mouth.

"I donna. Maybe another few hundred metres,"

I rolled my eyes. She was meant to know exactly where this place was and-

The Hunters appeared. Someone else joined them. Their shadowy form flickered.

The Hunters disappeared.

I whipped out my swords and carefully went over to the corpse-like thing they had dropped.

It looked like a young female, wearing heavy white armour with her long brown hair, bright red skin and something around her neck. Probably a necklace.

She jumped up.

Her necklace glowed.

Throwing Abbic in the water. Holding her down.

I raised my swords.

I flew at her.

She disappeared.

I stopped.

She appeared behind me.

Putting me in a headlock.

"Now, now dear sister play nicely. Daddy wouldn't like that?" the woman said.

This was exactly what I didn't want to happen, I didn't want to run into any of my half-brothers and -sisters, and I sure as hell didn't want to run into a magical one.

"You are not my sister!" I shouted.

Abbic floated in the air. Taking a deep breath. She dropped back in.

"Do you want your friend to die?" she asked.

"I'll kill you,"

"Ha! Sister, you are not one of us anymore. The All-Father has gifted us with more powers then you possibly could imagine,"

I shook my head and my hands tensed around a

sword.

"That might be true. But I will always be the First-Born,"

I jumped back.

Knocking us over.

I flicked my sword.

Cutting her leg.

She hissed.

Her grip loosened.

I headbutted her.

She let go.

I jumped up.

Spun around.

Thrusting my blades into her chest.

I ripped off her necklace.

Throwing it against the wall. It shattered.

As Abbic popped up, I pulled her up and slapped her back as she coughed for a few minutes, taking long deep breaths as she recovered.

Whilst she coughed, I couldn't help but worry about the person I had just killed. My own half-siblings were after me now, typical Overlord always using others to do his dirty work. I might not have known how many more half-siblings I had to deal with, but at least something was now making sense.

My father make sure his so-called prized children were kept in reserve to protect him or kill the Rebellion when they got here, but now if he was sending them out to die. Then he knew for a fact what I was doing and how dangerous it was to him.

I helped Abbic up. "Please. We need to go quicker,"

Abbic smiled and started running off. "Come on then, it round tha corner. I remember now,"

With my hands tightly on my swords, I ran to keep up with her.

And I dreaded to know what was coming.

At some point I would have to face my father, and I had no idea if I could win that fight.

CHAPTER 10

Coleman flat out hated the Overlord.

As Coleman led the Rebels towards the City, he frowned at the Capital's massive brown iron walls but his focus shot towards the massive Gate. It was at least two metres thick but it was higher now, easily twenty metres high.

Two massive catapults stood firmly next to the Gate. Coleman had to get there.

He rode his horse faster and faster and faster. Sand was thrown into the air. The horse breathed heavily. Coleman's heart pounded.

This was the moment. Coleman led the Rebels this far. Now the faith of everything rested on the plan.

Bells rang out all over the City.

Black dots lined the massive City walls.

Archers fired.

Launching thousands of arrows.

Coleman kicked his horse. It shot forward.

The arrows left behind him.

Screams filled the air.

Coleman kept riding.

The Catapults were loaded.

They fired.

Massive chunks of flaming rock flew at them.

The rock was getting closer to Coleman.

Coleman forced his horse away.

They moved.

The rock smashed next to them.

The warmth licked Coleman's flesh.

He kept riding.

Rebels screamed as they were burnt.

The Archers fired again.

More arrows flew at them.

An arrow hit Coleman.

Coleman flew off his horse.

The arrow dented his armour.

His horse ran off.

The Rebels rushed past Coleman.

Hands grabbed him.

Richard threw Coleman on his horse's back.

As the Rebels used their horses to form a protective barrier around Richard, Coleman clapped his hands and all the nearby Rebels raised their massive square shields. They easily interlocked forming an unbreakable barrier around Coleman, Richard and the all important cargo.

Coleman had almost forgotten about the cargo (the explosives) that were in the wooden carriage behind them.

One shield flew away.

Then another.

Then another.

Then another.

The shields were being ripped apart.

Rebels turned to ash.

People screamed.

Flames engulfed groups of Rebels.

Coleman grabbed a shield. Waving it about. Signalling the Rebels.

Everyone broke formation.

Everyone scattered.

Everyone charged towards the Gate.

The Rebels abandoned Coleman.

Richard kept driving the carriage.

Archers fired.

Attacking the horses.

Nothing happened.

The Catapults fired.

Flaming rock zoomed towards them.

Richard tried to steer away.

The rock got closer.

Coleman threw Richard out.

He tumbled on the ground.

Coleman kicked the connection between the horses and Carriages.

It broke.

The horse ran free.

The rock was too close.

Coleman jumped.

The rock smashed into the carriage.

It exploded.

Throwing Coleman through the air.

The plan had failed.

Utterly.

CHAPTER 11

Abbic led us to a small rusty door that was built into the sewer tunnels and knelt down and started whispering something. I really hoped whatever she was doing wouldn't take too long, the horrific smell of the sewage was overwhelming. I was starting to go lightheaded.

I hated the sound of the rushing sewages behind me and I just didn't want to be in the sewers anymore. I wanted to be killing, attacking and making sure the enemy couldn't never ever hurt me, the Rebels or Coleman again.

When I saw Abbic cock her head and frown, I just wanted to kick down the door but earlier Abbic had mentioned some nonsense about needing to show respect in this place.

Rubbish!

After a few more moments, Abbic gasped and the door opened slowly. The air stunk horribly of must, mummified flesh and dust, it smelt awful but at least it was better than breathing in raw sewage.

We went through the door and flaming torches turned on revealing a rather wonderful chamber. It was beautiful in a way, brown blood splashed up against the walls. Some walls were completely covered in blood. I was sure there were paintings, symbols or something else under the blood, but I wasn't interested in that. Because in the very middle of the grand oval chamber was an immense corpse.

The dragon corpse stretched on for hundreds of metres, it was beautiful in a way. Even after so long the bright red scales were still shiny, vibrant and full of life. The only real way to tell it was an actual corpse was because of the missing eyes, tongue and missing belly, as no scales were there to protect the underbelly.

"Wow! This is awful!" Abbic shouted.

"Why? Look at all this blood, the artfulness in this blood spray is great," I said.

"Sure girly," Abbic said walking over to the dragon corpse.

As much as I wanted to explore the chamber and learn about what had happened here, I knew my beautiful sexy Coleman was probably fighting up on the surface. I had to finish this, get rid of the Hunters and go and help him. I owned him that much.

I went over to the corpse and stood in front of the head with Abbic. Even the head was beautiful and terrifying, each dagger-like tooth was twice the size of me and the head was probably ten metres tall.

"Ya know to find tha Rod?"

I took out the journal that included in the map and frowned as it had all been turned to mush by the sewage. I swore under my breath.

"The map reader said about the dragon's resting place. A city of power and something about a rod of sacrifice," I said.

"Tha City of Power must be tha City. Sacrifice?"

"What if the City of Power reference isn't talking about a City as we know it. What other dragon stories do you know?"

Abbic shrugged and tapped the dragon teeth. Her hand shot back as the teeth cut her slightly.

"Come on, you must know some?" I asked.

"Just one other. Something about tha dragon's city high in the sky and within tha hearts of dragons,"

Now that got me thinking, this chamber was an oval shape without a domed ceiling so I doubt the map is talking about a sky city, but what about a city the dragons carry about with them?

What if to them cities symbolised their togetherness, love and admiration for each other?

I took out my swords and raised them. Abbic did the same.

"Ready!" I shouted.

We swung.

Swords smashed into the teeth.

They chipped.

I heard people outside.

We swung again.

The teeth cracked.

Guards stormed in.

They charged at us.

We swung again.

The teeth shattered.

I swirled my hands. Magical energy shot out.

All the teeth shards floated up.

I through them at the guards.

Slaughtering them.

"Get inside that skull. Go to its heart. Find the Rod!" I shouted.

Three tall men walked in. Necklaces around their necks. They glowed.

Three fireballs flew towards the dragon.

I thrusted out my hand.

Stopping them.

I threw the fireballs back at them.

The fireballs disappeared.

The three men whipped out their swords.

I raised mine.

The men flew at me.

Our swords clashed.

The air hummed.

Magical energy crackled.

One man ran broke away.

The other two kicked me.

A man ran towards the dragon.

I jumped into the air.

Kicking two men back.

I shot out my hands.

White fire shot out.

Vapourising the man.

I collapsed to the ground.

My body felt weak. Broken. Pathetic.

The last two people flew at me.

Leaping into the air.

Raising their swords.

I couldn't raise mine.

I was defenceless.

The Hunters appeared.

Ripping the other men apart.

I shot up. Grabbed my swords.

Pointing them at the Hunters.

But they didn't do anything and I looked round to see Abbic kneeling on the ground with something in each hand. I put my swords away and went over to her, to see she was holding two halves of a broke Oath Rod.

I wouldn't blame anyone for thinking she was holding a broken stick made from ivory, but I knew what it was as I could strangely sense the rest of the magic pouring out of the Rod and disappearing.

That's when I started to notice Abbic's hand. They were dripping more and more blood onto the ground. Her face grew paler and paler and paler.

I looked at the Hunters. "What did you do!"

"We did nothing. Whoever freed us would die. You said it yourself a Rod of Sacrifice. She freed us. We saved you,"

This time their voices were different. Instead of

their normal shadowy voices that sounded like logs crackling on a fire, they sounded more distant, like they were speaking more thousands of miles away.

Yet I never wanted Abbic to die. I couldn't let her die for my mission. It was my duty to protect her and I failed, I couldn't-

"She knew the risks. We explained them to her. She didn't care. She didn't care about dying. She wanted to save you,"

I looked back at Abbic and stared into her lifeful, deep eyes and I knew they were telling the truth. Abbic had always been a rebel, wanting to kill the Overlord and free everyone. To her this was just her duty, something else to do in the name of the cause.

But to me. It was losing a great person, fighter and probably friend. I never wanted to lose anyone.

She moved her mouth to say something but then her corpse fell. Landing with a thud on the ground.

I gently kissed her forehead and got up, I would be back here. I would collect her body and give her a proper burial, she had sacrificed herself for me and now I had to do my part.

I watched the Hunters disappear back to their own place and I stormed out of the chamber.

The Overlord was going to pay for killing Abbic.

And he was going to know my fury!

CHAPTER 12

Coleman felt his entire world crumble around him as he watched the disgusting rubble of the carriage fall down around him. Massive chunks of flaming wood pounded the ground.

He hated all of this, this was awful disgusting and utterly disgraceful. Coleman had failed. The plan was simple enough but it all relied on that damn carriage not getting destroyed.

Now it had. Coleman didn't know what to do, he had to do something. He had to fight.

Coleman forced himself up, his hand tightly around the hilt of his sword. He was ready to fight, kill and slaughter the enemy.

But that was half the problem. All around him the million of Rebels on their horses were riding around chaotically, the immense Gate in front of him had to go. He had to destroy it.

He just didn't know how.

An arrow hit him.

Denting his armour.

Coleman smiled. He charged towards the Gate.

Other Rebels joined him. They protected Coleman.

More and more Archers fired.

Rebels fell.

Corpses hitting the ground.

Coleman kept running.

More Archers focused on them.

Coleman ran as fast as he could.

The Catapult fired.

Coleman legged it.

The flaming rocks flew at him.

Coleman jumped.

The rock smashed into Rebels.

Screams filled the air.

Coleman kept running.

Making it to the Gate.

Knowing he only had seconds, maybe a minute until guards, soldiers and whatever monsters the Overlord had, came to stop him. More like kill him. Coleman ran his hands over the cold rough metal of the Gate.

He had to find a way to open it. He couldn't let his Rebels be stuck out here and picked off one by one.

It might take the enemy hours, even days to pick off everyone. But Coleman's friends were dying and he hated that.

As his hands searched the cold rough metal for a

lock, handle or some other type of opening mechanism, he swore when he couldn't find one. He had to open the gate.

Ropes dropped down behind Coleman.

Coleman spun around.

Soldiers climbed down the ropes.

They let go.

Landing on Coleman.

They smashed their fists into him.

Pain shot through Coleman.

He hissed.

Rebels fired arrows at them.

The soldiers got off Coleman.

Coleman didn't hesitate.

He whipped out his swords.

Ramming it into their chests.

Corpses fell to the ground.

Massive torrents of fire shot out of the wall.

Coleman felt the heat against his skin. He was tens of metres away. But he still felt it.

Rebels ran. Rebels burnt. Rebels melted.

Coleman focused back on the wall. His friends were dying. He felt useless. He searched the wall.

Part of the metal melted.

Someone's hand grabbed him.

Gripping his throat.

Coleman hissed.

He swung his sword.

The sword wouldn't move.

Coleman was trapped.

He hissed.

He gagged.

He was choking.

The hand didn't let go.

Richard rushed over. Grabbed the hand. Turning it to ash.

Coleman heard screams from behind the Gate.

Coleman and Richard spun around.

Rebel corpses littered the ground. This was a disaster.

Then Coleman heard the air hum with magical energy and he looked at Richard who was smiling at him.

Richard's eyes were shooting out golden light then it shot out of his mouth too. Coleman felt as if something bad was going to happen. But Richard placed a gentle hand on his shoulders.

"Get it done, my friend. The new Lord Castellan," Richard said, as Coleman felt something slip into his body.

Coleman wanted to speak but he couldn't. He couldn't imagine losing Richard, his powerful Ruler, ally and friend. He didn't want to lose anyone but Coleman knew it was the only way.

Richard walked out into the open and stared at the Gate. Coleman carefully walked away from the Gate and stuck close to the walls, so the enemy couldn't see him.

Richard shot out his hands and started muttering ancient words. The entire world darkened, the sun was dimmed and Coleman felt his eyes strain just to see Richard.

Slowly Richard started to rise into the air and golden light shot from every single part of his body, and the air hummed, crackled and sang with magical energy. The entire battle stopped as everyone just stared at the Lord Castellan.

Then Richard flew at the Gate.

It exploded.

Shattering.

Ripping the City wide open.

Ripping out sections of the Wall.

Soldiers screamed.

Soldiers were smashed.

Soldiers died.

Richard was dead.

Coleman didn't have time to morn. The enemy was injured. The enemy was down.

Coleman raised his sword.

He charged into the City of Power.

Hundreds of thousands of Rebels followed him.

Now Coleman was one step closer to killing the Overlord.

CHAPTER 13

I loved explosions!

As I walked along the massive stone wall that went around the entire City of Power, I was forced to grab onto it as I felt a massive explosion. I hated the feeling of the wall's warm smooth surface, but I hated the soldiers even more.

In front of me for what looked like miles upon miles there were lines upon lines of black armoured soldiers all armed with swords and bows and crossbows as they prepared to smite the Rebels where they stood.

It was flat out outrageous. It was disgusting. It was why the Overlord had to die. Especially after causing the death of Abbic, I had to get revenge for her, even if it killed me.

Loud explosions, collapsing buildings and screams filled the air as I realised that explosion had annihilated the Gate and ripped massive chunks out of the protective wall around the City. I was easily a mile or two away but it was still a glorious sight.

So much death, destruction and chaos. Now that was perfect.

I pulled my long black cloak and hood tighter as I knew it was finally time for me to reveal myself. Coleman and the Rebels might be riding through the capital, but I had to draw as much as attention away from them as possible.

Granted the City of Power was beautiful in a strange way with its crystal, bejewelled houses and massive crystal spires. But these people inside the city loved their houses and spires too much.

If I wanted to get their attention all I had to do was destroy some of them.

A large chunk of rock smashed down in front of me.

I gently poked it and thankfully it wasn't too warm so I picked it up.

Below me were a few crystal houses where people were standing out with stunning knives and pots and pans. All looked beautiful but they would be utterly useless against an attacker.

I threw the rock at them.

It smashed into the house.

The crystal cracked.

It shattered.

Screams filled the streets.

People rushed out of their houses.

They were screaming as loud as they could.

Soldiers saw me.

They hesitated.

I did not.

I whipped out my swords.

Charging at them.

I jumped into the air.

Whirling around.

My blade chomped into their flesh.

Hacking their bodies apart.

I landed.

I grabbed their heads.

Throwing them hard at the houses.

The heads slammed into them.

Painting the houses red.

More people screamed in outrage.

More soldiers charged.

I slaughtered them.

I kept throwing the heads.

The crystal houses cracked.

More and more.

They collapsed.

Crossbows fired.

I spun round.

Ducking.

Soldiers were storming over to me.

I had to act.

I jumped off the Wall.

Into the City.

They kept firing.

And firing.

Arrows smashed into the crystal houses.

Crystal shards flew at me.

I kept running.

Soldiers turned a corner. Stepping out in front of me.

I ran faster.

The soldiers raised their swords.

I jumped.

Ramming my swords into their heads.

This was me. I was an Assassin.

And I was free to kill an entire City full of my enemy.

I planned to do just that.

CHAPTER 14

Coleman followed by his amazing Rebels stormed the City of Power, their swords were wet with blood, the streets ran red and the entire City was filled with the echoing screams of the Overlord's soldiers.

As Coleman passed each of the large crystal houses that lined a massive street that led right to the bottom of the crystal spires, he couldn't understand where all the soldiers were.

He had been walking down this awful street with his forces for an hour and yet after the initial slaughter, there were no enemies to be seen. Something was off.

Something was extremely wrong. And Coleman hated not knowing what was happening.

When they were close to the bottom of the crystal spires that rose like daggers into the sky, Coleman went out into a massive stone square that was easily the size of twenty football pitches and there was where the enemy was.

Hundreds upon hundreds of black armoured soldiers stormed out of the streets all around the hundreds of thousands of rebels with their swords, bows and crossbows raised.

But no one fired.

Coleman didn't know why but it surprised him when he saw twelve tall young people with glowing necklaces walk down the steps that led up to the spires. They were different skinny, slightly muscled and life filled, yet they all looked so fake. As if each one of them had been augmented so many times that they weren't even human anymore.

As Coleman focused on them more and more, he noticed that there were six men and six women, but the person walking in front and leading the others was a tall elegant woman. She wore an awfully tight white robe, black shoes and had two black swords at her waist.

Coleman knew they were just for show. The real danger was of course from the necklace. He recognised it from books. He didn't want them to use it.

"Lay down your arms," the woman said, her necklace growing bright.

No one put down their weapons. Coleman loved that.

The woman frowned and clicked her fingers. Three others' necklaces glowed. "Lay down your arms!"

Nothing again.

"You have no power here," Coleman said walking towards them.

"We are the Children of the Overlord. We have all the power. We serve him for his divine protection," they all spoke as one.

Coleman forced himself not to be shocked. These monsters couldn't be related to the Assassin, she was beautiful, sexy and adorable. These twelve were far from that.

"If you think you're so powerful then why does your father cower?" Coleman said.

"Kill him!" they all shouted. Their necklaces glowing bright white.

Coleman heard some people move, metal slashing against metal and bodies drop. He was glad he was protected but he didn't know how much longer his forces could resist their corrupting magic.

"Kill them all!" they shouted.

Coleman charged.

The Soldiers stormed towards him.

Coleman whipped out his swords.

Raising them.

The Soldiers attacked.

Swinging their swords.

Coleman ducked.

Jumped up.

Slashed their throats.

Magical energy gripped him.

Coleman dusted it off.

Soldiers punched him.

Whacking their fists into him.

Coleman fell.

The Soldiers kicked him.

Again.

And again.

Coleman leapt up.

Swinging his sword in a bloody arc.

Corpses dropped.

Fireballs flew at him.

They burnt him.

Coleman ran.

The Rebels attacked.

Swinging their weapons.

Slashing the enemy.

Blood flooded the ground.

The sound was deafening.

Ten crossbows fired.

Coleman ducked.

More soldiers stormed.

Pointing swords at his chest.

He couldn't fight alone.

The soldiers raised their swords.

They bought them down.

Someone tackled Coleman.

Knocking him away.

The Assassin kissed his cheek. Jumped up.

Flying at the enemy.

Her swords sliced the enemy.

She slashed their chests.

Magical energy filled the air.

Ice formed around them.

Coleman looked.

They were cutting him off from the Rebels.

An ice cage grew around them.

Cutting off the square from the rest of the City.

Then the twelve sisters and brothers of Coleman's beautiful Assassin fanned out into a straight line, the tall elegant woman still stood in front. She extended her hands.

Fire shot out.

The Assassin raised her hands. Her face unsure.

The fire hit it.

A torrent of white magic shot out of the Assassin.

She hissed.

More and more necklaces glowed.

More half-siblings shot out their hands.

The fire grew in intensity.

Coleman ran at them.

One of them flicked their hands.

Ice covered him.

Coleman couldn't move.

The Assassin screamed.

She sunk to her knees. She couldn't stop the torrent of fire.

She was growing weak.

She collapsed.

The fire engulfed her.

CHAPTER 15

A horrific icy coldness gripped me as the immense torrent of fire engulfed me and burned me to... death? I actually didn't know if I was dead because as I looked around nothing seemed out of place.

I was still in the City of Power with the horrible crystal spires in front of me, my awful twelve half-siblings were standing there smiling as they killed me, and the ice cage around us was standing strong.

It was honestly impressive how powerful my siblings were with their magic, but I guess it was all a part of learning. They had probably been using their magic since the day they were born, I had only been using mine for a month or less.

But the strangest thing about all of this was how cold it was, my skin felt icy and now I realised it, everyone wasn't moving. Even the massive torrent of fire that was just engulfing me, yet I could walk about.

So I went over to Coleman and saw the pain,

agony and rage in his eyes as he watched the fire engulf me. I wished I could tell him I was here, but I didn't know what I was.

Was I dead? Alive? Dying?

"Strange isn't love?" an elderly woman said.

I spun around and went to raise my swords when I realised I didn't have them. I didn't even have my long black cloak and hood. I was actually naked!

This was just embarrassing!

"Oh relax honey I've seen it all before," the woman said.

The woman seemed familiar as if I should have known her but I couldn't place her. But her strong cheekbones, long greying hair and her slim figure reminded me of someone.

"Do I know you?" I asked.

That question seemed to pain the woman, her eyes started to wet then they dried.

"I guess not. I was dead before you were thrown into the river. But I take we had a few hours before the Overlord ripped us apart,"

A memory popped into my head about me and my mother cuddling after I had just been born, she was telling me something about magic, dragons and power, and that I needed to remember something important for the future.

"You can't be my mother," I said.

My mother laughed. "Course not love, I died. I sacrificed myself. He was scared of ma power, I just planned some stuff,"

I gestured towards the torrent of fire, my siblings and Coleman. "What is all this!"

"This was always my plan. You see the True Master in the City of Pleasure as he was infecting me with his Pleasure gave ma the ability to see,"

I shook my head as I remembered that horrible creature called the True Master. It was wrong about it had sex with humans to make them his sex slaves. But somehow my mother had survived.

"Then I see ya death love. Ya would be killed by a half-sibling. So I learnt from the True Master how to infect people during sex,"

This wasn't happening. This couldn't be my mother. This was just a delusion caused by the flames killing me.

"I infected the father with a shard of my soul. It infected his body so whenever he passed on his material to another woman, it infected her. I am in each of those awful half-siblings. I am in their magic,"

My glaze hardened on her. "So when they used their magic to kill me. You could interfere,"

She nodded. "I think if I was still alive I would be proud. But time is running out. I have saved you for now but when I act, you must act. You must kill them. I love you,"

The entire world vibrated, jerked and crumbled around me.

I ran to Coleman.

The world started moving.

Coleman shrieked.

He smiled.

My Siblings screamed in rage.

They raised their hands.

Magic energy crackled around us.

White cracks appeared in the air.

Reality was breaking.

Their rage was immense.

The streets exploded.

The ice cage cracked.

The crystal spires were shattering.

They were ripping apart reality.

They thrusted out their hands.

They froze.

I had to act.

I was scared.

My siblings struggled.

They were regaining control.

I slapped Coleman. Freeing him.

We stormed over.

Whipping out our swords.

I stabbed, slashed slaughtered my siblings.

Their necklaces broke.

Their blood flooded onto the street.

And as I rammed my swords into the last two, I felt something inside my mind click. This was why the Overlord had wanted me dead, I was somehow the most powerful child he had ever had and he wanted to make sure I could never be used against him.

He failed.

And I was going to storm into those Spires. Find

him. Kill him.

I was so close to my goal.

CHAPTER 16

As Coleman wiped the thick coating of blood on his sword on his armour, he felt relieved that his beautiful sexy Assassin was safe. He didn't know, he didn't care, he just wanted to stay alive.

The sounds of screaming, slaughter and clashing swords filled the air and Coleman spun round. Seeing a massive army of black armoured soldiers storming into the City of Power.

He had no idea there were forces outside the City coming back to reinforce it.

Coleman looked at all the disgusting enemy corpses and the sad corpses of his friends. They were spent already, people were tired, injured and hungry.

They couldn't fight anymore. And these stupid reinforcements dared to attack and slaughter his forces. He wasn't having this!

Coleman had to hold the Rebellion together. He couldn't let it fracture. He couldn't let it die.

He just had to hold it all together long enough

for the Assassin to do her thing, kill the Overlord and free everyone.

The screams grew louder and louder as the reinforcements stormed into the City, slaughtering anyone who wasn't one of them. They didn't care about the innocent, they only cared about extermination.

That's when Coleman realised, he had to not only protect his own forces, friends, but the innocent people who supported the Overlord. It killed him inside but that was one of the things about being a leader.

Sometimes you just had to do the right thing, no matter how badly you didn't want to.

The Assassin kissed him and ran off.

Coleman watched her run into the crystal spires. He went to follow her for some reason, but the crystal around the Spires started to become thicker and impossible to break. And the crystal turned blood red.

He didn't know what the Overlord was planning but whatever he wanted with the Assassin, she had to fight it alone.

And that terrified him.

CHAPTER 17

I wanted to burn this place to the ground!

This massive oval chamber made from solid crystal looked disgusting and it was such a testament to my father's arrogance, idiocy and just him being so stupid. I would happily smash it all up.

I went over to the massive iron throne on the far side of this chamber which was clearly a throne room of some kind. And there was my father just sitting there smiling at me.

I wish I could just gut him. I hated seeing his massive seductive smile, long white robes and his long golden hair. I listened to the magical energy humming, popping and crackling in the air. This wasn't going to end well.

Then my long black cloak and hood started flapping in a wind that wasn't there. I took another step closer but froze. Bright white energy wrapped around me like ropes.

"I didn't think you would be this scared so

quickly, father,"

"Now, now daughter. You did not think at all. You haven't won,"

I wanted to cock my head but the ropes were too tight. "We have won. Your forces are dead. Your forces were weak. You have lost,"

The ropes burnt around me. I hissed.

"See daughter, you cannot do anything. Let me show you something," the Overlord said, making me float in the air as he walked over to the other side of the throne room.

"This room hasn't seen any love for years, has it?" I asked.

"I do not need the likes of Lords, my puppet Kings or anyone to help me deliver my vision,"

"Your vision? Your vision of what? Lies? Tyranny? Corruption?" I asked.

We were almost at the other side of the throne room and I watched the foggy crystal walls turned see-through and I could the raging battle below. The Rebellion was trapped. My friends were dying. I had to get free.

"See my daughter. You have not won. Your friends will die. My remaining forces will grow stronger and stronger. I will scourge the City of Martyrs from the map. You have lost,"

"You cannot do that,"

The Overlord extended his hand and aimed it at the floor. The ground crackled, hummed and vibrated as he did something. After a few moments he stopped and smiled.

"What did you do?" I asked.

"It is simple. Whatever was left in that dragon's resting place is alive once more. The Dragon lives,"

I forced myself to stop smiling as I just realised me leaving Abbic's body there might have just saved us. I was now glad I beheaded all the other bodies in the resting place.

"So what are your plans for me?"

The Overlord forced the ropes to turn me and stare at me in the eye. For the briefest of seconds I actually wondered if I was staring at a father. His eyes were soft, loving and almost caring, this might have been the kindest I had seen him in my entire life.

Then his eyes hardened. "You. You betrayed me. Your mother betrayed me. I failed to kill you once, I killed your brother, I will not fail to kill you,"

Stupid man!

I flicked my hands. The ropes burnt away. The Overlord's eyes widened.

"Witch!"

My hand shot out.

Torrents of fire roared at him.

The Overlord jumped back. Whipping out his swords.

I whipped out mine.

He flew at me.

I flew at him.

CHAPTER 18

Coleman flat out hated the Overlord.

He whipped out his swords. He raised them high in the sky. Everyone looked at him. Coleman pointed his swords at the enemy reinforcements.

Everyone charged.

The remaining hundreds of thousands flew at the enemy.

Coleman heard their rage.

The Rebels smashed into the enemy.

Coleman looked around. The crystal houses were close together.

He ran over to one. Climbing up onto the roof. He ran across the rooftops.

The enemy surged forward.

They slashed the Rebels artfully. Their movements elegant. Precise.

They kept killing.

Slicing through the Rebels like they were nothing.

Coleman ran quicker. He had to get to them.

Rebels' heads smashed.

Shattered.

Crumbled.

The enemy kept attacking.

The Rebels fell back.

Magic hummed in the air.

Crystal sealed the side streets and square.

The Rebels were trapped in the main street.

The enemy pressed their attack.

Coleman jumped into the air.

Raising his swords.

He landed.

Swinging his swords.

Slaughtering the soldiers.

The enemy grabbed him.

Pinning him against the wall.

The Rebels roared.

They marched forward.

Rushing to Coleman.

Coleman kicked the soldiers. Their grip loosened.

Coleman snapped their necks.

Flaming rocks flew through the air.

Smashing into the City.

Annihilating Crystal houses.

Innocent people screamed.

Innocent people died.

Coleman flew at the enemy. He wasn't kidding about.

His swords chomped on flesh. His kicks dented metal. He kept going.

Rebels became more savage. They charged past Coleman.

Becoming raging berserkers.

They ripped into the enemy.

Tearing out flesh.

Drinking blood.

They pressed their fingers into the enemy's eyes.

Their rage filled them.

Coleman heard something. Something strange. Something different.

The ground vibrated. Cracked. Moved.

Coleman felt something coming out of the ground. He shouted a warning.

The ground exploded. Something shot out of it.

Coleman stared at the object.

A massive blue dragon stretched its wings. It roared. Unleashing black fire.

The dragon stared at Coleman.

It zoomed towards him.

CHAPTER 19

I hated the Overlord! That bastard was going to die. My long black cloak and hood tightened around me.

The dragon roared outside.

I flew at the Overlord.

We jumped into the air.

I swung at him.

He swung at me.

Our swords clashed.

Sparkes shot out.

Thunder echoed around us.

His swords buzzed.

My swords shattered.

Deadly shards sliced my cloak.

He punched me.

He kicked me.

I landed with a thud.

The Overlord flicked his hands. Throwing me across the room.

I slammed into the crystal wall.
My head whacked it.
He flew at me.
Kicking me.
Again and again.
He kept kicking.
He slashed his sword at me.
Cutting my cheek.
My body ached.
Crippling pain filled me.
The Overlord thrusted out his hands.
Black fire charged at me.
I rolled away.
I jumped up.
Charging at him.
Fireballs shot at me.
I dodged them.
The Overlord disappeared.
I spun around.
My father tackled me.
Smashing my head into the floor.
His hands wrapped round my throat.
He squeezed.
I couldn't beat him.
His hands burnt hot.
I screamed.
My neck burned.
My lungs burned.
Everything was burnt.
He kept squeezing.

I struggled. I kicked. I punched.

He was too strong.

The air moved.

A sword swung at the Overlord.

He ducked.

Jumping off me.

Abbic stood there. She was alive. She was strong.

She threw me a sword.

The entire spire shook.

The Dragon smashed into the spire.

Massive flaming rocks smashed too.

The Overlord cursed.

As the spires shook more and more as the massive flaming rocks smashed into it, I knew this was the end. The Rebellion would survive and-

Abbic screamed as the Overlord thrusted his swords into her. Turning her body to ash.

How dare he! She had saved me, protected me, given me a second chance. This wasn't on!

I roared.

I flew at the Overlord.

He disappeared.

Reappearing by the crystal wall.

I charged at him.

Thrusting out my hands.

Torrents of fire shot out.

The Overlord hissed.

I kept running.

I kept charging.

I tackled the Overlord.

Pushing him against the crystal wall.

The wall cracked.

It collapsed.

I gripped him.

We flew out of the Spire.

Plumping towards the ground.

The Overlord screamed.

I gripped his throat.

Torrents of fire pouring out of my hands.

He screamed.

He tried to escape.

He couldn't.

He wasn't strong enough.

I was. I was an Assassin.

I grabbed a knife off his own belt.

I slashed it across his throat.

He smiled. He bled. He died.

More fire shot out of my hands.

Annihilating his body.

I was so close to the ground.

I almost wanted to hit it.

But as I waved my hands I felt magical energy circle me and create a cushion between me and the ground so I landed gracefully.

My father was dead. Abbic was dead. So many good people were dead.

A dragon roared.

Immense fire roared out of its mouth.

Catapults were fired.

Smashing into the dragon.

Rebels burnt.

Rebels died.

Rebels were slaughtered.

The dragon kept attacking.

It kept killing.

I saw Coleman. He was in trouble. The Dragon had him.

The Dragon was going to eat him.

I ran.

I ran towards them.

I swirled my hands.

Shattered crystal floated up.

The entire crystal Spires broke away from the ground.

I whistled.

The dragon stared at me. It smiled. It dropped Coleman.

It opened its mouth. Fire was about to pour out.

I thrusted out my hands.

As all the crystal shards and the entire crystal spires shot into the dragon, it screamed in utter agony. It threw the crystal shards, Spires and dragon so hard that they would all crash outside the City of Power.

Dead.

I ran over to Coleman.

But thankfully he just laid there on the ground smiling at me, he was happy to be alive (hell I was happy he was alive), yet I sort of knew he was more happy to see me, and that I was okay.

And as I looked around taking in all the death, destruction and chaos the City was in, I actually had to admit that I was okay. The Overlord was defeated, the Rebellion was safe and my beautiful Coleman was safe too.

But my glaze turned back to Coleman, I knew there was something else that had to be done first, before everything was truly over.

There had to be a coronation and I had to know my future.

CHAPTER 20
Two Weeks Later

Coleman took long deep breaths of the crisp clean air of the City of Martyrs after his coronation speech and he walked off the large wooden stage and stood in the archway of a little shop. He didn't know what shop it was, but that didn't matter.

Coleman couldn't believe that everything was truly over, and an immense wave of pleasure, excitement and happiness was washed over him. He had led a Rebellion, almost destroyed it and then rebuilt into the unstoppable force that had conquered the Capital.

Of course Coleman knew that everyone else had been a major part. His amazing Rebels that had been with him from the start, the brilliant three million people who had left the slavery (and safety) of their homes to him, and his amazing sexy Assassin.

Without her none of this could be possible, so Coleman had made his speech where the millions of people all over the Kingdom had voted him in as their new King. But what truly surprised Coleman even more than him actually being ruler, was that every single man and woman over the age of 18 had come out to vote.

Not a single person didn't vote.

And even more surprisingly, only one man didn't vote for Coleman, but he was exiled by his friends, City and the entire Kingdom. Coleman didn't want that but he had to respect the wishes of his people.

As Coleman stood there and listened to the cheering, laughing and happiness of everyone as the parties started, wonderful plates of food were bought out and bands started playing. Coleman just stood there amazed that this was all happening.

Sure it had happened two or three months ago after the City of Martyrs was freed, but what delighted Coleman was that this was happening all over the Kingdom. Every single City, village and town was partying, celebrating and wishing the future was as bright as they dreamed.

In all honesty it wouldn't be hard for Coleman to dazzle these people, anything would have been better than the decades of the Overlord's rule. But Coleman still wanted, needed to do his subjects proud. He would serve each and every one of them and make sure they would be proud to have voted for him.

And maybe he'll get in again in five years' time.

The air smelt amazing of fresh sweet fruit, rich pies and so many more amazing sweet and savoury flavours that Coleman didn't want to wait to find out what everyone had cooked up.

Coleman started walking through the City of Martyrs, smiling and waving to anyone he saw. Apparently these were pockets of Overlord soldiers scattered throughout the Kingdom, but after rewarding Dragnist with the title of Lord Commander, he had dispatched him to kill them all.

As a new ruler it may have made sense to arrest them, put them on trial then kill them. But Coleman didn't need votes to know that everyone just wanted to move on and look to the future, and Coleman was no fool. The longer those Overlord soldiers were alive, the more time the Overlord's ideology had to spread, corrupt and lead to a new force that would enslave the Kingdom once more.

Coleman wasn't going to let that happen.

Coleman shook some people's hands, thanked them for their help and started to walk over to the horses. His beautiful Assassin had left this morning for a town about two hours ride away, she wanted him to join her and Coleman wanted to join her.

He had no idea why she wanted him to go somewhere else, but a tiny part of Coleman just wanted them to have some private time. Time where they weren't leaders, freedom fighters and now King and King's Consort.

He just wanted them to be a man and woman deeply in love.

So Coleman took another look around and

couldn't stop himself from smiling. This was all amazing, he had done what no one thought he could do. He had freed millions of people from a tyrant so they could live a life they wanted, how they wanted.

Sure he might never get into power again, but Coleman didn't care. He never wanted power, he wanted Richard to take over the ruling part of the Kingdom. All because Coleman had done his part, he had freed everyone.

And that was more than enough to him.

CHAPTER 21

Sometimes I honestly shock myself, I wasn't surprised so much by the fact that Coleman had gotten elected, or that the election had taken place, but I was actually amazed at how pleased I was. I couldn't be happier for Coleman, the Kingdom and even myself.

I was no longer just an Assassin with the evil Overlord as my father, I was something more. I was loved, cared about and I was a hero.

I wasn't sure if I wanted to be a hero, I was just doing my job but for some reason, I knew that was a lie. If my job was just to kill the Overlord, I would have done that years ago. But my job as an Assassin, a female assassin at that, is to kill the guilty and protect the innocent.

And if I had killed my father years ago then someone else would have just taken his place and punished the innocent for killing him. Simply because I was so good at killing they never would have known it was me.

With the sound of music, laughing and happiness filling my ears, I stared down the massive street. I stared at amazement at all the dishes of fine sausage rolls, crispy golden lamb and succulent juicy pork. And thousands of the other dishes.

The air smelt amazing with hints of thyme, rosemary and chilly. Crisp meat, juicy bacon and sweet fruit. The entire town was an amazing explosion of wonderful smells, tastes and colour.

But there was a reason why I was here. I didn't just come to a random town, I came to the town where it all began. Sure the large wooden houses were different and they were painted in the blood of the Overlord's soldiers that these people had killed.

Yet the massive stone wall with raising towers was still there. I remember running towards them, fighting on them and releasing the birds. All in an effort to get my message about the Overlord's invasion to Coleman. That simple message had started it all. I had come here to try and save the Rebellion when the Overlord launched an attack out of the City of Death.

It all seemed so strange now and even though it was only a few months ago, it felt like a lifetime ago.

The music stopped as everyone sank to their knees for a few seconds before my beautiful Coleman ordered them to stand, party and keep celebrating. Then he said this was their victory as much as his.

I actually agreed with him, before I joined the

Rebellion properly, I really thought I could do it all on my own. I thought I could kill the Overlord, free everyone and keep being an Assassin.

But now I was something more, something better. I had found my family, not a family of blood, but a family of love and brotherhood. A family I would happily die for (technically did) but I wasn't going anywhere.

I would like to think (and I do know) that my beautiful little brother who the Overlord killed when he attacked the Assassin Temple would be proud of me. I knew he would be but I wished he was here, my sweet little brother was amazing, he was the only blood family I had left, and he was dead. It killed me when that happened.

But he would be proud that I overcame my assassin training and learnt to love again and find a family.

I would be Coleman's King Consort, probably marry him because it's tradition and I would serve by his side for all the years we remained in power. Because like him, governing the Kingdom was only part of the mission now, the real mission that no one would ever see would be to stop another Overlord from rising and wanting to turn the Kingdom back to the *good old ways*.

It sounded ridiculous and when Coleman first mentioned it to me, I didn't believe him. I couldn't understand how someone might want to turn the Kingdom back into the corrupted, tyrannical and slave state that it had been. But as Coleman pointed out, people always tell themselves that the old ways were better if the current ways were lacking.

I agreed.

So my mission was to protect everyone, stop another Overlord rising and kill any dangers to our freedom.

I felt Coleman wrap his strong arms around me and he started to kiss my neck. I couldn't help my smile because this was what I had always wanted but never allowed myself to think about it. I had always wanted a man to love me, care for me and want to be with me.

And now I had one.

I turned around and kissed Coleman's soft sexy lips. Hard. And as we kept kissing, I knew the future was going to be bright. Because there were no more threats to everything, the entire Kingdom could celebrate, love each other and live without fear.

As me and Coleman walked hand in hand and spoke to our people, I just smiled at him, because I truly did love him.

And I know my life was going to be amazing.

Just as I always wanted.

AUTHOR'S NOTE

Thank you for reading, I hope you enjoyed it.

Like in all my other Author's Note in my books, I wanted to quickly tell you about some of the inspiration behind this book. Therefore, for the City of Power book, I knew I wanted to do the final book based on the Capital, but the problem with that was to keep with the titles of the series. I had to give the Capital a City name so hence the map reading and the Capital being called the City of Power.

Then the book became a part of tying everything together. Like exploring more about the Hunters, the history of the Assassin and the half-siblings that the Assassin has. As well as this was really the last chance for us to explore the Assassin's mother and what happened to her as her storyline had been revealed in major ways in City of Pleasure.

So it had all had to happen in this book and the main inspiration behind this was a strange mixture of the last Hunger Games book, because the entire thing was based on attacking the Capital (even though I haven't read that book in years) and another series that I stopped reading but liked the titles, and I can't remember the series now for the life of me.

Overall, I hope you really enjoyed the book and please check out the rest of my fantasy, science fiction and other books on my website or at your favourite book retailer.

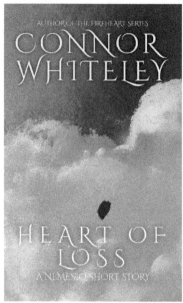

GET YOUR FREE AND EXCLUSIVE
SHORT STORY NOW! LEARN ABOUT
NEMESIO'S PAST!

https://www.subscribepage.com/fireheart

Keep up to date with exclusive deals on Connor Whiteley's Books, as well as the latest news about new releases and so much more!

Sign up for the Grab a Book and Chill Monthly newsletter, and you'll get one **FREE** ebook just for signing up: Agents of The Emperor Collection.

Sign Up Now!

https://dl.bookfunnel.com/f4p5xkprbk

About the author:

Connor Whiteley is the author of over 60 books in the sci-fi fantasy, nonfiction psychology and books for writer's genre and he is a Human Branding Speaker and Consultant.

He is a passionate warhammer 40,000 reader, psychology student and author.

Who narrates his own audiobooks and he hosts The Psychology World Podcast.

All whilst studying Psychology at the University of Kent, England.

Also, he was a former Explorer Scout where he gave a speech to the Maltese President in August 2018 and he attended Prince Charles' 70th Birthday Party at Buckingham Palace in May 2018.

Plus, he is a self-confessed coffee lover!

OTHER SHORT STORIES BY CONNOR WHITELEY

Blade of The Emperor
Arbiter's Truth
The Bloodied Rose
Asmodia's Wrath
Heart of A Killer
Emissary of Blood
Computation of Battle
Old One's Wrath
Puppets and Masters
Ship of Plague
Interrogation
Edge of Failure
One Way Choice
Acceptable Losses
Balance of Power
Good Idea At The Time
Escape Plan
Escape In The Hesitation
Inspiration In Need
Singing Warriors
Dragon Coins
Dragon Tea
Dragon Rider
Knowledge is Power
Killer of Polluters

Climate of Death
Sacrifice of the Soul
Heart of The Flesheater
Heart of The Regent
Heart of The Standing
Feline of The Lost
Heart of The Story
The Family Mailing Affair
Defining Criminality
The Martian Affair
A Cheating Affair
The Little Café Affair
Mountain of Death
Prisoner's Fight
Claws of Death
Bitter Air
Honey Hunt
Blade On A Train
City of Fire
Awaiting Death
Poison In The Candy Cane
Christmas Innocence
You Better Watch Out
Christmas Theft
Trouble In Christmas
Smell of The Lake
Problem In A Car

Theft, Past and Team
Embezzler In The Room
A Strange Way To Go
A Horrible Way To Go
Ann Awful Way To Go
An Old Way To Go
A Fishy Way To Go
A Pointy Way To Go
A High Way To Go
A Fiery Way To Go
A Glassy Way To Go
A Chocolatey Way To Go
Kendra Detective Mystery Collection Volume
1
Kendra Detective Mystery Collection Volume
2
Stealing A Chance At Freedom
Glassblowing and Death
Theft of Independence
Cookie Thief
Marble Thief
Book Thief
Art Thief

Other books by Connor Whiteley:
The Fireheart Fantasy Series
Heart of Fire
Heart of Lies
Heart of Prophecy
Heart of Bones
Heart of Fate

City of Assassins (Urban Fantasy)
City of Death
City of Marytrs
City of Pleasure
City of Power

Agents of The Emperor
Return of The Ancient Ones
Vigilance
Angels of Fire

The Garro Series- Fantasy/Sci-fi
GARRO: GALAXY'S END
GARRO: RISE OF THE ORDER
GARRO: END TIMES
GARRO: SHORT STORIES
GARRO: COLLECTION
GARRO: HERESY

City Of Assassins Urban Fantasy Collection

GARRO: FAITHLESS
GARRO: DESTROYER OF WORLDS
GARRO: COLLECTIONS BOOK 4-6
GARRO: MISTRESS OF BLOOD
GARRO: BEACON OF HOPE
GARRO: END OF DAYS

Winter Series- Fantasy Trilogy Books
WINTER'S COMING
WINTER'S HUNT
WINTER'S REVENGE
WINTER'S DISSENSION

Bettie English Private Eye Series
A Very Private Woman
The Russian Case

Miscellaneous:
RETURN
FREEDOM
SALVATION
Reflection of Mount Flame
The Masked One
The Great Deer

All books in 'An Introductory Series':
BIOLOGICAL PSYCHOLOGY 3RD
EDITION
COGNITIVE PSYCHOLOGY THIRD
EDITION
SOCIAL PSYCHOLOGY- 3RD EDITION
ABNORMAL PSYCHOLOGY 3RD
EDITION
PSYCHOLOGY OF RELATIONSHIPS-
3RD EDITION
DEVELOPMENTAL PSYCHOLOGY 3RD
EDITION
HEALTH PSYCHOLOGY
RESEARCH IN PSYCHOLOGY
A GUIDE TO MENTAL HEALTH AND
TREATMENT AROUND THE WORLD-
A GLOBAL LOOK AT DEPRESSION
FORENSIC PSYCHOLOGY
THE FORENSIC PSYCHOLOGY OF
THEFT, BURGLARY AND OTHER
CRIMES AGAINST PROPERTY
CRIMINAL PROFILING: A FORENSIC
PSYCHOLOGY GUIDE TO FBI
PROFILING AND GEOGRAPHICAL
AND STATISTICAL PROFILING.
CLINICAL PSYCHOLOGY
FORMULATION IN PSYCHOTHERAPY

City Of Assassins Urban Fantasy Collection

PERSONALITY PSYCHOLOGY AND
INDIVIDUAL DIFFERENCES
CLINICAL PSYCHOLOGY
REFLECTIONS VOLUME 1
CLINICAL PSYCHOLOGY
REFLECTIONS VOLUME 2
CULT PSYCHOLOGY
Police Psychology

511

CPSIA information can be obtained
at www.ICGtesting.com
Printed in the USA
BVHW030941100323
660077BV00023B/222